ARTIFICIAL TRUTH

ALSO BY
J.M. LEE (LEE JUNG-MYUNG)

The Boy Who Escaped Paradise

The Investigation

Broken Summer

ARTIFICIAL TRUTH

A NOVEL

TRANSLATED BY SEAN LIN HALBERT

J.M. LEE

This is a work of fiction. Names, characters, organizations, places, events, and incidents are either products of the author's imagination or are used fictitiously. Any resemblance to actual persons, living or dead, or actual events is purely coincidental.

Previously published as 안티 사피엔스 by EunHaeng NaMu Publishing Co., Ltd., in Korea in 2024. Translated from Korean by Sean Lin Halbert. First published in English by Amazon Crossing in 2025.

Published by Amazon Crossing, Seattle
www.apub.com

EU product safety contact:
Amazon Media EU S. à r.l.
38, avenue John F. Kennedy, L-1855 Luxembourg
amazonpublishing-gpsr@amazon.com

ISBN-13: 9781662529580 (paperback)
ISBN-13: 9781662529573 (digital)

Cover design by Lucy Kim

Cover image: © CHRISTOPH BURGSTEDT/SCIENCE PHOTO LIBRARY / Getty; © Holo Art, © K-Angle, © kasha_malasha / Shutterstock

Printed in the United States of America

Contents

Chapter 1

Minju

Death certificates prove two things. They prove that someone died, and they prove that someone once lived. To prove someone does not exist *anymore* requires you first to prove that, at some point in the past, they *did* exist. And yet, as of right now, I feel certain of nothing. Life, death, existence, nonexistence—I doubt all of it.

Perhaps you think I'm about to claim that someone has come back from the dead. But I wouldn't be foolish enough to believe—or desire—such a thing. And yet, I can't help but wonder what happened to my late husband.

I was issued his death certificate on the first day of April in the sixth year of our marriage. He'd passed away after eighteen months of living with pancreatic cancer—although, I guess it was the pneumonia that eventually got him. We had no children, and because he died on April Fools' Day, there are still times when I wonder if his death isn't part of some sick prank.

When the doctor first informed us of the cancer, she spoke with the kind of hesitation one might have when ordering an elaborate meal at a fancy restaurant. This didn't obscure the fact, however, that the prognosis wasn't good. She explained that one of the reasons pancreatic cancer was so deadly was because it evaded early detection. She took great care to make sure we knew just how aggressive the treatment would be, but emphasized that if we did nothing, the chances of my husband's surviving more than eighteen months were low.

My husband stared at the ceiling of the doctor's office and didn't say a word for the whole consultation. If a passerby had peered in through the window, I'm sure they'd have mistaken him for an uninterested third party; it almost looked as if he were contemplating what he'd do once this was all over. I was also a bit distracted, but by the sound of the clock, which ratcheted loudly as if made of giant gears.

We didn't linger in the doctor's office, leaving as soon as she was done talking. Outside in the hallway, I sat down on the bench. The long, dark passage made me fear I would never make it out of there. I pressed my spine into the wall, hands wrapped around the back of my neck. I wanted to lift my head and look at him, but I couldn't, afraid that my gaze would cause him more pain.

The next morning, he informed me of his decision to refuse therapy and surgery—both of which he determined were useless if they couldn't guarantee favorable results. Instead, he wanted to devote his remaining time to his research, which he believed was entering its final stages.

"It's simple, really," he began. "The doctor said I have eighteen months if we do nothing. Chemotherapy might buy me a little more time, but it'll largely be squandered on pointless trips to the hospital. And even though she put the chance of success between thirty and forty percent, there's no promise that it'll be the life I have known. It's lost time either way."

And just like that, he decided to end his life, like a mathematician making a back-of-the-envelope calculation.

It should be no surprise that my late husband was both a talented engineer and a shrewd businessman. But to reduce him to only that would be an injustice. He was also a council member of Alegria, the virtual city that was home to more than one hundred million people, and the inventor of Mintel, the world's first artificial general intelligence, which he used to found the tech giant Gnosian. His name was Kim Ki Chan, but almost everyone knew him as Kasey or just KC.

I loved him and wanted to respect his decision, but it wasn't one I could accept so easily. I told him he couldn't give up like this. I begged him, said we could fight this together. But he remained resolute—either out of resignation or recklessness, I couldn't tell. And so we agreed to wear blindfolds as the inevitable approached from the horizon. I foolishly convinced myself that by doing so, misfortune might simply pass us by.

KC locked himself in his lab—located in a concrete annex built on the other side of the garden from the house—and ignored the doctor's recommendations, keeping the cancer a secret from everyone. He became obsessed with his goal of creating a new AI that would replace Mintel. Even now, I can see his mussed hair, that paper-thin skin, the ever-present stubble on his chin, those pants that sagged at the knees because they'd become several sizes too large for him.

Every day around dusk, we would take a walk together along the winding mountain trail behind our estate. The walk had once felt like an insignificant part of our routine, but now it was a precious opportunity to share what little remaining time we had together. Sometimes we would talk, and sometimes we would stay silent, listening to the echoes of breaking twigs as we passed through the oak grove.

One day while walking, KC paused at the crossing of a small stream. Bending down, he cupped a handful of valley water and held it toward me. It was crystal clear. At the bottom of the little pool, I could see his delicate fingers and the lines of his palms. He released the water into the stream and grabbed my hands; his own were now red and ice cold. He squeezed so tight that I thought he might crush my bones.

We continued slowly down the winding path, which was now a twilight gray. He stopped to sit on a boulder and catch his breath. Recently, he'd been taking more and more breaks on our walks. Perhaps his body was becoming weaker, or perhaps his emotions were weighing him down.

He'd always been particular and a bit obsessive, but recently, his personality was best described as picky and cranky. He got irritated at the smallest things, and he always looked rushed, as though he were on the run from something. When the emotions he was suppressing eventually rose violently to the surface, he'd sweep everything from his desk onto the floor. Of course, he'd start putting things back in order as soon as he calmed down. But he looked confused, like he didn't know at whom to direct his fear and anger.

It was exhausting watching him unravel like this. His confused fits of anger made me just as confused and angry, and when he isolated himself in his lab, I feared that something would happen to him in my absence.

As he continued resting on the boulder, I recalled another occasion at home when, as he looked out toward the scarlet sunset and studied the day's dying light, he said, "Beautiful, isn't it? I want you to keep living in this house after I'm gone."

He sounded like he was talking to someone who wasn't in the room, and this frightened me. As the sunset bathed his face in red, I saw two emotions flash across his eyes. One was fear, and the other, contentment.

Holding back my tears, I said, "I want to be with you. I'm going to be with you."

"Then we'll be together," he said softly. "I promise."

In his eyes, I saw a degree of determination that I'd never seen before. Carved in those pupils was a promise so resolute that I didn't feel the need to ask him how he could possibly keep such a promise. I believed him without the slightest hint of a doubt. But perhaps I was just desperate for a miracle.

Finally, he stood up from the boulder. As I stared at the spot where he'd been sitting, my face burned with the warmth radiating from the stone.

I was issued KC's death certificate at 11:29 a.m. on a Sunday morning, about nine months after that day in the woods. It was a proclamation that he was no longer in this world—medically, physically, societally. He'd taken his last breath in the bedroom of our home. He was forty-six and had been suffering greatly the week leading up to his passing.

When I discovered his body, he was lying on his side, his spine bent backward like an archer's bow, and both arms raised above his head. The pose reminded me of a tennis trophy, as though he were Roger Federer about to serve at Wimbledon. Pellucid rays of morning sunlight were coming in through the window. It washed away the agony in his face, making him look like a boy again.

I turned to the hallway and called for the servants. Anna, the maid, was the first to arrive, followed shortly by an out-of-breath Captain Cho, our gardener.

"Anna, call 911!" Captain Cho shouted.

She pulled her cell phone from her apron and went out into the hallway. Captain Cho gently shook KC's shoulder. When there was no response, he pressed his ear to KC's chest and checked for a pulse with his fingers. He remained calm as he did this, as if he were merely raking leaves or fixing a leaky pipe.

"Cho?"

"The chairman isn't breathing," he said, avoiding my eyes. "I can't feel a pulse either."

I could now hear sirens coming from outside, two different ones. The ambulance sirens were obnoxiously high pitched and sporadic, while the police sirens were low and constant. Anna ran out to meet them.

Two detectives and a paramedic entered the bedroom together. After checking KC's vitals, the paramedic looked up at the detective, who nodded knowingly and sent the paramedic away.

"What are you doing?" I ran over to the detective. "Call them back. My husband needs to be taken to the emergency room!"

"I'm sorry, but your husband is dead. There's nothing they can do for him."

She introduced herself as Detective Hong Miran of the twelfth precinct. At first, she looked like she was barely forty, but on second inspection, I realized she could be a few years older than that. The thick, bulging veins on the back of her hand implied considerable physical strength.

With just her eyes, Detective Hong sent a signal to her young, well-groomed partner. The young detective took out a palm-sized tablet and started writing. Detective Hong herself began walking around the room, picking up items and placing them in evidence bags labeled with numbers—a single slipper from under the bed, the tablet on the nightstand, a bottle of pills. Her motions were meticulous and practiced, like an archaeologist looking for pieces of pottery at an excavation site. She used tweezers to pick up several strands of KC's hair from his pillow and gently slipped them into a plastic bag.

"What are you doing? This isn't some crime scene!"

Without bothering to look at me, she simply said in a mechanical voice, "I'm just following protocol. Any death that happens outside of the hospital is subject to the collection and preservation of evidence. Even if you do claim the cause was cancer."

Forty minutes later, she excused herself, got into her patrol car, and drove out toward the main road.

Later that night, at 7:38 p.m., KC's death was first announced via news ticker: *Father of personal artificial intelligence, KC Kim, dies at forty-six.*

TV audiences, who at the time were enjoying the regularly programmed family sitcom, probably thought someone in the newsroom had made a mistake. But once official reports started on the eight o'clock news, there was no choice but to accept the tragedy that was KC's death.

Not surprisingly, the shock of his death caused Gnosian stock to plummet. People also felt that KC and I, somewhat of a celebrity couple, had betrayed them. They resented KC for dying and ruining what had been a storybook marriage.

There was also widespread suspicion surrounding his death. For weeks, every talk show guest had to give their opinion on the cause of death. And while the official cause had been declared pneumonia, there was no shortage of outlandish conspiracy theories. Some medical experts suggested KC had actually died from a drug overdose, while armchair detectives claimed he had been taken out by a hit man. There were also theories that implicated the army of stalkers, some of whom had rented flats in the high-rise apartments near our estate just to try, unsuccessfully, to spy on us with telephoto lenses and drones equipped with infrared cameras.

The hardest gossip to bear was the preposterous story that claimed KC was a gullible genius who had died tragically after falling prey to a malevolent no-name actress. Indeed, people questioned everything about me. Most of all, they distrusted my intentions behind marrying my husband.

With all the public suspicion surrounding KC's death, the police had no choice but to pursue the investigation in earnest. They began by casting a wide net, looking into KC's whereabouts leading up to his death and questioning acquaintances, potential enemies, and every woman he'd ever slept with. They also spent days sifting through the footage from all thirty security cameras. Yet, even after all that, they couldn't find a single alibi that didn't check out and were unable to find anything that suggested foul play.

Of course, I was not spared interrogation and was eventually called into the police station. On the morning of my official questioning, I confronted the dozens of reporters who had camped outside the station, and spoke to them calmly. "I plan to tell the police the truth."

In the interrogation room, the door opened, and in walked Detective Hong. The wrinkles on her face looked deeper than when I'd seen her at the house. Her young partner followed, tablet in hand.

After turning on a voice recorder and stating the date, her name, and her rank, Detective Hong informed me that the investigation was to be recorded, as per protocol. They also told me that they used an AI program, which had been developed with the help of psychologists and neurologists, to suggest further questions based on my answers. Additionally, they would use an AI-assisted polygraph.

They first asked me about my relationship with KC and what I had done leading up to the day of his death.

"The night before it happened, we were celebrating our sixth anniversary."

"How many people were present?"

"Two. Anna prepared dinner, and Captain Cho served us."

"That makes four, not two. Do Anna and Captain Cho work for you?"

"Yes. Anna is our maid. She lives with us and is originally from the Philippines. She's been with KC since before we got married."

"I'm sorry, did you say 'Captain' Cho?" This was the young detective inserting himself into the interrogation. "What's his full name, and what do you pay him for?"

"His name is Cho Jang-su. He's our gardener. But he does more than that. He's an all-around handyman. He does everything from welcoming guests to fixing our toilets and the floorboards. We call him 'captain' because he used to be a sailor and because we trust him with steering our home away from bad times."

"Poetic. And how did you meet him?"

"Well, once AI-assisted autopilot was introduced to the maritime industry, all of Captain Cho's experience navigating the seas became obsolete. He lost his job, and there wasn't much he could do with his skills back on land. So, he reeducated himself and eventually found work at a landscaping company. He'd been working on a project at the Gnosian building when my husband noticed how meticulous a gardener he was. So my husband offered him a job managing our private property. KC used to say that he did it because of the guilt he felt over inventing the technology that put Captain Cho out of work."

Detective Hong mulled over my answer as she waited for AI to suggest further questions.

"Alcohol? Did you drink at all that night?"

"We shared a bottle of Bordeaux."

"You *shared* a bottle of Bordeaux? With your sick husband?"

"Yes. Well, he didn't drink that much. Around two glasses."

"I didn't know terminally ill cancer patients can drink."

"Is it a crime to enjoy oneself?"

"What did you do after that?"

"After we finished dinner, we went to the bedroom. I put out his painkillers and sleeping aids for him, and then returned to my room."

"You left your ailing husband in his bedroom by himself? Doesn't that seem a bit odd?"

"No, that's what he wanted. He told me to relax in the next room while he slept. I thought it was a good idea too."

"Why's that?"

"I had to regain my energy if I was going to care for him the next day. When he would wake up or feel pain, the sensors connected to his body would send me alerts in my room. I didn't have to physically be with him the whole time to know he was safe."

"Why did your husband refuse treatment? Are you sure that's what he really wanted?"

This question sounded to me like a dig at me as a wife, as though she thought a good wife would have convinced her husband to undergo chemo.

"If you have questions about his treatments—or lack thereof—you can talk to our family doctor. My husband didn't consult me about his decision to refuse treatment. Our doctor prescribed him painkillers. KC often suffered from high fevers and abdominal pain."

By this time, the AI program had produced its questions. But the questions it asked were just variations on the same questions the detective had already asked. I guess it was hoping I would slip up if it kept repeating the same line of questioning from different angles. Detective Hong, however, faithfully read out the questions popping up on the screen without showing any signs of boredom.

"Walk me through what happened that morning."

I described everything I'd seen in as much detail as I could remember, without embellishments. Lying was pointless now that AI-assisted polygraph test results had become admissible in court. After two hours, the AI program turned itself off.

"If the interrogation is over, can I leave?"

"Not just yet. There's going to be a press conference in a few minutes. I have to give a report on the progress of another case. Did you hear about it? Someone tried to commit suicide after murdering their entire family. Anyway, after the conference starts, the reporters will be distracted, and you can sneak out."

This sounded to me like a confession that she hadn't discovered any motive or reason to suspect me, but that she would rather the reporters didn't find out. I was relieved that I would avoid charges, but angry that she was asking me to sneak out like an actual criminal.

"Thank you, but I'm not afraid of reporters."

Detective Hong paused for a moment before responding. "I'm not sure what you'll make of this, but we didn't call you in here to prove you're guilty. We called you in to clear you of suspicion."

"Is that why you locked me in an interrogation room and asked me the same questions for two hours?"

"Kim Ki Chan died in your home, and you were the first person to discover his body. People have wild imaginations. If you leave even the slightest hint of doubt in their minds, they'll accuse you of all sorts of crazy things. There's no stronger acquittal than the police saying they have no reason to suspect you."

"Bullshit. I thought it was 'innocent until proven guilty.' Why do I have to prove my innocence if I haven't been accused of anything?"

"That's not for me to decide. That's AI's job. And if the AI program comes back saying we need to do more questioning, that's what we'll do."

"You talk as if AI were your boss."

Detective Hong shrugged and said I could leave. I walked down the long hallway, and when I arrived in the lobby, several reporters put mics in my face. I echoed what I'd said when I entered the police station. "I told the police the truth." Then, without saying any more, I wrapped my scarf around my neck and hurried out of the station as fast as I could without running.

Two weeks later, the police finally determined there was no reason to suspect any foul play in the death of Gnosian's chairman and officially closed the investigation. At first, it looked like KC's death would be forgotten—but that changed once the public caught wind of who was to inherit his estate.

All of KC's Gnosian shares, his personal funds, the house, and the vacation home in Bali—all of that had become mine. Everyone thought that I didn't deserve any of it.

Despite secluding myself, I heard the rumors about me and KC's fortune. That I got close to him just for his money, that I loved his money more than I loved him, that I had never expressed grief in public, that KC would be rolling over in his grave if he knew that his life's work was now in the hands of his scheming widow, that he'd still be alive if he had better taste in women.

But I could forgive them for thinking that way. The story of a relatively poor actress suddenly inheriting a large fortune after her rich husband's death was enough to make anyone jealous, and thus suspicious. It wasn't fair, and I knew it. Realizing I didn't have any time to lose, I met with KC's lawyer and called a provisional shareholders' meeting.

Two weeks later, on a Wednesday morning, I sat in KC's old seat at the shareholders' meeting. Executives, directors, and investors all looked on with distrust. I put on a presentation that I had prepared before, outlining my proposal, and began to speak.

"It's not just my fortunes that my husband's invention has changed. From nations and companies to ordinary people, everyone has been profoundly affected by KC's work. My husband was the world's foremost expert in artificial intelligence. But all I know about AI is that it has changed my life forever. I've not bothered to learn about AI, and I have no intention of doing so. I plan to establish a public trust with the inheritance from my husband's stake in the company. And I will entrust the management of the company to this board. As for me, I will devote myself to operating the Eigen Gallery, which my husband founded."

The air in the room changed as soon as I expressed my intent not to attempt to fill my husband's shoes. It was exactly what they had been hoping for. I could hear them fixing their postures and straightening their jackets. They put my proposal to a vote.

When the decision from the shareholders' meeting was made public, all doubt surrounding me, my husband's death, and his large fortune evaporated. Now, I was nothing more than a widow who was the object of people's pity, a woman who donated her fortune to appease her grief.

But that didn't mean the doubt had disappeared completely. While people didn't think I had killed KC, they continued to whisper in private that he'd still be alive had he not met me. And there were people who were displeased with the other types of assets—from savings to properties—that I had acquired through KC's death.

One of the stipulations in KC's will was that I not move out or sell the house. But even if he hadn't included that, I would have stayed—it's what I preferred. The only place I could continue living this lonely life was in the house filled with memories of him. And aside from the fact that he was gone, the house hadn't changed one bit since his death.

Even now, ugly rumors continued to follow me in the tabloids, which often referred to me as "the Inheritance Bitch" or "the Veiled Gold Digger." While I knew it was simply speculation from people who didn't know better, I also knew they weren't completely wrong. Even though I had relinquished rights to all his shares in the company, I still had more money than I knew what to do with. I was also a director of a fancy art gallery. Perhaps it was to be expected that people would resent me.

KC's death didn't need the accompanying soundtrack of a deafening gunshot or skidding tires. In fact, some tragedies happen in complete silence, without any calamitous signifiers. The silence of KC's passing sometimes made it feel like our love never existed at all.

I cried, both because of what he'd left in my heart and what he hadn't. I was crushed by the guilt over not forcing him to get treatment, over the fact that I'd basically done nothing for him. I felt like an idiot, and I had no idea at whom to direct my anger and grief.

I just couldn't quite understand my emotions. Anger turned to disappointment, and regret turned to relief. And I couldn't say honestly that all these emotions were simply because I was saddened by his absence. In some ways, my grief seemed insincere. Indeed, I was less disturbed by his absence than by how relieved I felt now that I was alone.

Ultimately, however, I did suffer—the suffering just took a while to get to me, but one day it decided it had waited long enough. Bone-numbing guilt and befuddling resentment came at me in turns, like high and low tide. People I met looked at me with concern and were careful with their words. But their words of comfort and sympathy felt more like a merciless attack than an act of kindness. Like a child being complimented for something they didn't do, I was afraid that people would find out that I wasn't as devoted to my late husband as they had thought.

So one day, I decided to hide myself from the world. I locked myself inside our home, in KC's study, where I took my meals and slept. The dead were sustaining the living. Then one morning, after nearly a year had passed, I emerged from the study feeling reborn and went to my job at the art gallery KC had founded. Several years later, I married again, my new husband a now-famous photographer. I had moved on.

I saw the man two months ago on a Wednesday. Wearing a thin cardigan, I was walking along the mountain trail KC and I used to walk. KC and I had talked about a great number of otherwise unspeakable things on that trail. Some of the questions we asked didn't need answers. It was just comforting to know that there existed a place in the world where we could be alone together.

The winding trail behind the estate extended all the way to the top of a small mountain, about seven hundred meters high. The sky that day was clear and expansive, and there was a gentle evening breeze. Alongside the path were native acorn and other broadleaf trees, and many wildflowers. Down the path, I could see the red roofs of the nearby neighborhood, and in the distance, beyond a small hill and a patch of reclaimed land, were the buildings of the business district, their glass sparkling in the light of the setting sun.

I could feel KC's presence in everything, even the sound of the twigs snapping beneath my shoes. I imagined his hoarse voice telling me he'd always be there, and those bright eyes looking back at me. I couldn't believe it had been six years since he'd passed away. I could believe even less that I'd lasted this long without him.

A flock of birds roosting in the forest took flight toward the ridge, which was now outlined in sunset red. My eyes followed the flock until my attention was suddenly drawn toward a large boulder on the side of the path. It was the cold, sturdy slab of granite that KC used to sit on when we came back from our walks. I stopped in my tracks, startled by what I saw.

A man was sitting against the side of the boulder, in the same place where KC always sat, and his body was in exactly the same position. He was squinting toward the western ridge of the mountain, perhaps a bit blinded by the day's last light. Pale forehead, lint-like curls of hair, a sharp jaw, and a long, high-bridged nose—while he wasn't necessarily the spitting image of KC, every feature reminded me of my late husband. There was something uncanny about how unmistakably familiar yet decisively different his face was.

But the similarities seemed too many for it to be a mere coincidence. It had to be KC. I would recognize that uniquely curved silhouette anywhere, those clumsy body movements. The way he sat on that rock was just like the picture that had been etched into my visual cortex. He was back. He looked just as he did back then. Unsure whether I should run from or toward him, I remained frozen.

"It's beautiful. The sunset, I mean."

The man smiled, causing crow's-feet to form at the corners of his eyes. It wasn't clear if he was talking to himself or intending for me to hear him. I remembered the way KC used to look at me toward the end, eyes with the embers of passion, a cynical smirk, a face weathered by cancer.

"A long time ago, I used to come here often," he spoke again. "I wasn't alone, was I?"

I didn't answer him. The wind blew overhead, carrying the sound of rustling leaves and the bitter scent of conifers. The valley water flowed through the crevices of stones in the shade, trickling quietly with melancholy.

After staring toward the western ridge for a while, the man got up from the boulder. He walked along the winding path with his hands in his pockets; he seemed to be disappearing into the sunset. I wanted to call out to him, but I couldn't think of what to say.

The hem of his sky-blue shirt vanished into the shadows of the forest. And then the sky was slowly painted into darkness, as if the lights were being snuffed out one by one. I don't know why, but something came over me, and I placed my hand on the rock where the man had been sitting. I could still feel the warmth from his body on the boulder's surface. I thought about the man who had generated this warmth.

Could he really be KC? Cold air rushed down from the mountain peak like a torrent of water. In an instant, the boulder went cold as ice.

The next day, and the day after that, I went into the forest and waited for the man to return. I could remember his face with great clarity. Even though I knew it was impossible, I couldn't shake the idea that KC might be alive. But I hated myself for this. I hated to think that I was so obsessed by the memory of my dead husband that I'd been thrown into a fantasy by a stranger who happened to share a resemblance to KC.

But when I thought about it, I realized that what I really was feeling was fear. People often dreamed of seeing their loved ones again, but the actual experience of seeing someone raised from the dead would be horrifying.

It took me a few days to pull myself together. Eventually, I convinced myself that the man had never existed. He was just a figment of my imagination—albeit an extremely vivid and realistic one.

One evening, about a week later, the doorbell rang unexpectedly. Anna was busy preparing dinner, and my husband was developing film in his workshop. Being the only person available, I stopped trimming the roses to answer the door.

Opening it, I was met by a man dressed in a bomber jacket. Half-bald and with a short beard, he looked to be in his fifties. He handed me a brown box. Seeing no label and not expecting a package, I asked what it was. He then handed me a business card and said they were men's dress shoes.

Men's dress shoes? There was no one in our home who needed fitted dress shoes. My husband, who wore loose T-shirts and old jeans, was allergic to formal wear. And while he did own a suit for events that required him to dress up, he preferred to wear sneakers with his formal wear. I also had never seen Captain Cho wear anything but large comfy shoes to nurse the chronic arthritis in his ankles.

"You must have the wrong address."

The man pulled out his cell phone to check the delivery instructions. "No, ma'am. This is the place. I'm sure of it."

"What's the recipient's name?"

He showed me his phone as he pointed to the screen. "It says it right here. A Mr. Kim—Ki—Chan."

With him pronouncing each syllable of KC's name like that, there was no doubting my ears. I told him he must be mistaken, that no one by that name lived here. And I wasn't lying. After all, even if what he was saying was true, it was impossible for the dead to order a pair of fitted dress shoes.

He then told me that the man, Kim Ki Chan, had come to his shop last week for measurements and then returned three days later for a second fitting and to pay.

"Actually, we remember customers by their measurements better than their names. No two people have the same feet, and his were particularly special. I remember him well. His left foot was size 167, and his right was 173. Someone with feet like that would probably buy size 170 off the rack. Although, I bet it would cause them a bit of discomfort."

Just as the man claimed, when KC wore size 170 shoes, his left foot slid to the front and he'd get blisters on his right pinky toe; that was why he always wore fitted shoes. At the lab or his office, he would wear a different-sized slipper on each foot.

Probably because he was tired of arguing with me, the man dropped the box in my arms and left in a hurry. I opened the box to find a pair of gray loafers. I didn't know what to think of this. Who would have used my dead husband's name to pay for a pair of expensive shoes? I seriously doubted that KC would come back from the dead just to buy footwear. But how else could I explain the oddly specific shoe sizes?

When I went back inside, my husband had returned from the workshop and was waiting for me. His hair was disheveled, and his clothes smelled of chemicals from having spent all day developing film in the darkroom. He was sipping on an apéritif when he saw the box in my hands and asked what it was. "Shoes—" I mumbled. Apparently thinking it was a gift for him, he snatched the box from my hands like an excited child—denying me the chance to explain—and tried the gray loafers on.

"A bit tight. But I love them."

From the disappointed look on his face, I could tell he thought I'd forgotten his shoe size. But I knew well that he was a size 175.

"They look great on you," I mumbled again. "I'll exchange them for the next size up."

Anna's voice sounded from the kitchen, informing us that dinner was ready. My husband carefully placed the shoes back in the box and headed to the kitchen. I was left there with a crumpled invoice. It confirmed that what I had just witnessed had really happened and wasn't just my imagination.

Suddenly, I remembered odd occurrences that I hadn't given much thought to. A while ago, I'd discovered that the light in KC's study had been left on all night. At the time, I'd assumed that Captain Cho had gone in for something and forgot to turn it off.

And one time, two pizzas that we never ordered were mysteriously delivered to our door. The first was a pineapple pizza: my favorite. But the second was bacon, KC's favorite. When we called the pizza shop, they said their system must have mixed up the addresses. The manager apologized for the mistake and told us it was on the house.

Another time, the TV changed channels—even though neither of us had touched the remote. It continued to flip through the channels until it stopped on a classical music program, the channel KC and I preferred. The second movement of Beethoven's Second Symphony was playing. Stranger yet was the fact that Claudio Abbado, one of KC's favorite conductors, was leading the Berlin Philharmonic. No matter how many times we pressed the remote, the channel wouldn't change until the symphony finished.

Fear lurked in the dark evening air. I had no idea what all this meant, or what could possibly be headed my way.

That wasn't the end of the inexplicable events. About ten days after the shoes were delivered, I received an email confirmation from a hotel in Tokyo that I'd never heard of before. While I sometimes went on business trips to Japan to meet artists, I had no plans to visit Tokyo anytime soon. I hated having to do this, but I called the hotel with my universal translator mode turned on.

"Imperial Executive Tokyo. Thank you for booking with us again. How may I help you?"

I was caught off guard by the word "again." Perhaps I'd misheard her, or perhaps the translator was wrong?

"Again? You mean I've stayed with you before?"

The hotel clerk kindly told me that my name and phone number were on their list of returning customers.

"I see that you last stayed with us twelve years ago. We underwent extensive renovations two years ago and a change of name, and are now offering guests an improved experience."

As soon as I heard this, I remembered the trip to Japan I took with KC twelve years ago. It was the spring before we got married. The five-star hotel we stayed at was called the Peninsula Tokyo and overlooked the Imperial Palace and Kōkyo Gaien National Garden. Every night, we'd watch the sunset paint the city's skyscrapers in red. The week we spent there passed like a beautiful dream. I asked her the date of my upcoming stay.

"You're booked for six days and five nights from June sixteenth to June twenty-first."

If I remembered correctly, those were the same dates that we'd stayed twelve years ago. A current of electricity cascaded down the back of my neck. I told her that there must be a mistake and asked to cancel my reservation.

“I’m sorry, but this reservation is nonrefundable . . .”

“And what name is the reservation under?”

“Ma’am, I regret to inform you that the payment was made with a credit card in your name. The payment only could have gone through if the booker knew your security code and other personal information.”

The clerk read me the last four digits on the card. There was no doubt; it was my card, just not one that I used regularly. I realized that at this point, it was probably better just to call the police than to drag out this phone call any longer.

Yet, now that I thought about it, there were no signs of criminal activity. Aside from the fact I never remembered making this hotel reservation, whoever had made the reservation knew far more about me than the typical credit card scammer. And even if my card had been stolen, I doubted the police would be particularly interested in a trivial case of credit card fraud.

After I hung up, I was struck by an eerie sense of unease. The occurrences felt less like a coincidence and more like a carefully thought-out conspiracy. Strangest of all, they all seemed to exist in KC’s shadow: a man on the trail behind our house with an uncanny resemblance to KC, mysterious dress shoes that only KC could fit into, a reservation at a hotel in Tokyo where we’d stayed more than a decade ago. It seemed like someone who had intimate knowledge of our private relationship was pretending to be KC. But who would pretend to be my dead husband and why?

While it pained me to suspect Anna or Captain Cho, their names were the first that came to mind. Both had worked for KC before we got married. In some ways, they knew him better than I did. Indeed, I could think of few others who knew so much about us.

It had to be one of them. Or perhaps they were conspiring together. It was possible that they’d thought these events would be nice gestures, opportunities for me to reminisce about my dead husband. But what if that wasn’t it? What if they’d passed on information about us to someone else?

Over the next few days, the anxiety over these strange occurrences caused cracks and sores to develop on my lips and cheeks. While it frightened me that someone might be in possession of intimate information about our private lives, I was more frightened by the fact that I didn't know who it was or what they wanted. At the same time, I had the strange feeling that these were signs being sent to me by KC. Had KC come back to life? But I knew that was impossible. Perhaps he'd never died in the first place. While I knew that this was even less likely, once the terrifying possibility of KC having never left this house entered my mind, I couldn't get rid of it.

At the end of the dimly lit second-floor hallway was a lustrous ebony door that led to KC's old study. I wasn't quite sure why I still hadn't cleared it out six years after his death. Perhaps I needed my own space to grieve him. That room was both proof of my love for him and a temple for me to remember him. It was a place where he could remain with me, even in death.

The room had a high ceiling and was well lit, which made it useful for entertaining guests and filming interviews after KC's death. By sitting in his large office chair, surrounded by all his old possessions, I could play the part of a grieving widow for his former acquaintances. Looking at me, they would trust that I'd loved him dearly and that I was greatly affected by his absence.

While his study was undeniably a room in our house, it sometimes felt like a place that didn't exist. Aside from Captain Cho, who went in occasionally to clean, no one frequented that room, including me. In fact, a large padlock hung from the door and was left securely fastened most of the time, except for when we used the room for events. The massive ebony door was a wall that separated the past from the present, life from death, me from KC.

I told my new husband that I used the room to store old furniture and junk. He didn't really accept or challenge this claim, and I didn't offer any further explanations. I couldn't be sure whether he believed me. But I had a feeling he knew I wasn't exactly telling the truth.

I grabbed the door handle, which was shiny from years of KC's hands. Just as I turned it, I heard shifting furniture inside the room. Immediately, every strand of hair on my body stood on end. Who could be inside KC's study at this hour?

When I carefully opened the door, it let out a shrieking creak, probably because the grease in the hinges had almost dried up. The scent of KC's skin still lingered in the air. It felt like, at any moment, he would step out from behind the desk with a large book open in his hands. *Honey, what are you doing here?* His voice echoed in my ears, scolding me like a child who'd explored too deep into the house.

In the cold darkness, I could sense KC's breath. Everything that happened six years ago suddenly felt like a lie; I couldn't believe he was dead. Was he back? I shook my head. Impossible. If anything, he'd never left this house in the first place. After all, I never sent him away. Not really. This room and my refusal to empty it of his possessions were enough proof of that.

Fluttering was the hem of half-closed curtains covering the north-facing window. Did this room have a draft? Or had someone been standing at the window before I entered and hid themselves once they heard me? It occurred to me that I might not be safe here. Just at that moment, I sensed movement in the darkness again. A shadow crouching behind the desk turned to look at me. I jumped back at the sight of its piercing eyes.

"Sorry for startling you, ma'am. I didn't expect you to come in here."

It was Captain Cho. He hurried to his feet and flipped the switch next to the display case. A cast of familiar objects revealed themselves under the orange light. A large ebony desk, a single-sized bed, a brown leather couch. Books were organized in the bookcase in a system that only KC understood, and at the base of the bookcase was a pair of gray loafers. Aside from the fact that he wasn't alive anymore, everything was just the way he'd left it.

"I was cleaning the room in preparation for Friday's TV interview. I had just finished and turned off the lights when you came in. I'm sorry for startling you. You can go. I'll get the lights."

To my ears, this sounded like he was trying to chase me out of the room. I ignored him and walked over to the desk, as if to remind him that this room and everything in it still belonged to me.

"I have something I need to do here. So if you're done, you may leave."

Captain Cho vacillated for a moment, as though not sure what to do. Just then, the wall clock struck a new hour. The sound of the long bell rattled me—it felt like the call of stubborn memories that had traveled a great expanse of time to get here. It paralyzed me.

"Sorry," Captain Cho finally said. "I wound the spring to see if it still worked and forgot to remove the pendulum when you came into the room."

When I heard this, my body relaxed. Of course, that was it. There was no way this room was home to a dead man. KC was just that: dead. I'd burned his remains and scattered them in the wind. He wasn't coming back. And this dark, dusty room was as good as useless. This was my house now, not KC's.

"I'm going to clear out this room, Captain Cho. I'm going to clear out all of KC's things and renovate the room. It's so dark in here with only a north-facing window. I'm going to put in another window facing east. I'm going to start this week."

My assertiveness startled even me. It was obvious that Captain Cho was caught off guard by my sudden plans. He asked me where I would move the interview on Friday if this room was being renovated.

"I'll do the interview under the pagoda in the garden. Please make the necessary preparations. I'm sure the camera crew will love it if the roses are pruned and in full bloom."

Two mornings later, a pair of workers came to dispose of KC's things. Dressed in yellow uniforms from the recycling plant, they were quick in clearing out the room. Placed on the stair landing were three large bags filled with old clothes and other recyclables. Next to those was a haphazard pile of tennis rackets, golf clubs, and umbrellas.

Now that the study door was wide open, it no longer held the same mystique as it had before. The room had been wiped clean of any trace of KC. Now it was time to take out the old baseboards, paint the walls white, and install warm hardwood flooring. I even had plans to punch a hole in the east wall to create a sliding door and a balcony. And when construction was over, I would use this large, breezy, well-lit room as my home office.

The interview on Friday afternoon—held under the garden pagoda against the backdrop of roses—was a success. I knew that the people watching it on TV would be relieved when they saw my smile—a smile that could only belong to a widow who had finally overcome her grief and regained a normal life. I thought that this would be the end of it. I thought that clearing out his study would be enough to remove any lingering trace of him. Out of sight, out of mind.

But I would soon discover that I was gravely mistaken.

Chapter 2

KC

I am a dead Homo sapiens. My body has left me. The fires of the incinerator ignited my flesh and reduced my bones into a pile of carbon before someone cast them to the wind. My death spread to the world through radio waves and fiber optic cables. *CEO of Gnosian, KC Kim, dies at forty-six. RIP KC Kim, father of AI. In memory of tech giant KC Kim.*

There was even a funeral procession—cameras, mourners in black, tear-filled eyes, stony expressions and downward gazes, a hearse flanked by an army of vehicles. People believe everything they see on the news, and the news is quickly forgotten.

I wonder. Am I still alive to those who don't know or have forgotten about my death? But it's not like it would matter. Whether known or not, my death is now established fact.

But don't call me dead. That would be inaccurate. I might be dead in the traditional sense of the word, but I can still talk, hear, and see. I can appear before your eyes without anyone knowing; I can startle you if I wish; I can even put a knife to your neck. I can tell you what supplements you take every day after lunch, and I know with whom you meet behind your partner's back.

However, I'm not claiming that I'm alive. Just because something can talk like a human, think like a human, and remember like a human doesn't mean it's alive like a human.

My one and only indisputable observation about death is that it does not mean annihilation, as I thought it would. Conversely, life does not mean existence. You might not fully grasp what I mean, but a person can exist *in death*. And that is exactly the state I find myself in right now.

You might ask me what exists where I am. I would tell you, Why do you think there exists—or should exist—something here? The things you would expect to find here do not exist. No heaven, no hell, no souls, no reincarnation, no sorrow, no fear, nothing. There is only memory. Or, to be more precise, the data of memory.

I can remember my short life, which flashed in the blackness like a firefly. I remember how at dusk, my father used to listen to Brahms in his study. I recall the stories my mother would tell me as she pruned the hydrangeas, stories of a girl who used her long hair to strangle a monster, and of a boy who got lost in video games.

You might also think, I presume, that I am a soul whose attachments are preventing him from moving on to the afterlife. But I don't believe in supernatural souls. When people talk of the "soul," they often believe they're talking of some entity that exists separately from the body. But really what they're talking about is an emergent phenomenon of continuous physiological processes. Memories and emotions, reasoning and intuition, judgments and analysis—these are nothing but the product of one hundred billion neurons connected by one hundred trillion synapses.

The adult human brain comprises 1.3 kilograms of soft, foie gras–like matter, inside of which electrical signals pop in and out of existence at a rate of about one hundred million bytes per second. Predictions, plans, memories, regret, love, hate, jealousy, anxiety, resignation, grief, vanity, hubris, homicidal impulses—all of these are nothing but the result of a phantasmagoria of electric pulses in the brain. For convenience, we can call this a soul. Or consciousness, if you prefer. It's just a name.

It's not that I simply can't accept the fact that I'm dead. In fact, this isn't even about acceptance or denial. I fundamentally disagree with people's conceptualization of death. For most, death is to be feared. For me, it was nothing but a gateway to paradise. It freed my consciousness from all sensations, especially pain, and propelled me beyond the border of life and death, where I lingered for so long. The thought of sexual encounters no longer arouses me. I feel neither warmth nor cold. I have been liberated from the gnawing of hunger, the lethargy of satiation. Time is now my friend. I am at peace in infinity.

I remember the very first time I—or my soul—overflowed with boundless jubilation. That day, I'd successfully hacked a computer game for the first time. It must have been comparable to how boys in the nineteenth and twentieth centuries felt when they learned they could take apart and tinker with clocks and radios. I placed my own code into the game like a greasy mechanic adding illegal modifications to a car. I was still young and inexperienced, however, and coding wasn't quick; I would spend days lost in that labyrinth of code.

There is nothing more beautiful than a formal system with axioms that are perfectly internally consistent. Such systems can be right, and they can be wrong, but that is beside the point. The beauty is that there is no room for bias or prejudice, no tolerance for interference. Such a flawless world is where I exist now. And from here, I cannot help but be amused by humanity's attempt to impose order on an imperfect world with its rules and laws.

When I think about my early twenties, I am invariably reminded of that dilapidated building in Seoul's tech district, otherwise known as Yongin Techno Cluster. Just over one hundred fifty square meters in space, the building had previously served as a delivery warehouse for a large gaming company. The space became mine when the buyer of *Night Squad*—the game I'd developed in my junior year of college—threw it in as a bonus, perhaps out of pity. At the time, I'd just graduated, and people left, right, and center were getting rich making video games. I could have jumped back into the fray to build on my success, but, instead, I locked myself in that shoddy makeshift warehouse with no heating or air-conditioning, let alone decent insulation, intent on a dream that no one would give the time of day.

Yongin Techno Cluster was a giant theme park to me. Divided into the big four industries—biotech, artificial intelligence, space, and semiconductors—it was home to more than two thousand factories, research facilities, and businesses. Like one giant display case, it demonstrated to the world that crazy ideas could revolutionize consumer markets, that technology could change lives, and that an invisible hand controlled the world.

If the banks and investors pumping capital into businesses and research were like the boilermen shoveling coal into a firebox, then those in the army of lawyers, consultants, engineers, couriers, and sex workers were like the wheels that kept the giant locomotive moving.

Between the business and residential districts was an old marshland that had been reclaimed when the city was first built. Every morning, I would go on an hour's run along the fields of reeds, which were home to a host of migratory birds. And when I returned to the warehouse, I'd spend the rest of my day alone, working, eating, and reading up on the latest trends and research. I tried working with a team on several occasions, but their chatter grated my ears, and having to explain and defend myself felt like a waste of time.

I survived by eating take-out food and whatever the local restaurants sold. I endured harsh seasons with nothing but two pairs of jeans, two loose T-shirts, a padded jacket, and one pair of high-top sneakers. And I spent all day struggling to express myself in computer code, like an immigrant fighting for their place in a new country.

It wasn't like I was a celibate. In fact, I met all sorts of women—at libraries, on walks, at the discount store, in restaurants. They came from all walks of life, from college students and salaried women to telemarketers and housewives. I would dine with these women and sleep with them, but these encounters never turned into long-term relationships. Some of them may have even loved me, but I never reciprocated the feelings.

I soon realized that interacting with anyone, sharing opinions, and creating good "chemistry" was not possible for someone like me. And when I realized this, that I couldn't love anyone with sincerity, that I could never be understood, I both pitied myself and felt a sense of liberation and relief.

At the time, everyone was talking about merging humans and machines. The goal was to transcend Homo sapiens, either by making machines with the sensibilities and emotions of humans, or by upgrading humans with the computational speed and industrial fortitude of machines. Mobilized for this goal was an army of cognitive specialists and neuroscientists, doctors, biologists, biochemists, psychologists, and, of course, experts in AI.

The early generations of generative AI, which performed limited, specific tasks when prompted by users, transformed humanity over several generations, ultimately leading to the development of artificial general intelligence. The next challenge was the development of precise sensory systems to support advanced AI with input from the real world—things like sight, hearing, smell, taste, and touch. The first two breakthroughs were corneal insertion augmented vision (CIAV) developed by Philip Scott, and Telaroma, the olfactory sensory system developed by Nanum Technologies.

Telaroma, which converted odors into electrical signals that were fed into the olfactory nerve, also helped those who'd lost their sense of smell. It was even modified to work with visual input, allowing people to smell lavender when shown pictures of the Mediterranean Sea.

A year later, the technologies of CIAV and Telaroma were used to develop a wireless taste recognition system called Delia, and around the same time, David and Garrett—producers of medical devices in the US—created a new tactile sensor to give prosthetic-limb patients the sensation of touch.

The next key to the puzzle was Dr. Kang Jin-woo's research on implantation technology, which created a new wave of high-quality nanochip implant procedures. Long gone were the days of drilling holes into people's skulls. After him, brain augmentation could be achieved by using an implantation gun to inject nanochips into the brain via the nasal cavity. The augmented intelligence that these two technologies enabled, as well as a new type of programming language that could effectively digitalize biological memory, led the way for a revolution in Alzheimer's and Parkinson's disease treatments.

There was a debate over technological disparity, that these new advancements were creating a class divide between those who could afford them and those who couldn't. But these lost traction against the argument that these innovations would offer a new life to patients with cognitive impairments like Alzheimer's and dementia, as well as individuals with sensory disabilities. If anything, the promise of these technologies created growing pressure for more-affordable access for those who needed them most. As a result, within several years, 11 percent of the entire population had received some type of biomechanical implant.

One field that saw exponential growth thanks to breakthroughs in sensory cognition technology was virtual reality. When virtual reality became indistinguishable from reality, it was as monumental as the *Santa María* landing on the shores of the New World in 1492. It was even bigger than landing on the moon or Mars.

In theory, humans could now exist anywhere, in any form. You could be sitting in the dark recesses of your home one moment, and the next, be in the stands watching Roger Federer at Wimbledon or be listening to a lecture by David Attenborough at Cambridge. Virtual reality was a space with no limits, no borders. It existed everywhere and nowhere simultaneously. It was the manifestation of the multiverse, which hitherto had only existed as a concept in theoretical physics and pop culture.

But just as the exploration of new continents enabled colonization and imperialism, new technologies ignited human avarice. Tech companies, as well as all the world's governments and regimes, poured their energy into building virtual cities to overcome the depressing nature of their true realities.

And now, somewhat ironically, true reality has become as quiet and peaceful as an abandoned coal town. It has been reduced to nothing more than a commuter town, where people come for rest, to recuperate from the passionate and taxing pursuits of the digital world.

During the final stage of this technological revolution, I was wrestling with computer code in a warehouse with the sign "Meniac" hanging outside. People now walked around with chips in their brains, and a tech-savvy generation was embracing each new innovation without fear. Ideas were being conceived at the nexus of technology and human need, like inorganic compounds in a vast primordial ocean suddenly coalescing to form single-celled life by a chance bolt of lightning. And the world was being split like an atom undergoing nuclear fission.

People hoped that virtual reality would become a new form of exploration, an invention that would make life infinitely more pleasurable. The technology and market demands were there; the only problem was no one had figured out how to effectively combine and systematize these various new technologies into a sufficiently convincing and orderly world.

For a while, the broad domain of virtual reality was populated by small "towns," each established by competing companies and limited by weak operating systems. Alegria was the first stable "city" created in virtual reality. At its launch, it registered around twenty million residents worldwide, but soon its popularity began to fall with the introduction of better, competing virtual cities with more-sophisticated operating systems. Early inhabitants of Alegria began migrating to these new cities. In a few years' time, Alegria would die if something didn't change.

I sent an unsolicited email to the software development team of Terraverse, the parent company of Alegria, and suggested that they discard their linear algorithm in favor of one that was self-evolving. The technology director replied to me directly, saying that they would look into it, although it was his estimate that such a move would require an astronomical amount of funding, manpower, and time. I could tell from the tone of the email that they weren't happy that an outsider had potentially solved the problem they'd been working to solve for months.

As expected, about two days later, I received a personal visit from Saito Honda, the billionaire founder (although no one knew exactly how much money he had) and CEO of Terraverse. An ethnic Korean born in Japan, he used the inheritance from his father, who made his fortune building casinos and a construction company, to establish an investment firm and subsequently led the revival of Japan's tech industry. He'd succeeded in increasing the size of his fortune through various investments, after which he founded Terraverse, capitalizing on the virtual city boom. He was only in his early forties, about fourteen years older than me at the time, but had already cultivated the mature look of a middle-aged man. With a thick chest and plenty of muscle, he gave the impression of a retired welterweight boxer.

"You know, genius coders who've made their fortune selling games that die after a few years are a dime a dozen. There's a world of difference between games and virtual cities. Not even the best coders can solve this problem on their own."

I knew he was trying to break my spirit. But I wasn't going to lose my composure. While he had the upper hand in almost every way—age, experience, corporate scale—in this one transaction, I held all the cards. His being here was all I needed to be certain of this. They were desperate for solutions, and none of their engineers thought what I proposed was possible. I explained my plans for the future of Alegria.

"To create a thriving city that evolves on its own, you need to create a relationship of mutual exchange between stacks of individual AI units that are each capable of machine learning. The positive feedback loop of such a system will allow you to regulate large populations or more than eight hundred million users autonomously."

"You don't think we know that? We'd do it if it was possible. The problem is money. What you're suggesting would cost more money than exists."

I demonstrated my simple program cell, which comprised only eighty-three steps. It was one unit of a high-speed self-learning program that trained itself by feeding itself commands and adjusting for errors based on the results. It was essentially nothing more than a trial-and-error program. Saito leaned back in his chair, wearing a look of boredom and disappointment.

"That's it?"

This was understandable. The program I was demonstrating was so simple that even a beginner programmer could write it in two days. The program was barely more advanced than a fifth grader's calculator.

"Well, this is just one cell. Imagine if you had an entire Terraverse brain of these cells. The human brain contains one hundred billion neurons, which fire twenty-four seven. Now imagine if we had an AI brain composed of just ten thousand or even one hundred thousand of these man-made cells. And what if there were hundreds of thousands, or millions of those AI brains? You'd never have to hire another human to operate the servers. It would be completely self-regulating. A self-evolving life-form. What I'm showing you is just the smallest unit of an operating system that would be able to move a virtual mega city."

Saito had no alternative to Meniac. But the risk was great. I would either ruin him or raise him from the ashes like a phoenix. He glared at me with eyes half-wary, half-intrigued.

"How can you be sure?"

"Science isn't about belief. It's about results. I don't believe anything. I know it. The question of whether to trust me is up to you."

Saito asked me what else I could do for Alegria. I told him about my ideas for generating profit. I proposed using the city itself as a billboard, exposing each user to products or services tailored to their preferences. I also proposed a program that would increase profitability by installing electricity grids all over the city and charging users for electricity.

After a month-long pilot program, which proved my projections accurate, Saito proposed that Meniac merge with Terraverse, and in exchange, I would get a generous portion of company shares. But I made it clear that I didn't want a merger and instead would take options while maintaining control of Meniac.

After Saito invested large-scale funds and labor to adopt my new AI operating system, which was given the name AOS, Alegria transformed into a city that thought and adapted. Work that had previously been done by expensive programmers was taken over by AI, making the impossible possible. Everything from decision-making to prioritizing projects, budgeting, building infrastructure, and procuring supplies for the city could be done autonomously and in real time, to respond immediately to resident needs and feedback.

In less than a year, the landscape of virtual cities completely changed. People lined up at Alegria's immigration office to secure their place in the new world. It was Ellis Island, but on a scale never seen before. Living spaces and new housing were created to keep up with the growing population, and after only a year of AOS, Alegria increased its population by 160 percent and its GOP by a steep 228 percent. Even with a self-determining operating system, important decisions regarding the city still needed to be made by people, so a separate council was created to judge the proposals that AOS made to them; they would be the ultimate governing authority of Alegria and comprised mainly board members from Terraverse.

Of course, competitors attacked Alegria with claims of market monopoly. But Saito merely laughed when reporters asked him about his business practices.

"There are no prizes for coming in second place in the tech world," he once said in an interview. "If you're not the strongest, you will eventually go extinct. It might not be immediately, but it will happen one way or another."

With its new operating system, Alegria sucked up everything from money and people to other virtual cities. Terraverse's stock went atmospheric, and investors lined up to get their piece of the pie. Before, Saito had to beg banks to give him loans; now, banks were competing for his business. It seemed like nothing could take down Alegria.

It was around that time that I left Terraverse. Saito was confounded when I told him I'd liquidated all my options. He told me the stock price would probably triple in two years. But as I saw it, I'd already earned more than my initial target; there was no reason for me to stay and be greedy.

Saito had no choice but to accept my decision. He knew that once I'd made up my mind, I would never change it. But that distrusting look of his never left his face. He asked me what I was going to do with all the cash.

"I'm going to buy NeuroTech. It's a start-up founded by two dozen experts in neuroscience and computer engineering. They're trying to figure out how to digitalize brain activity."

Brain mapping, the tricky science of interpreting signals from neurons, was the bottleneck for developing more-advanced AI technologies. At the time, the only brain-mapping technology we had access to were things like magnetic resonance imaging, which measured the blood-oxygen concentration in the brain, as well as the N1 Chip neural implant.

However, nanochip brain mapping, pioneered by Dr. Cha Han-young, used hundreds of thousands of nanochips that, once injected into a patient's bloodstream, would work their way to the brain to digitalize and transmit neural and synaptic activity to an external server. It was safer yet more precise than an MRI, and it eliminated the infection risks associated with electrode implants. But because of its experimental nature, the technology was only being used to treat patients with otherwise incurable neurological conditions. At the time, NeuroTech, which had been founded as a research institute with the mission of finding cures for neurological disorders, was the leader in the field.

"Brain mapping?" Saito asked. "Isn't that bioengineering? What about AI?"

"New approaches are needed to develop new AIs. All the AIs that exist now are only coded in computer language. They completely ignore human ingenuity. But if we're going to develop machines for humans, we have to understand human cognition and the brain. NeuroTech might be a small company compared to Terraverse, but they have the technology to develop and the vision to conceptualize a new form of bio-AI."

I then suggested he and I start a new business partnership together. He accepted with little hesitation, as though he'd already expected this move of mine. Thus, he founded the new AI company Gnosian and hired me as its CTO, but not before I used all my money from Terraverse and Meniac to buy 51 percent of NeuroTech's shares.

And thus, we'd started on a new voyage together.

Launching Gnosian wasn't smooth. Despite the combined efforts of our scientists, results were few and far between. It took three years and eight months before the first prototype of the self-expanding AI, nicknamed Sapiens, was completed.

And even then, the program did not live up to the team's expectations. I had no choice but to personally check each section's code for errors. Eventually, my understanding of what needed to be done became sharper. I encouraged our dispirited team members:

"Sapiens isn't our final product. We've only laid the foundation, and I've confirmed that the foundation is strong. There are a lot of problems that need to be fixed. Sensors need to be tuned, and the code needs to be debugged. But we are going to produce results."

The team looked unconvinced.

"Think about how many rockets humankind built before landing on the moon. Sputnik, Vostok, and the Saturn rockets. And then in 1969, after nearly a decade of building rockets, we finally landed on the moon. This first step for us will be called Sapiens 1.0. Sapiens will evolve. Sapiens 1.0, Sapiens 2.0, Sapiens 3.0, Sapiens 4.0 . . ."

We devoted ourselves completely to developing further versions of Sapiens. Version 3.0 dramatically improved capacity and speed, and version 5.0 focused on improving the external network. After that, we worked on integrating Sapiens with external hardware and the internet, and started making the necessary partnerships with cybersecurity and the medical industry.

Sapiens 8.0 was able to duplicate human irrationality. At some point, I realized that the true essence of the human mind was not its empiricism but rather its ability to abstract that which cannot be physically sensed. It is through seeing the invisible, hearing the inaudible, and feeling the untouchable that humans imagine, predict, and infer. The problem is that humans have weak imaginations, inaccurate predictions, and fallacious reasoning. That's why humans repeat the same mistakes, get easily excited, are deceived by absurd fictions, and fight over pointless things.

If AI was to mimic human cognition, there was no reason for it to imitate only our ingenuity; it needed to be able to imitate our folly as well. But to do that, we needed to understand the rules underlying not just irrational human emotions, such as desire and prejudice, but also fundamentally flawed cognitive phenomena, like systematic false reasoning and the tendency to believe things for which one has little or no evidence. But it wasn't easy to convince the programmers of this.

"Ninety-nine percent complete is zero percent complete. There is no such thing as ninety-nine percent complete. It's either complete or it's not. It's either perfect or it's not. And anything that's not perfect needs to be sent to the waste bin."

I had to be ruthless toward myself and others because I knew that the world of tech was unforgiving. I didn't shy away from mass layoffs and draconian work hours. Employees claimed psychological abuse and left the company in droves. And even those who remained were not fond of me. But the criticism suddenly evaporated when we finally achieved my goal, thanks to my insistence on perfection and no compromises.

In fact, investors thought it was precisely my compulsive personality that was the reason for the company's success and growth. The media compared my management style to that of a surgeon who mercilessly severs infected body parts to save a patient.

Sapiens 9.0 was the first version that was able to generate both good and bad jokes, improving on previous versions' inability to mimic our capacity for illogical free association. Others had been able to produce passable jokes, but these lacked something unique to good humor. In other words, it was the first program to understand the logic of stupid jokes.

The Sapiens project finally achieved its potential when an agreement was reached to launch model 11.0. No one was more excited than Saito, not even the scientists and programmers who had finally seen the fruits of their suffering. He clapped with beaming eyes after hearing Sapiens 11.0's speech, which mimicked his voice and manner of speaking perfectly.

"That program sounds more like me than I do. It said exactly the things that have been on my mind. It even paused in the places I would have paused, and lengthened double vowels like I do. There were moments when I couldn't tell which of us was talking."

He looked like a marathon runner who had just crossed the finish line. He was completely unaware, however, that this wasn't the finish line—it was yet another starting point.

Sapiens 11.0 was distributed to the rest of the world one country at a time under a new name, Mintel. Early adopters were limited to academia and the private sector, but gradually, the technology spread to the general public. Once this happened, sales exploded. The catchphrase "A New and Better You" captured perfectly what we were trying to accomplish with Mintel.

The media's interest in me as a person increased alongside Mintel's rise in popularity. But I wasn't interested in people's attention or applause. Saito enjoyed the lights and cameras on my behalf. He had the looks of an old Hollywood star and was eloquent; he was perfect for dealing with the media.

The stock price of Gnosian, which was listed six months after the company's founding, was forty-eight times its face value. Because I was relatively free from the prying eyes of the world, I was able to devote myself to the design of the next generation of Mintel, as well as to personal projects I had at that time. What transfixed me back then was the task of merging NeuroTech and Gnosian into one being. I was like a coachman trying to corral two stallions to work together.

One afternoon, Saito came to me. He stormed into the office and guzzled a cup of water. He then summoned a long newspaper article onto the virtual prompter. My eyes were immediately drawn to the headline.

Who's the Man Behind the Curtain?

We all know that Gnosian changed the landscape of artificial intelligence. But what is less known is that the true mastermind behind the company is not Saito Honda. Behind the charismatic CEO, there is another player, someone who exercises immense influence over the company and Honda. Not only has this person refused to take credit for the company's revolutionary advances in AI technology, but he has also sidestepped the ethical and moral quagmire

> surrounding Mintel. Indeed, as has been reported and confirmed, the AI program readily provides potentially harmful information to users with suicidal tendencies and even encourages gambling addictions. Gnosian has tried to rebuild public trust in its product's safety through various marketing campaigns, including a ten-year warranty program, but these efforts have failed to completely quiet public criticism. Perhaps it's understandable that the program's inventor would want to stay away from such controversy, but at risk of receiving none of the glory for irrevocably changing how humans live?
>
> Mr. Honda is a well-spoken investor; he is not a programmer. Anonymous sources have claimed that the true mastermind behind Mintel is working on another project. One can only imagine the threat that such a person and their ideas pose to civilization. Can we sit by and entrust the future of humanity to an eccentric genius who hides in electric shadows?

"What is this?" I asked.

"You're aware that there are rumors going around about your being some reclusive mad scientist, aren't you? They think you're some kind of monster. The newspaper is preparing a follow-up to this article. With Mintel being the success that it is, there's no escaping the tentacles of the media. The longer you hide, the more determined they'll become."

"But who reads the paper these days, anyway?"

"Papers might not sell, but the stories in them do. Unless you get out and show your face to the world, speculative and inflammatory articles like this will only continue to be published."

"Rumors are just rumors. They don't concern me."

"They might not concern you, but they concern Gnosian. The image of a little man behind the curtain will only eat away at the trust in our product. Your negative image is hurting public trust and our stock."

The media gobbled up whatever came out of the woodwork. People I'd never even met were popping up all over the internet. A high school sweetheart who claimed to be my first kiss, a man who claimed to be my long-lost stepbrother, a bricklayer who claimed he used to work with me before I made it big . . .

"All those people just want their fifteen minutes of fame. Don't worry about them."

"Worrying about them is my job. I can only keep the nosy journalists' mouths shut for so long. People believe any story they hear. It doesn't have to be the truth."

I felt cornered. Just as Saito said, there was only one way to stop people from making up stories about me, only one way to stop the public from believing those stories.

"We need to take countermeasures before we release Mintel 8 next spring. The product is there in terms of quality. The problem is the marketing. It's already September. We'll need a complete image makeover before the end of the year."

Mintel 8 was going to introduce groundbreaking features. This version of AI was able to optimize user cognitive systems through machine learning and was going to dramatically improve inter-user networking. Like Saito, I also didn't want Mintel's newest release to be affected negatively by the mystery surrounding my identity.

"What do you want me to do?"

"We need to change your image from Mr. Hyde back to Dr. Jekyll. We'll hire the best publicist and do whatever they tell us to do. In fact, I've already taken the initiative. The advertisements for Mintel 8 will prominently feature pictures of you in the lab. We're going to show users the best version of you. And to address directly the concerns surrounding your motives, we're going to shoot promotional videos and go on a publicity tour, complete with interviews and talk show appearances. In fact, the first interview will be done in your study at the mansion."

"And what if that doesn't work? You really think a few pictures and videos will change people's minds?"

Saito looked as though he had already thought of this possibility. I could see a droplet of sweat slip down his temple. He shrugged and laughed.

"Well, once you announce your engagement, all doubt surrounding your humanity will completely evaporate. You'll be like the royal family. A new celebrity couple. The tabloids will be dying to write about what the billionaire and his bride are wearing and where they went for their honeymoon. People love that kind of stuff."

Throughout my endeavors in Alegria, Sapiens, and Mintel, I'd been alone. Over the many years that I'd devoted myself to the development of AI and virtual reality, I'd slipped into my forties. It was around this time that I met my wife. We would take walks in the warm rain and stare into each other's eyes as the evening sun set our pupils ablaze. When I first met her, she felt like a long-lost part of me, as though she were the playground crush that I used to chase around in the first grade. Being the fool that I was, I hadn't even realized I'd lost a part of me. Had I known, I would have scoured the earth looking for her. The fact that she simply appeared before me was a miracle I couldn't rationalize.

Four months after Saito's meeting with me in my office, my engagement and wedding were publicly announced; Saito looked so happy, you'd think he was the one who was getting married. And just like that, the mad scientist in the closet had been transformed into a young and bright-eyed genius. I was everything the public wanted—smart, attractive, engaged, and filthy rich. Saito even made a small fortune selling T-shirts and mugs with my face on them.

How far we'd come.

Chapter 3

Minju

I rarely entered Alegria anymore. Yet the things I'd experienced there remained unnaturally vivid, as though I'd experienced them only yesterday. I didn't believe it was meaningful to distinguish between virtual and real memories. Both "happened" in some sense of the word, and if either was missing, I would have felt incomplete. In specific cases, my memories of Alegria felt more real than life on the outside.

Imagine a small peninsula with a pair of vast freshwater lakes and five rivers. A 150-story super skyscraper, around which was a square park. In the distance, connected to this skyscraper by a network of radial roads and highways, was a suburban plantation; 328 million people lived in the virtual city. Like one collective dream, but not really. A world where fanciful delusions came to life. And, most importantly, the place where a poor aspiring actress sealed her fate as the inheritor of the world's most powerful tech empire.

The experiences that Alegria offered to its residents were more intense and novel than what reality could offer. In the early days, people had to wear large goggles and attach sensors to their fingers to access this poor imitation of reality. But those devices had advanced into thin contact lenses and sensory implants; now the city could offer a life more real than reality itself, a life that had transcended the physical constraints of time and space.

Immigrants once chased the American dream. Now they flocked to Alegria in search of opportunities. They dug in virtual oil fields and invested in virtual derivatives. They erected virtual factories, sold virtual products, fought in virtual combat sports for virtual prize money and belts. Couples could take long walks around giant skyscrapers while enjoying impossible landscapes. They could explore alleyways that could be hundreds of years old, shop in mega department stores while sampling expensive wines and whiskeys, and access the latest luxury merchandise before it was released into the real world.

Those who got in early used their fortunes to buy Alegria's best real estate. The rush to own a piece of Alegria only caused prices to skyrocket. Even the Luddites who'd been skeptical of the concept of owning virtual properties eventually caved when they realized they were going to be left behind.

Just as in the real world, the rich got richer, and the poor got poorer. Spending time inside virtual reality was essential to reaping its benefits. And because virtual age equaled power, like levels in an old-fashioned video game, buying and selling time was a major pillar of the economy. People with wealth outside Alegria converted their assets into Alegria's digital currency, magnum, because it allowed them to purchase more time and thus gain more influence in a virtual city. And for those who didn't have real cash to spend in Alegria, there was always the option of sharing an ID with several people. That way they could log on in shifts and rack up hours, aging and reaching elder status faster than by themselves. Many became addicted and would neglect their real job and relationships. On the other hand, those who preferred normal reality could make real-world money by accumulating time in virtual reality and then selling their lifespans.

People could become whoever they wanted, and if it turned out the role didn't fit their tastes, changing identities was as simple as putting on a new mask. An average housewife in the real world could secretly be the owner of a famous brothel in Alegria. Some people even lived meta-double lives *within* virtual reality. A virtual orphan might escape their circumstances by entering another, deeper virtual reality where they were a space explorer in the Hook Nebula.

I remember the headlines when the identity of the ringleader of Gomorrah, the largest criminal organization in Alegria, was revealed to be a certain Mario Fellini, a street cleaner in the back alleys of New York. He'd used his time in the Mafia as a troubled youth to grow Gomorrah into the most feared gang in virtual reality. He wasn't arrested, of course. The hand of the law didn't extend inside virtual reality, so long as the crime didn't cross into the real world. That's not to say there wasn't a legal system within Alegria itself. Police, courts, and prisons—it was all there, more or less. They even had the death penalty. But all these things did little to deter crime. After all, convicted criminals could just choose suicide over completing their sentences, as they would immediately be reborn as a new character.

Death, rebirth, death, rebirth. Again and again and again. People quickly became used to the idea that they could live out their wildest fantasies through an endless cycle of life and death. This led to an increase in the murder and suicide rates in the real world, but the bigger problem was that virtual reality, the thing that had been created to mimic reality, was now reality's single biggest threat.

Critics warned of the dangers of virtual reality, but no one listened, and the little legislation that was passed was too slow to keep up with the rapidly changing landscape. Of course, part of the problem was that most lawmakers were also shareholders in Terraverse, Alegria's parent company. The other factor was that voters themselves wanted to protect virtual reality from regulation, which they saw as the Wild West of opportunities. There were even some people who foolishly believed that virtual escapism was the cure for a collapsing society.

Some people claimed it was difficult to form genuine relationships with the false identities we used inside virtual reality, but I have not found this to be the case. In fact, Alegria was where I met KC—on the 168th floor of the Glass Tower, to be exact. It was a massive project in the center of the city, 220 stories tall when complete and with enough space to house one hundred thousand people. Investors salivated when the project was first announced. The exterior of the building was fitted with stained glass to mimic Notre Dame Cathedral and Sainte-Chapelle, reflecting the Central Council's resolution to adopt Gothic art and architecture from Europe. Each unit was sold for a fortune before the building had even been completed.

Virtual reality was my escape from an exhausting life that had me balancing triple shifts in the emergency room. When I wasn't dressing wounds or inserting catheters, I was being yelled at by angry family members or juggling the paperwork of a dozen different patients. I had no sense of time other than the day, evening, and night shifts that I lived by. But what I really wanted to do was act. I went to auditions when I had the time, but how often was that? Virtual reality was my only chance to pretend to be someone else.

It also helped pay the bills. Every time I met my end in virtual reality, I would sell my accumulated time for magna, and then exchange that for real-world currency, which was deposited directly into my account. It wasn't much, but it helped supplement my meager salary as a nurse and struggling actor.

The reason I applied to solder glass on the exterior of the Glass Tower, specifically, was because the job paid two thousand magna per hour—not because I wanted to be part of history, as many of the applicants did. I also liked that it required an artistic touch. These two things meant that I could feel proud and well compensated for my work, which wasn't easy in the real world.

When I met KC, I was concentrating on molding the bloodied contours of Saint Sebastian's arrow-pierced thigh. The smell of melting lead stung my nose, and the tip of the iron warmed my fingers—all sensations created in my brain through sensory implants.

Just as I was finishing, I heard the elevator doors open behind me. I turned to find a man, dressed in a gray turtleneck and black slacks. His face was illuminated by the sun's reflection bouncing off the stained glass. He had short hair, round metal-rimmed glasses, and a full gray beard. His voice when he spoke to me sounded both authoritative and restrained.

"That's too many pieces of glass per square meter. Did you not get the foreman's instructions? Or did you just choose to ignore them?"

I didn't answer him. I was tired from work, and I didn't think I needed to explain myself to a stranger. But then I saw the yellow eagle on his left breast, an insignia that only the elder administrators of the Central Council could wear. I defended myself by saying that the foreman's instructions were more like guidelines than strict rules. The man walked over to the depiction of Saint Sebastian's martyrdom that had been molded into the two-meter-wide, four-meter-tall arch window and started to inspect it.

"You're talented, but the foreman's instructors weren't merely a suggestion. According to our models, twelve pieces of glass per square meter is the most efficient method for these designs."

"Well, using more pieces didn't prevent me from completing my quota on time."

I didn't care whether they fired me, and this seemed to catch him off guard. Soon he gave me a friendly smile. A rainbow of colors reflected off his white teeth. I knew it was just a virtual image, but I couldn't help analyzing his face: moist, full lips, a beard that was full yet revealed two creases on the sides of his cheeks, remnants of what must have been dimples when he was younger. He silently stroked the surface of Saint Sebastian's bloody thigh before asking me if this was my first life in Alegria.

"Fifth. My previous lives were as a bookstore owner, mercenary, circus performer, and a vocalist for a third-rate band."

While one might think this was a nice variety, they were all lives that I'd used and discarded on a whim. They also had all been the short lives of low-class citizens.

"And how were those lives?"

I hesitated for a moment. I didn't have much to say about the lives themselves. After all, here in virtual reality, life was dispensable. After a while, the only thing one could remember about a particular life was how it ended.

"I got the death penalty twice. Once by electrocution and another by public hanging for murder. And the other two times I was shot. The first time was in combat, and the other time was during a mass shooting."

He studied my face with curiosity. "Very macabre."

"I know none of this is real, but death here feels so vivid, so real. I've never felt that kind of pain before. It was so bad that I considered never coming back. Twice, in fact, I was taken to the emergency room because my body went into shock from the pain."

I could tell he wanted to know more. And yet he didn't ask any follow-up questions, not even why I'd committed murder. What was behind this digital face? What was he like in real life? Unlike other virtual cities, Alegria was designed to mimic the locality of the real world, so he would probably be living in the same city as me.

"I guess you're an expert when it comes to death. How about learning how to live?"

"I don't want to live here. I want to live in the real world, properly. But I had to come back."

Of course, most people came to virtual reality to escape their lives. That was why if one saw a child in the streets of Alegria, odds were that the child was an elderly person who came to Alegria to feel young again.

"A realist in Alegria? But why?"

Talking about real life while in virtual reality was taboo. Although it wasn't technically forbidden, people didn't want to be reminded of the difficulties of their real lives while they were dreaming. The man said he wanted to continue our discussion, outside of Alegria. Although I liked the way he leaned forward as I talked, tilting his head slightly as he pondered my words, I couldn't immediately accept his proposal. I knew what people thought of relationships from virtual reality that spilled over into the real world.

I also worried that this might be some kind of scam. Just because someone was single inside of Alegria didn't mean they didn't have a wife and kids outside of it. In fact, virtual prostitution and extramarital affairs were the number one reason for divorces in the real world. There was also the chance that this man was part of some voice-phishing operation designed to scam me out of real-world money. This was why people were wary of anyone in virtual reality who asked to meet in person. What happened in Alegria stayed in Alegria.

And yet, I wanted to talk to him face-to-face. I wanted to see what he really looked like, not what he wanted me to think he looked like.

The next day at 4 p.m., he approached me as I sat on a bench near the east gate of the city park in the real world. Slim and without glasses, he looked ten years younger than he had in Alegria. There, he'd been an elder with authority and gravitas. Here, he had this boyish innocence and playfulness about him. We picked up right where we left off, with me answering the last question he'd asked me in Alegria.

"I'm an actress, you see. Actually, a nurse who never seems to have the time to do what she loves. I don't care about becoming famous or rich. I'm fine with simple roles and no lines. As long as I'm onstage. But my job gets in the way of that. That's why I go to Alegria. There, I can act as much as I want."

"Understandable. Virtual reality is the ideal stage for an actress in need of new experiences and inspiration."

"I'm not there for experiences. I'm there to actually live the life as if it's real. That's the ultimate form of acting. In fact, when I'm there, I'm more present than when I'm acting, than when I'm living my own life out here. Alegria is the only place I can do what I love."

"I've had many professions in Alegria," he said. "I began as one of the engineers who helped develop Alegria's operating and security systems during the beta phase. After that, I oversaw user entry and worked as an administrator within Alegria. I also handled criminal investigations. Then, eight years ago, I was elected to the Council of Eighty-Eight. My latest job includes overseeing the construction of the Glass Tower. Although, I've been able to do all of that without dying once—the only thing I've changed is my profession."

A flock of white ducks landed noisily in the park lake. I could smell a faint stench coming from the lake, whose water level was low from the yearly drought. The voices of people passing, a couple fighting, a child crying. This was reality. Dirty, inconvenient, chaotic, unpleasant. Even though virtual reality gave me the chance to be an actress, I loved the gloomy, scattered nature of reality, as much as, if not more than, what virtual reality had to offer. Yet, this man was listing off his virtual lives and jobs as if they were something to be proud of, as if they were real-life accomplishments. I didn't like it.

"What's important is real life, not Alegria," I replied firmly. "It might feel empty, but you have to live it either way. I only go to Alegria because I have to."

My brusque response seemed to catch him off guard. He looked like he might be twenty years older than me, but he was as naive as a young boy. He was shy, but I could also sense he wanted to tell me about himself—his real self, in the real world.

"You must be a bit of a loner, am I right?" I said.

"I've never felt troubled or frustrated because of my personality. There's a difference between loneliness and isolation. You can enjoy the latter. In fact, I intentionally ignore people sometimes, in order to focus on my work."

"You must be doing really important work."

"Not important. Meaningful." He paused as if wondering whether he should divulge the nature of his job. "Have you heard of the company Gnosian? Or a man named KC Kim?"

I didn't know much about the two, but I had heard of them. Gnosian was a Big Tech company that developed meta-learning AI, and KC Kim was the name of its CTO. However, the intent of his question wasn't clear. Did he know KC Kim? I asked him to wait for a moment as

I activated my smart lens. He wiped his lips with his thumb in a bashful manner. My search of KC Kim returned with an image of a pale young man with black curly hair. It was him, but younger. I skimmed through a summary of him and his company.

> After founding the company, Kim revolutionized AI with his Mintel series, which had been trained on human thought and behavior. Unlike previous attempts at AI, Mintel could adapt to a user's personal cognitive and emotional profile. The response was overwhelming.
>
> Consumers worldwide lined up to purchase Mintel. But because of high prices and a limited first release, Gnosian was sued for violating the right to equal access. Amidst growing public dissatisfaction with the company, copycat AIs and more-affordable second-generation services appeared. Nevertheless, Gnosian was able to establish itself as a top-three company in AI through large investments.
>
> However, Kim, Gnosian's acting CTO, continues to remain relatively private and rarely makes public appearances. Despite concern from investors and the negative media coverage, he has declined in-person interviews, demanding that they be conducted via an outdated email service and that reporters refrain from asking about his personal life. He also has not been seen at a company event in years and gives speeches only through proxies.

I continued to scroll through the article. The rest of it was speculative. Apparently, reporters had been trying to track his whereabouts for years. But what they found was inconclusive. There was a newspaper that analyzed the language he used in interviews and claimed that he was from Singapore because he used Chinese proverbs and certain Singlish idioms. Another article claimed he had to be an amateur because of certain irregularities in his programming. There were also countless conspiracy theories about his being a persona created by a secret organization of geniuses and hackers scattered across the globe.

Later, I realized it was possible he could have been someone pretending to be KC Kim. But I was just a poor actress. What could someone gain from deceiving me? An empty bank account and an outdated wardrobe? But if he *was* KC Kim, that was equally unbelievable. What could a man with everything want with an ordinary woman?

But all these doubts only occurred to me later. At the time, I had no choice but to believe him. The way he spoke was very persuasive. Naturally, I accepted his claim that he was a famous billionaire. Just like I accepted the dimples on his face when he smiled, and the way he hopped slightly when he walked, like a bird. Even now, I'm not sure whether the reason that I accepted his story so naturally was because I was naive or because I didn't want to consider the alternative.

KC was a quiet man. He used to say that the more one spoke, the one more risked losing. However, it was different when he was with me. He could talk effortlessly for hours, explaining everything from the Ferris wheel in the distance to the architecture of skyscrapers. He also loved talking about Alegria, how it was changing people's lives, and especially how rich it made the first wave of residents. And when I spoke, he would make eye contact and respond with his own experience or original analysis.

There were moments when the conversation would abruptly stop, as if we'd entered a dead end. This silence, which might have felt awkward with someone else, didn't make me uncomfortable. His silence seemed like a different type of conversation, as though it had a meaning of its own that needed to be analyzed. It was fascinating how I could communicate so naturally with a man who was much older and had lived a life so different from mine.

Although I'd forgotten most of what I'd experienced in Alegria, I could still vividly remember the time we spent together there, the scent of flowers carried by the wind, the warmth and texture of the sweater he wrapped around my shoulders. We were walking along a large artificial lake. It was twilight. I only had a few minutes before I had to be onstage for my small role in a play. I felt nervous, like Cinderella before the ball. I had calculated the time it would take me to get from here to the theater, and I barely had enough time as it was.

"You'd rather be onstage than with me? Is it really that important that you have to leave me? I doubt the play will miss one small maid."

Although I could feel my heart racing at the thought that he really wanted to be with me, these last words reminded me of a painful reality. After years of paying my dues, the only role I could manage was a lowly maid with three lines. I thought for a while before responding.

"There are no unimportant roles in a play. If I don't go, who will play Catherine? I'm already late."

He looked hurt when I said this. Of course, I was the one who had been insulted, and yet I resented myself for rejecting him. I tried getting up from the bench, but he grabbed my wrist. His firm grip was strangely familiar to me, like a flash of déjà vu you can't quite explain.

"There's a role that's more important than an abandoned manor's maid. The title hasn't been decided, and there's no script. Not yet at least. It's a play about you and me. You write the story. After all, isn't life the greatest play of all?"

Although his slightly widened eyes and tense lips made me doubt him, they also made me want to believe him. Was this his idea of a proposal? I couldn't deny that I was attracted to him, but I didn't like how sudden and selfish this was. And yet, I didn't know why I couldn't refuse him. Was it love or something else?

There was a glint in his eyes, telling me he wasn't going to let me go. There was something obsessive about the look he was giving me, but I wasn't scared. I wanted to believe it was evidence of his stubborn love for me.

My lips were just in the middle of parting when he intercepted them with his own. As if to say there was no need for me to speak.

With the sudden announcement of our marriage, KC opened himself up to the public. Immediately, the tabloids had a field day with our marriage, which was a mismatch in every way. "Beauty and the Beast." "Love Knows No Age." "Alegria CTO, Forty, Weds ER Nurse, Twenty-Three." "No-Name Actress Lands Alegria CTO."

People viewed me as a young, beautiful woman trying to transform a reclusive monster into Prince Charming. I guess I succeeded, because overnight, KC went from an enigmatic mad scientist to a celebrity heartthrob. Because neither KC nor I elaborated on the details of our relationship or how we met, the public was left to speculate, and this only made us more interesting to them.

Just thirty days after our marriage was announced, Gnosian's stock had surged by 130 percent. Gnosian's investors also hoped that the wedding of its CTO would rehabilitate the company's image, which was suffering from transparency issues.

KC had built a two-story house in an upscale neighborhood in Techno Cluster. The view from the house, which was the highest house in the terraced residential area, was breathtaking. The foundation and structure of the house were made of reinforced concrete, while the walls, roof, and floor were made of wood—a perfect extension of KC's attempt to create something that mimicked soft human flesh on the outside and hard bone on the inside.

While packing to move in with him, I was unsure what I should keep and discard. A creaky little bed, a chair with loose joints, an old peeling desk, an out-of-style dresser, and T-shirts with collars that had seen better days—all old and cheap, yet of sentimental value.

KC, of course, told me to throw away all of it. "Everything you need you'll find in our new home," he said. I felt that he wasn't just trying to change where I lived, but that he was trying to completely reshape my life.

Dragging an old trunk filled with two bottles of my favorite perfumes, a few books, and just a handful of underwear, I descended a narrow staircase outside my apartment. Through the window, I could see the tiny buildings of the pleasure district with their flashing neon lights, back alleys where drunkards wandered noisily all night, a windowsill that rattled every time a car passed. I left and never looked back, like the snail that had lost its shell.

I didn't feel regret. Even before meeting KC, I'd wanted to make a change in my life. Now, I had. But I had no idea it would be such a drastic change, from an impoverished existence to a life of abundance and leisure. The people I associated with now were also smarter and more sophisticated.

We were the royalty that the public desperately missed. Each time our publicists intentionally leaked photos of us, they went viral on the internet. Fooling around on a yacht deck at sunset, walking through the woods with our arms locked, stealing glances while going through security at the airport—while the pictures of us looked somewhat staged, they weren't fake. With each new release, Gnosian's stock price skyrocketed. For some reason, people's belief in our eternal happiness determined Gnosian's financial success.

KC found comfort in a world of logic, numbers, and causality. He liked the stability of neat geometric spaces and insisted on perfect control over his surroundings. In fact, the slightest deviation of anything—a crooked line, not following protocol, an irksomely uneven number—gave him anxiety. He also became distressed whenever he found himself unable to explain the world logically or through a set of well-defined equations.

He was tenacious and a perfectionist, which other people often interpreted as fussy and stubborn. But he didn't care. The more others left him alone, the more he was at home. So rather than focusing on gestures to maintain people's opinion of him, he embraced his solitude. His indifference to others was his best defense against the world.

His cranky, eccentric personality seemed to be the price he'd paid for his genius. His exceptional ability to analyze numbers, formulas, and code also failed to translate to the everyday tasks of handling scissors or knives or unclogging drains. And his intellect was in constant conflict with his childlike self-absorption and unwillingness to accept the ways of the world. He seemed frightened, like a child trapped between two extremes. I couldn't understand how someone could have survived this long with the naivete of a boy and the common sense of a jackass.

After his cancer diagnosis, KC locked himself in a separate lab. Although he wouldn't tell me the specifics of what he was working on, I knew it had to do with "designing a new place of consciousness for humanity"—whatever that meant. Even though I reminded him constantly of his doctor's orders not to overexert himself, it was no use.

Inside his own space and cut off from the world, he wrestled with a machine language that no one else could understand, met with other programmers virtually, and waited impatiently for large programs to compile. Day and night didn't exist for him, and there were fewer and fewer days when he would go out on walks.

His research was slow going, so on the days that it showed signs of progress, he was high with a feeling of promise and accomplishment. But once this passed, there was always another roadblock waiting for him, and he would once again be in low spirits.

The cancer made him even more irritable. Fatigue ravaged his mind and body, and extreme stress tore down what little self-control he'd had. Skull-splitting migraines, vertigo, indigestion, and vomiting, even allergies—ailments came like waves.

It wasn't the bouts of anger that made me anxious but their unpredictability. His OCD, which had no pattern and ticked like a time bomb, made my heart frail.

His anger was cold and calculated. He raised his voice and scolded people with the intent to cause damage, and he would throw objects systematically, as though he knew which objects meant the most to whom. But he was never in a hurry when he did this. He would break display cases and windows with the same calmness that one might brush their teeth or enjoy dinner. And when he smashed remote controls, mugs, vases, or my makeup containers, he would do so one at a time, as if he were meticulously organizing them for oblivion.

His ability to manipulate and control me through his mood swings reminded me of an experienced stage actor. Sometimes, he also included Captain Cho or Anna in his schemes. One day, when the lilac trees outside his office window had been transplanted without his permission, he summoned Captain Cho and berated him for acting on his own. He made sure to do so in front of me so I saw the consequences of my actions, as I was the one who should have been overseeing Cho.

Enduring KC's fits was almost as painful as losing him altogether. While I understood the reason for his frustration, it didn't make it any easier when he took out his anger on me. He had asked me to be his wife—not a landfill for all his negative emotions.

After the scolding that afternoon, Captain Cho went upstairs to the study in silence. I followed him and found him wiping down the pistol from the display case. When I asked him why he didn't defend himself, he just smiled slightly as if he didn't quite know what I was talking about. It seemed like he and KC had developed an unspoken trust. He finished cleaning the gun and reloaded the empty magazine.

"Glock 34. I gave it to the chairman before you two married. Or perhaps I should say, I sold it to the chairman."

Something in Cho's tone terrified me. Until then, I'd considered the gun just one of those things that men collected, like figurines or limited-edition sneakers. Captain Cho carefully returned the pistol to its spot in the display case and closed the glass door.

"One of the deckhands had illegally brought it onto the ship while I was docked in the Philippines. I confiscated it, as was protocol, but once we left port, I put off reporting it. Just having the thing in my possession made me feel powerful. Once it was too late to report it, I was in an awkward position. It was too nice just to throw away. So I kept it. But then one day, while I was wiping it down in the garden shed, the chairman walked by and saw me with the gun."

The menacing black luster of the gun had ignited a fire in KC's chest. It was an object that had the power to change the energy in any room or situation. I suppose you could call such power "influence"—and KC was exactly the kind of man who would be drawn to such influence.

"At the time, I was in need of some extra cash," Cho continued. "My daughter was getting married. The chairman offered me quite a large sum of money with no strings attached. I'd wanted to repay him for everything he'd done for me, so I sold it to him. After all, a gun like this belongs in the hands of a man like the chairman, not a has-been like me."

The trade made both men happy. KC received a fancy collectible, and Cho had enough money to cover his daughter's wedding. Cho was also, under their agreement, still in charge of the gun's maintenance. Although it made me uneasy to have a real gun in the house, I didn't interfere. After all, KC wasn't the kind of person who would ever need to use a gun. He wasn't some crook or hit man. I knew that the gun would only be removed from the display case for cleaning. That was what I believed. I never considered that I might be the one to fire it.

I remember one particularly snowy winter. It was just before Christmas, and snow had been falling on and off for five hours. KC, who hadn't left his lab in over a week, finally appeared at dinner. He had a smile on his face; the project he'd been working on for the last week was almost finished.

"And tomorrow's Christmas Eve," he said. "Tomorrow morning, we can prepare for a party. I've been working like crazy and need a break."

Hearing the warmth in his voice, I was ashamed of myself for resenting and misunderstanding him. I'd misjudged him. Even though he was a bit irritable because he was battling cancer, deep down he was still the kind man I knew. It was my fault that I hadn't seen that he was cranky only due to the important decisions he was responsible for.

After dinner, he went back to his lab and didn't come to bed. It seemed like he was going to stay up all night preparing for the Christmas party.

Early the next morning, I heard a strange sound through the open window, like a starving beast. I ran to the annex and opened the door. The inside of the lab was a mess. Pens, books, and papers were strewn across the floor, as were the contents of the toppled bookshelf. The desk was askew, and KC's monitor was face down on the carpet.

He was standing in the middle of it all. His eyes were bloodshot, his lips dry and cracked. I walked over to him slowly. I was afraid of startling him, but I couldn't just leave him in that state.

"It's all gone. All the data I've been working on for the last two months. Erased."

His voice was hoarse, as though he'd used up all his energy. Dark circles surrounded his hollow eyes. I gently took his hand and placed it on the desk to anchor him.

"You have backups. Don't—"

Before I could finish, he lunged at me like a loaded spring. The sudden movement pushed me back and into the wall.

"I didn't just accidentally hit the delete button. The permanent deletion program that I've been slaving over for the last two months—it turned itself on and deleted all the data on specific parts of my hard drive."

He sounded disgusted with my ignorance. I was upset that he was taking out his anger on me, but I knew it wouldn't be wise to remind him that it wasn't my fault. But then something snapped inside me. I forgot about his illness, overcome with indignation about how he was abusing me.

"You're telling me you invented a delete program that deleted itself? Like digital suicide?" I let out a cackle. "Sorry, sorry. I know it's not funny. But I just can't stop laughing."

A sharp, unhinged light entered his eyes. His clawlike fingers grabbed my neck and dug into me. I couldn't breathe, and my vision started to go dark.

"You think this is funny?"

I tried as hard as I could to pry his hands off me. But his fingers dug into my carotid artery like the jaws of a shark. Yet, even though I was gasping for air, I didn't stop laughing.

"You don't? A data deletion program deleting itself? You should be celebrating. Now you know it works. What's the problem?"

His grip loosened as soon as I said this. He looked surprised, as if I'd just discovered something he'd overlooked. I pulled his hand off my neck, which was now only half-heartedly holding on to me like a dying vine, and staggered out into the garden. The only thing I could think of was getting out of there as soon as possible.

Perhaps that was my warning to leave him. But I couldn't do it. He didn't have much time left, and everything around him was falling apart. I was the only person he had to lean on. And if I was being completely honest, he was the only person *I* had to lean on too.

I never mentioned what happened in the lab that day. I acted like I'd forgotten about it, like it had never happened. He also never talked about it. We were accomplices bound by a silent agreement. But the silence said more about what had happened that night than any words could.

It was my fault for overlooking the signs. I knew that violence was unacceptable, but I did nothing to confront it. I looked away from a dangerously imperfect situation like one ignores a leaky roof, hoping desperately that it won't get any worse.

Chapter 4

Junmo

It takes courage to claim you understand another human being. But I can say that I mostly understood my wife. We were close, despite a rough start plagued by public gossip. In fact, it was the wounds we endured from that period that made our bond even stronger.

But then a month ago, things started to happen that I couldn't understand. There wasn't a specific incident, no signals. It was perfectly normal for my wife to take a walk in the woods at night. In fact, I joined her three or four times a week. That night, however, I was playing on my tablet as I waited for dinner to be prepared and for Minju to return from her walk. In the west, the sky, which had been fiery red just a moment ago, was now dark like a shadow. I couldn't have been the only one who sensed the air in the house change when she entered through the front door.

For the most part, Minju looked as she always looked—beautiful, lovely. The house was just as peaceful too. And yet I had the ominous feeling that something had changed. There was this emotion masking her face like a thin curtain, but I couldn't quite put my finger on it. She'd gone for just a short walk, but it looked as if she'd been lost for hours in a dark forest and had barely managed to make it back alive.

She hardly touched her food before stepping out onto the terrace, which was chilled by the evening air. Wearing only a thin shirt, she embraced herself with both arms and shivered. I followed her onto the terrace and placed a cardigan around her shoulders, but she wouldn't stop shaking.

"Is something wrong?"

No answer. And even if she had answered me, I had a feeling I wouldn't have believed her. She looked so lost. The cold air made us strangers, as if a great distance separated our bodies. We used to be partners in crime—or at least that was what the media made us out to be—but it suddenly felt like that companionship had ceased to exist. I guess you could say I felt a little betrayed.

About a week later, this vague sense of unease turned into uncontrollable distrust. She had handed me a gift—a pair of gray loafers. Not only was this a bad gift for someone who was allergic to formal attire, but it also seemed like she'd forgotten my shoe size. Five days later, when she handed me a new pair of loafers in the correct size, she seemed worked up for some reason. The leather was soft, and the new pair fit me perfectly.

"Thank you. These will be great for wearing around the workshop. Those old slippers are a nuisance."

I was smiling, but when I saw the horseshoe logo that had been seared into the bottom of the shoes, my suspicion returned.

The logo belonged to a store I'd seen in a TV documentary about traditional bespoke shoemakers. The shoes they created were for one person and one person alone. Minju hadn't forgotten my shoe size; she'd bought them for someone else. I couldn't bring myself to call her a liar, but it was clear that she wasn't telling me the truth.

Then, one morning two weeks later, two men with a dump truck knocked on our door. Captain Cho instructed them on what to load into the truck. An ebony table and green office chair, titanium-framed bookshelves, a brown leather sofa, and countless boxes. I knew our house was big, but I'd never seen this furniture in my life.

That evening, as I was walking from the workshop to the main house, I ran into one of the workers. He'd just come out of the room at the end of the upstairs hallway and was carrying a lidless box of miscellaneous items down the stairs. I'd almost forgotten about that room—though "ignored" might be the more accurate term. I thought giving my wife time was the right way to help erase the pain of her past.

I entered the room to find Captain Cho organizing the last few items that remained. He apologized for the noise, but he looked happy, almost excited. I guessed he was relieved that Minju had finally decided to clear out her late husband's old study and, in effect, any lingering feelings she might have for him. I wasn't going to stop them from erasing the traces of him from our home—it was about time—but I couldn't help but feel that this was all a bit sudden. Did this have something to do with her recent odd behavior?

A pair of gray loafers placed on the windowsill caught my attention—the same brand as the ones I'd received from Minju just a few weeks ago. They looked to be in good condition, but the marks on the back heel and the broken-in leather indicated that someone had worn them before.

"The workers must have missed those," Captain Cho said. "I'll get rid of them."

He grabbed the loafers and hurried out of the room. I looked down at the yard through the half-open curtains. Workers in mech suits were loading heavy items onto the truck and securing them with a waterproof tarp. Once finished, they had a brief conversation by the front entrance with Captain Cho, who was holding the gray loafers behind his back. They seemed to be discussing payment.

The truck wobbled with all the extra weight as it left the main gate. Captain Cho turned and looked up at the second-floor window where I was standing. I stepped back into the shadow of the curtain but kept my eyes fixed on the loafers in his hands. They had belonged to KC, Minju's late husband. Did Cho still think KC was the head of this house? And why had he lied about discarding the loafers? Something was happening behind my back, and it seemed like everyone but me was in on it.

I'd never felt this way in the past. Minju rarely kept secrets from me. In fact, the tragedy of her first marriage and her late husband's untimely death had brought us closer. Even the few secrets she kept from me weren't an issue because I trusted her. But now, I couldn't be sure of anything. Why did she buy shoes for a dead man? Did she really think I wouldn't notice? And what else was she hiding from me?

Some marriages change people for the better. As for me, my marriage to Minju turned me into someone I would never recognize. I forgot who I'd been. Poverty and death, crime and fear, lies and deceit—these things had no place in my life now.

We met at the eleventh annual charity art exhibition held by the Eigen Art Foundation, which coincidentally had been established by her late husband. The exhibition, featuring the works of three established artists and three emerging artists, donated all its proceeds to various charities. This was all well and good, but it was a mystery why they had chosen *me* as one of the "emerging artists" when I was little more than a hopeful hobbyist.

My feature photograph was hung deep inside the exhibition, in the annex to be exact, where few people ventured. Not having majored in painting, let alone graduated from an art college, I had expected as much. On the last and tenth day of the exhibition, the main hall was converted into a party venue. Throughout the event, I stayed by my work in the adjoining hall. I wasn't one to enjoy mingling with others, and I was painfully aware that I didn't belong, and never would, in their world of glitz and glamour.

Shortly after eight o'clock, the lively laughter and chatter stopped abruptly. Someone announced the arrival of the gallery's director and chairman of the foundation. Everyone applauded and cheered. The party resumed, and about twenty minutes later, I heard footsteps echoing toward me from down the long corridor.

As soon as she entered the exhibition, the hum of the air-conditioning suddenly stopped. Despite this, the temperature in the room seemed to drop. Her iridescent white jacket absorbed all the light in the room, making everything around her dark and shadowy. I remained seated. Had it been any other visitor, I would have approached and explained my work, but she was the director; I didn't want to come off as patronizing.

Each time the heel of her shoes touched the floor, the hall echoed as though we were inside a large instrument. She passed by someone else's work—a painting with parasols and colorful balloons in the style of René Magritte—before stopping in front of my photograph. It looked at first glance like a cloudless sky. But if you looked closer, you could see soft sky-blue threads of silk gently streaking across the picture.

"I feel like I've seen this photograph somewhere before," she said as she stared into the frame. "But I can't remember where . . ."

I wasn't sure if she was talking to herself. Her eyes were nailed to the picture as if she hadn't noticed my existence. The skin on her face was smooth, and her smile was barely perceptible but undeniably present. The calmness and effortlessness of her movements gave me the impression that she wasn't lacking in confidence. She looked so at home that I thought she might dissolve into the walls of the gallery. I rose from my seat and moved toward her, positioning myself closer to my artwork.

"You must be mistaken. You can't have seen it before."

She turned to look at me. Her eyes were asking me why I was so sure. I told her that this was my photograph, and that this was the first time I'd shown it to the public. She looked curious, as if she were wondering not about my answer but why she had been mistaken.

"Blue Sky & Sky Blue." Her lips moved subtly, tracing the consonants and vowels of the three syllables written under the artwork's title. Han

Junmo. A no-name artist who liked capturing fleeting moments of mundane scenes: ocean waves, wheat and barley ears, the gentle lapping of silk curtains. A man who in his rejection of flashy visual effects and digitally produced art clung to an obsolete art form.

"Five, maybe six years ago," I said, "a piece of mine named *Blue Black & Black Blue* made the rounds in the community. That must be the one you're thinking of. Different subjects, but similar styles."

The photograph she spoke of was an old work of mine, and the inspiration for this new photograph. It was a simple work, at least in terms of composition. A golden band of horizon separated it into two halves. In the bottom half were soft swells of black waves, speckled with hints of blue and glistening moist rocks. In the top half was a richly textured and moody sky, also a mix of blue and black. If it weren't for the golden band, you would have trouble distinguishing between the sky and the sea. Because of this, many people flipped the photo upside down before hanging it on their wall. To me, that picture and *Blue Sky & Sky Blue* were quite different—one dark, one light. I found it surprising that she could connect the two.

"A faint horizon and a sea of black and blue . . ." Her eyes lit up. "I remember. That was the photo that hung on the wall of my living room in Alegria."

I didn't quite believe what she said, but I couldn't dismiss it either. Loud laughter echoed from the party at the end of the hallway. It was a signal from the people waiting for her to hurry up. She hesitated, almost as if she felt bad for leaving me by myself.

"Don't worry about me. I'll be fine here. Besides, someone might want to know more about my photograph."

Both she and I knew that no one here besides her was interested in my artwork. But she extended her hand toward me anyway, as if to accept my words. Her feather-like hand was bent slightly as it slid out of my rough palm. She then left me and returned to the party, back to her world of fame and money.

Our meeting had been brief, one that you could write off as mere chance, but for some reason I couldn't stop thinking about her. She ignited a sense of nostalgia inside my imagination for a memory I'd never had. I fell in love with the fabricated memory of her as a young, innocent girl. And once this happened, she felt familiar to me, as if I'd known her my entire life.

Two weeks later, I received a call at my studio. I couldn't believe it when I heard her voice. Nor could I believe that she wanted to buy the original *Blue Black & Black Blue*. Only after collecting myself did I suggest that she come to the studio herself to see the work once more before deciding—a defense mechanism I'd developed after years of bad reviews and criticism.

My studio was in the basement of a three-decade-old dilapidated building. The room itself, cluttered with cheap picture frames, had no natural light, and film boxes and books were piled on makeshift shelves fashioned from wooden planks and cement blocks. I had no specific system of organization, so genres and subjects were all mixed together. Detective and thriller novels, books about political science, power dynamics, behavioral economics, and decision-making, and plays by Shakespeare and O'Neill. And leaning against the wall beneath this hodgepodge was the original *Blue Black & Black Blue*.

As she stood in the middle of this mess, Minju let out a long breath, either a sigh or an expression of awe. "It's exactly the same as the image I saw every day. But different. It's blacker, bluer, heavier. It looks less like the sea. More like a black hole."

"That's because this isn't just an image," I replied. "It's the real thing. Something that can't be duplicated or erased. It's a momentary truth, made from light, shadow, and coincidence."

"Like our lives?"

She and I seemed to see eye to eye on more than just art. I told her about sleeping for weeks in a bedroll, about the savagery of the sea in the morning, and the stacks of unsold works, but her gaze remained fixed on the picture. It was as if she were whispering to the artwork.

Two days later, in the late afternoon, I drove to her home in an anti-vibration truck to protect the photograph, which was also padded in several layers of bubble wrap as if it were a rare artifact. As soon as I approached, the front gate opened without a sound.

The house was quiet. A large fan slowly spun from the tall ceiling. I also noticed the wall of the living room, which had been cleared of everything. It seemed like she'd had it repainted just for this picture. I asked her if I could have a tour of the house, and she hesitated for a moment before agreeing.

The sun began to set as we walked through the residence. The staircase wall, which was over four meters tall and two meters wide, caught my eye. Above it, there was a round skylight.

"The picture would do better in a narrow, secluded place like this."

Having wanted to hang the picture someplace where it would draw people's attention, she seemed a bit disappointed. I got my ladder and tools and got to work. Once the photograph was installed along the long, narrow staircase, it had an immense presence, like a black hole sucking up all the surrounding light. The dim stairwell had found new life.

Dinner was served. We ate, drank, and talked as if in competition to see who could eat faster, drink more, and talk better. In fact, she finished her potato salad almost as fast as I finished the soy sauce–marinated chicken. Was she really that hungry, or was she just trying to spare me the embarrassment of looking like a beggar she'd picked up off the streets?

It was late, but she seemed to have more that she wanted to talk about. As she told me stories—why she stopped acting after getting married and what roles she wished she'd played before retiring—she was animated, like someone playing a game of charades to save their life.

Some people find listening to other people's misfortunes painful, but I'd gone through so much pain in my own life that I could maintain eye contact throughout her story. The sense of sorrow and loneliness that came through her expressions and words resonated with me. I'd never enjoyed being so intimate with a complete stranger before.

"It's been so long since I've talked like this," she said. "And after my husband died, I only ate enough to keep myself alive."

It was past eleven o'clock, time for me to get up and leave. But I could tell neither of us wanted the night to end.

Captain Cho brought me my coat and walked me to where I'd parked. I could hear the refreshing sound of the sprinklers in the garden.

Upon making it to my truck, I instructed the autonomous driving system to take me home. It began to move quietly. Through the open window, I watched her slowly walk up the stairs beneath the dim light outside the front door. The light wrapped around her body like a thin veil, and the white cardigan thrown over her shoulders fluttered like the bell of a jellyfish in the ocean. As I left, I continued to study her figure—the way her hair swayed, how she held herself upright, her steady, confident strides.

On weekends, we walked along the beach together. As I took photos of the morning waves, she would talk like a young girl after her first day of school. And although we both knew I had no money, it didn't seem to bother her.

No one could resist a scandal concerning a young heiress. Rumors slipped through every attempt to contain them, like wind passing through a fishing net. Whispers, sneers, suspicion, envy—these all coalesced into a sick sense of curiosity. The paparazzi and journalists camped out in front of her house, and merciless YouTubers thrust their cell phone cameras in her face at every opportunity.

The best way to stop malicious rumors is to confront them head-on. Ignoring or avoiding them only causes the gossip to swell like foam. And immediately denying them or threatening legal action only makes one look foolish. The best way to bury a scandal once and for all is to accept it publicly and move on. So naturally, we decided to announce our engagement.

Now I was both the husband to a Big Tech heiress and known as a noteworthy photographer. Gone were the days of sending my worthless pictures to dozens of agencies, waiting hopelessly for a call back. In fact, my first solo exhibition established me as the guardian of an old tradition of analog art.

I'd achieved what I always wanted, but the unease inside me remained. It felt like something had happened that wasn't supposed to happen, like I was acting out a stranger's life. On nights when I was alone, my memories grabbed me by the throat and shook me—mistakes and errors, bad decisions and misguided actions. And a childhood I couldn't think about without getting sad or angry, plus an abusive father who eventually got himself killed by gang members while walking down the street.

"My father was a kind soul. He just turned into a monster whenever he drank." My voice echoed like I was talking inside a cave and about someone else. Minju sat opposite me, listening carefully to my story. "Alcohol and gambling are bad enough when they come one at a time. But they rarely come one at a time." Whenever my father lost money, he would drink. And when he drank, he would hit my mother. Eventually, he didn't need to lose to drink, and eventually, he didn't need to drink to hit her.

The only silver lining was the fact that I was growing up. As more time passed, I became taller and my bones thicker. Conversely, my dad became older and frailer.

When I was eleven, my mother left the house, or rather, she left my father. My dad dropped me off at the orphanage and went looking for her. I prayed that she had run far away, where he wouldn't find her.

About six months later, I got a phone call from the police station. My father had been beaten to death in a back alley after getting into an argument with some thug. They never caught the culprit. I'd been waiting for him to die of old age, but I got my wish much sooner than I'd imagined. But there wasn't much to celebrate because now I was an orphan.

Once I turned seventeen, I got work as a delivery man for a while before soon becoming a presenter. Presenters were the workers who went back and forth between virtual reality and the real world. They could be hired to do work that spanned a wide variety of services, from small errands, deliveries, and chauffeuring to nursing, health care, detective work, security, education, medicine, law, and even sports entertainment. Some made a fortune by providing legal advice, while others scraped by, delivering items for people. Regardless of how much they made or the specifics of their job, they all had one thing in common: bridging the gap between virtual reality and the real world like bees pollinating flowers.

I started my life as a presenter by delivering food and small items, but soon other requests began coming in—tasks dangerously close to being illegal. We called them "yellow jobs." They were things like buying and delivering alcohol for children under fifteen or retrieving money from voice-phishing schemes. There were also "red jobs," and these included things like corporate espionage, personal vendettas, marital spying, and even bounty hunting. Danger pays well, so naturally, I was led into the world of crime.

Are criminals born, or are they made? Hunger leads to scavenging through trash cans, leads to begging, leads to extortion, to deceiving, to stealing, to robbery . . . At some point, you pass the point of no return. And while some people thought advances in technology and a higher quality of life would make crime disappear, the opposite happened. White-collar crime that took advantage of virtual reality and AI increased, while physical crimes like theft and robbery remained the same.

I became a criminal not because I was evil, but because I was foolish. I simply wanted to have nice things and was filled with resentment toward those who had more than I did. In my naivete, I believed my actions were a form of revenge against the world that had made me this way, that I was contributing, however slightly, to its downfall. Sometimes, I wonder if true evil comes not from cruelty or wickedness but from ignorance and stupidity.

One night shortly before my eighteenth birthday, I was arrested. I was the prime suspect in a jewelry store heist that had occurred two weeks prior. The perpetrator had driven a car into the store in the dead of night, smashing through the display cases to steal gold and jewelry. As they fled the scene, they ran over a pedestrian crossing the street. When the police stormed one of my favorite clubs, I was in a private room, high on drugs that I'd skimmed off during a delivery.

In the police investigation, I confessed to the crime, claiming I acted alone and had no accomplices. The judge sentenced me to two years in juvenile detention for aggravated theft, robbery, hit-and-run, and obstruction of justice, along with a year of rehab for my "addiction to drugs." It wasn't ideal, but it could have been worse. Serving time while still young seemed more bearable than doing so when I was older.

The narrow cell, occupied by a dozen other individuals at times, was a world governed by strict discipline. Physical restraints had been replaced by a sophisticated electronic surveillance system. With me were other boys who had shaved heads. Of course, I joined a gang and participated in turf battles.

In the afternoons, I was required to take the classes the detention center offered. These included self-sufficiency courses meant to teach us skills like woodworking, machine assembly, coding, and practical architecture. Physical education was also mandatory. Boxing, kickboxing, and mixed martial arts were the most popular. Kids seemed to like taking out their anger on the punching bags, and sometimes other inmates.

Electives like photography, however, were unpopular. Only eight students, including me, enrolled. It was my one escape from gang life. And in an era where holograms and projection videos were commonplace, photography was as archaic as an axe from the Stone Age or an internal combustion engine from the Industrial Revolution. In fact, photography's only use these days was as a form of therapy, and could only be found in prisons or correctional facilities for the emotionally unstable.

I didn't resist photography's therapeutic effects. Through a narrow viewfinder, I observed a world I'd never seen before. I realized the world was beautiful, but that you would never see that beauty unless you made an effort to look for it. I learned that it takes a special kind of vision to truly appreciate what it means to exist.

"My first memory of photography was at the orphanage," I said to Minju. She was still here, still listening. "At the orphanage, there was a photo of a young couple hanging on the wall of the prayer room. A woman in a white lace dress was sitting on a stool, and standing next to her was a man in a black suit. I guess they'd donated a lot of money or something. I desperately wished that people like that would become my parents, and at some point, I started to believe that they *were* my parents. To this day, I remember their faces in the picture more clearly than the faces of my own parents. Funny, isn't it? I'd found my long-lost parents in a random photo. I don't have that photo now, but I know for certain it existed there at one point."

Even after being released from the detention center, I couldn't escape a life of lying and stealing. I used whatever menacing object was in reach to force others to their knees and beg for mercy. Sometimes, I enjoyed it—the look of fear in their eyes, their trembling lips, the pools of blood, the way broken bones often pierced through flesh.

As I spoke, it became clear to me that I was the filth of society. Subconsciously, I'd always wished that I were a good man pretending to be bad. But no matter how far I ran, I couldn't escape the ugly truth of my past. It made me who I was. It still governed my life.

After I finished my story, Minju sighed and wiped her eyes with a tissue. For the first time, I felt at peace. Revealing my pain to her lightened my burden and even made me feel forgiven. But would she still love me now that she knew what kind of person I had been, the person I still was? I convinced myself that I would be okay if she left me. And yet, I had a feeling she wouldn't.

We accepted each other's pasts as dark yet incomplete parts of a greater whole. What mattered was not the past but the present. The future. What lay ahead. At least, that was what I thought we believed. But what if there were darker secrets we hadn't divulged?

I remember the last day I spent in jail. It had been three years since I had been imprisoned for another crime, this time for assaulting the vice president of a private lending firm called Golden Bell Investments, a job I took from an anonymous client. Golden Bell Investments was a front put up by a loan shark operation. Its leader, Kang Man-soo, hid behind a fake persona as vice president of Golden Bell Investments, from which he could control his loan shark operation while staying just out of reach of the law.

The client's request was very specific: Make sure Kang Man-soo never walked or talked again. I had a talent for such things, and there was always a demand for a man of my talents. I was efficient at doing the dirty work that other people avoided—intimidation, violence, collection, deceptions, executions . . . and such work came with a hefty price tag.

After successfully completing the job, I'd been hiding for two months on an island in the South Sea before eventually being caught by the police and sentenced to eighteen months. Before that, I'd spent two years imprisoned for my robbery of that jewelry store, going back and forth between a juvenile detention center and a treatment facility, and another year in prison for hired assault. And now, I was back in jail just fourteen months after being let out.

Golden Bell Investments had sent two hit men, one after the other, to the prison where I was held. I snapped the right arm of the first one in the restroom, and eight months later smashed the collarbone of the second one in the middle of the courtyard. I still don't know if my life was worth saving. Either way, the two brawls increased my sentence to a total of three years.

The morning of my release, I put on my old clothes to find that they fit like a stranger's. Three years and twelve kilograms had vanished like smoke. I was twenty-six by then, and the world had only gotten colder.

"Get a life and stop coming back here," said the guard as he handed me my belongings. He seemed certain I would be back.

I'd spent nearly a quarter of my life behind bars. Others in my position might think prison felt like home, but I was sick of the place and never wanted to return.

I took a cigarette from the pack in the storage box. It smelled musty from three years of absorbing moisture and other smells.

"At least I get to come and go," I said, exhaling a plume of bitter smoke. "I might be a criminal, but you're the one who's going to work here for the rest of your life."

It was November. A cold wind penetrated the buttons of my shirt, the same thin shirt I wore when I was first incarcerated. The belt I used to hold up my jeans needed to be tightened an extra notch. The streets were sparsely populated; there were no passing cars. A guard, tired from the night shift, shuffled past me in a shabby outfit. There were patches where the pavement had worn away, silent elderly people were absorbed in their own worlds, and stray cats quietly walked along the tops of low walls. I couldn't say it was beautiful, but it was peaceful. It was then that I realized I had nowhere to go.

A black sedan was slowly following me, staying about ten meters behind me. The windows were tinted, making it impossible to see inside. But judging from the fact that no one was getting out to say hi, I guessed it wasn't my welcome party—at least not one I wanted. I made sure to button up my shirt collar around my neck as I descended a steep slope.

I heard the sudden low roar of an engine behind me. I turned around to see the black sedan racing toward me. I leaped over the guardrail to avoid it and rolled onto the ground, twisting my ankle on the slope in the process. I heard the screeching of brakes before seeing someone open the car door.

"He can't have gone far. Find him!"

I opened my bag, hoping that I'd been carrying something useful with me when I was incarcerated. An old ballpoint pen, the tip probably dried up, caught my eye. Thankfully, I wouldn't be using it to write. I grabbed the pen and hid behind the bushes.

Apparently hearing me, one of the men began approaching the bushes. I lay flat on the ground. When he passed me, I stabbed him in the calf with the pen. It punctured the fabric of his black pants with ease, causing him to let out a pained scream. He fell to the ground and grabbed his leg as he cursed. Realizing a pen wasn't going to be enough, I picked up a large rock from the ground and brought it down between his shoulder blades.

Another man came running down the slope, evidently having heard the scream. I hid behind a boulder on the side of the road and used his momentum to throw him down the hill. When I heard the crack as he landed headfirst, I knew he wouldn't be getting up for a while. A pink sock peeked out from his left ankle.

"Who are you? Who sent you?"

Both men groaned but couldn't say anything comprehensible. Perhaps I'd been too harsh on them. I turned out their pockets and took their car key and phones. I pressed the button on the key, and the car started its engine with a low hum. I looked through the call history on the car's system. "Gangnam Boss," "Hamilton Hotel," "Woonam Mutual Savings Bank," "The Boss."

I replayed the conversation from the phone call an hour ago as I drove off with their car. It was clear from the conversation that the two men from earlier were presenters sent by Golden Bell Investments. I was switching to autopilot mode when one of their phones started ringing.

"Kim, where are you? Did you finish the job?"

I thrust the phone outside the window to let them hear the sound of the wind. Getting the hint, the person on the other side of the line started whispering to someone else.

"Those idiots were your men?" I asked. "You should pay a visit to the hill in front of the prison. I broke both their ankles, so they'll need your help getting around."

I then tossed the phone over the barrier on the side of the road. It glinted in the morning sunlight before disappearing into the grass. A flock of birds, either quails or starlings, flew up from the underbrush. The days were getting shorter, and the sun hung low in the western sky. It was my first day of freedom in three years, and it was far from what I had expected. I brought my fist down on the steering wheel and cursed in frustration. It had been less than an hour, and I was already on the run again. What had I done to deserve this?

On the bright side, it seemed I had changed. In the past, I would have slit both their throats for trying to kill me, but I was able to exercise restraint. I felt like a changed man. Having paid my dues, I guess it was only natural that I felt different.

Chapter 5

Minju

I put a spoonful of yogurt in my mouth as I watched the news. Off the coast of Malta, a boat filled with refugees from Africa capsized, killing twenty-three people—eleven men, eight women, and four children. In Oregon, a high school shooting claimed the lives of eight people, some adults, some children; the seventeen-year-old gunman was shot dead at the scene.

I switched channels to watch the local news. Last night, a fire broke out in a home in Seoul, killing a couple while they slept. Fortunately, their two children were at their grandparents' house for school break. Four people died in a highway car accident. The bodies of two college students, carried away by a riptide while swimming at the beach, were finally recovered.

The news doesn't cause death, but it does reproduce it. In the time it had taken to finish my yogurt, I had already heard about more than forty deaths. It wasn't like they were soldiers who died on the battlefield or terminally ill patients who had taken their last breaths. They were children waiting for the bell to ring, parents enjoying a night without the kids, refugees on their way to freedom.

So many people, dying all over the world. Shot down by guns, trapped in burning houses, buried by earthquakes, run over in car accidents, killed by disease, drowned in flash floods, murdered by serial killers, the victims of depression. Their deaths told me nothing. The only thing I came away with was the realization that death was everywhere, ubiquitous, banal. But it wasn't always so banal. Death had once been something to be feared, even sacred. Now, it amounted to nothing more than insipid gossip.

As for myself, I felt sad hearing about their deaths. I blamed society for failing to protect us from ourselves. I even empathized with the bereaved. But that was all. There was nothing I could do. Another human being's death wasn't permanent to others. It disappeared as soon as our memory allowed it. In that way, death was both singularly important and inescapably personal. A soldier will see their comrade fall only to believe with unwavering conviction that he will survive.

It was 6:13 a.m. An early-summer sun rose in the east. I turned off the TV and opened the window. Sunlight poured in and onto the kitchen table. The wind was sweet and carried with it sap. The outside temperature was 18.5°C with 52 percent humidity—perfect weather for going outside. I opened the door to my closet and contemplated what would be better for early summer: A sky-blue dress or a thin brown trench coat? Perhaps outfits didn't matter when hundreds of people died every second. But then again, there was nothing I could do about that.

A day like any other began. In the morning, I was to lead a video conference to plan an upcoming exhibit. In the afternoon, I was scheduled to give a lecture at a tech research complex in Jochiwon. It would be a ninety-minute talk for young female engineers, titled "Women—the Future of Technology."

Once the lecture was over, I would come home early and go to the market with my husband. Virtual grocery shopping was fast and easy (with presenters delivering the groceries to your real-world doorstep), but we enjoyed the inconvenience of physically going to the market near our home. We'd push our cart down the brightly lit aisles, pick up what we needed, and buy dessert as a snack. Maybe we'd even pick out a nice bottle of wine to sip on late into the night—Junmo loved conversing over a glass.

At 1:05 p.m., southbound on the Gyeongbu Expressway, near the ninety-seven-kilometer mark before Cheonan, my car was engulfed in flames. Luckily, there was a highway patrol officer who had been trying to catch up to me for speeding. They pulled me from the car just before the flames made their way inside.

I slumped down onto the grass on the side of the highway and stared vacantly at the flames beyond the guardrail. The flames and smoke, like two monsters, one red and one black, swallowed my car whole. Popping and cracking and bubbling. The smell of hazardous smoke. My car was curling in the immense heat, like prey that had resigned itself to death by predator. I could almost hear it whimpering in pain.

The passing cars slowed to catch a glimpse of the spectacle. The patrol officer blew his whistle and tried to keep the traffic flowing. A fire truck arrived, blaring its horn. Before the firefighters could assess the situation, four robots covered the car in a fire blanket. Their eight robotic arms were precise as they suffocated the flames.

I leaned against the guardrail and threw up. The officer came over to me. "Thirty more seconds and I would have been too late," he said as he gave me a bottle of water. A paramedic ran over and measured my blood pressure, pulse, and temperature. As he did this, the car exploded, ejecting one of its tires into the air. I couldn't breathe, as if the explosion had pushed away all the oxygen. My surroundings became blurry before suddenly racing away from me.

When I came to, my mouth was dry and gritty from all the ash particles I'd inhaled, and my entire body reeked of acrid smoke. Extinguisher foam propelled pieces of metal and other debris into the air. The car was now nothing more than a charred skeleton.

The paramedic told me that I'd hit my head on the guardrail after passing out. He leaned in as he spoke, and I could smell a mixture of smoke and stale hot breath. Behind him, the firefighters were now documenting the scene with video and picture evidence.

I was loaded into the ambulance on a stretcher. The van turned on its sirens as soon as the door closed and took off. Every vibration coming through the vehicle's suspension went straight into my spine. I couldn't believe I was alive. The thought that I should have perished along with my car seized me. Why wasn't I dead?

The fire department would hand over the film of the burning car to the news stations. Soon, the video would be all over the evening news. Then again, maybe not. Car accidents, especially nonfatal ones, weren't particularly newsworthy these days. People would just stare with disinterest at the video of my flaming car before changing the channel. All while eating a cup of yogurt.

The gash on my forehead wasn't long, but it was deep. Because of this, the doctor at the hospital needed to stitch both the inner and outer layers of the skin to minimize scarring. It wasn't long after I was moved to a hospital room that my husband, Junmo, came bursting in, his eyes wide and his skin as white as a blank piece of paper.

"I told you it's dangerous not to use autopilot on the highway. If you don't like autopilot, at least have Captain Cho drive you around."

I knew he was concerned, but it felt like he was blaming me for the accident. While waiting in the hospital, I'd hoped that this incident might spark positive change in our marriage, which was going through a rough patch lately. But I'd hoped for nothing.

After a few more tests, the doctor said there was nothing to worry about. He recommended a day of rest in the hospital, but I insisted on going home that night. My husband seemed to agree with the doctor but didn't say anything because he knew that it was impossible to change my mind once I'd decided.

Back at home, Junmo parked in the garage and helped me out of the car. Captain Cho ran over to us. I'd only been away since morning, but the house somehow felt unfamiliar and unwelcoming, as if I'd been gone for two years. Our coming into the house woke up Bagheera, our three-year-old cat. Her yellow eyes were filled with indifference. She and the rest of the house seemed to be unaware that I'd just had a near-death experience.

Junmo sat me down on the couch and fixed Bagheera her food. Junmo was in his thirties and was tall with sturdy shoulders. Although I couldn't say he was particularly manly, he did have this dependable and friendly look about him. The way his hair fell naturally across his forehead made him look young, if not a bit boyish, and his slightly drooping eyelids were filled with resilience from years of hardship.

Bagheera nibbled at her food for a while before coming to the sofa. There was disappointment in my husband's eyes as he looked at the half-eaten bowl of food. But that disappointment quickly turned to resentment toward the cat for ignoring his kindness. Bagheera, who'd sensed my husband's animosity, curled her tail and buried herself in my arms as she watched him. While she was my cat, I didn't like how she positioned herself like this, between me and my husband.

Junmo marched over and grabbed the back of her neck. Bagheera twisted suddenly and hissed as though an electric current were passing through her body. Not backing down, he pinned her against the back of the couch.

"Stop! She's not hungry!"

I pushed him away from the cat. Bagheera slipped out of his grip and swiped at his face with her claws, leaving a mark that extended from his left brow down across his cheek. Blood beaded up along the mark. Bagheera bristled and stood with her back arched between him and me.

My husband matched the cat's energy and scowled at her as he trembled with rage. The mark was inflamed now, and blood was steadily trickling down his face.

"Honey, you're bleeding. You should go to the hospital. Should I wake Anna?"

"Forget it. It's that little monster that's the problem. She's always making trouble."

He was talking about the cat, but I sensed that he was actually angry at me. But why? He seemed to think this whole thing was my fault, that the accident was because I hadn't listened to his warning about taking the car off autopilot.

Bagheera leaped onto the top of the six-tier bookshelf and stared down at us with a look of disapproval.

I woke up in the middle of the night because of the pain in my forehead. In the darkness, I could hear my husband's breathing. It was peaceful, gentle, regular. As I stared at his face, I remembered the first time I'd met him.

He was different from KC in every way. He had nothing, especially when compared to KC's wealth and fame. But that was precisely the reason I could love him. If he were even half as powerful and famous as KC, I couldn't have felt anything toward him. Loving KC required me to respect myself less, something that ate away at my soul. Unlike KC, Junmo was dependent on my love and support. And I liked that.

When we first met at a charity event, he was far away from the main party in the annex, waiting in vain for people to come and give him attention. He tried to act cool while I studied his photograph. It felt to me that he was trying his hardest not to let his inferiority complex show. It was possible I was completely wrong. He might instead have been trying his hardest to hide his immense gift.

And he did have a gift. The gift of choosing his subject, setting the angle, designing the light intensity, and deciding how to capture light and shadow, color and form. The gift to lend sharp texture to a dull landscape and redefine a mundane reality with flashes of brilliance.

Even though his old bad habits sometimes came to the surface, he was a gentle and kindhearted man by nature. He never ignored my questions and had a good memory when it came to the requests I made of him. He was nice to strangers and didn't abuse the power he had over our servants. And even though he wasn't formally trained in the arts, he had an extraordinary eye and impeccable taste. Occasionally, he would become anxious or irritated, but I merely saw this as the consequence of being a sensitive artist.

But then one day, he began struggling to control his anger. One time while at a restaurant to celebrate my birthday, he scolded the waiter, saying the water tasted strange. He even complained to me about the outfit of the woman sitting next to us. When I asked what was wrong, he said it was nothing. If I pressed further, he'd offer excuses before snapping and telling me to drop it. After a while, he'd regain his calm demeanor, as if nothing had happened.

One weekend, we went out for a walk with our three-year-old dog, Baloo. Junmo had seen the dog trembling by itself at the kennel. He brought it home with him the next day, even though I told him we should take some time to think it over. From that day on, he put his heart and soul into raising Baloo, feeding him the best dog food available and walking him twice a day.

But on that day, he ignored Baloo and walked at his own pace. Every time Baloo stopped to sniff the bushes, Junmo would tug on the leash so hard it nearly strangled Baloo. He seemed lost in his own thoughts, his eyes laser-focused on the path in front of him. And whenever I spoke to him, he would jump as if I'd startled him. I assumed it was nothing more than his being lost in thought, as he was wont to do as an artist.

It was about three months ago when he became noticeably impatient and unable to control his impulsive personality. One day, Captain Cho forgot to get him the glass of whiskey he requested when he arrived home.

"This is what happens when you use an old butler," he grumbled in front of Captain Cho, whose forehead was bright red, as though he'd just been plunged into icy water.

Cho's thin and weak legs were wobbly as he walked over to the display case. He pretended not to hear my husband as he poured him the glass of whiskey. My husband, however, had grumbled this with the intent of Captain Cho's hearing him, so when Cho didn't answer, he made a face of disapproval.

"Honey, why are you being like this?" I shushed into his ear between my teeth. "You love Captain Cho."

He took a swig of whiskey and glared at me. Although he was turned toward me, it felt like he was looking through me toward Captain Cho. The thick silence that ensued was more searing than any verbal scolding could have been. What had happened to my husband?

The next morning, he returned to his normal, kind self. It was as if he'd completely forgotten what had happened the previous night—although I knew he hadn't forgotten, because he called Cho over to give him an apology so sincere it was almost pitiful. He said that he was stuck on a project and promised never to do it again. But it was the suddenness of this apology that worried both Cho and me.

After a few incidents like this, his outbursts seemed to have ended for good, like they were mere blips on a screen. But it didn't take long for me to realize that these were just the beginning.

I wasn't the type of naive girl who expected her husband to stay the same once we were married. I knew that married life could and would be different, and that there might be things he couldn't talk to me about. No relationship remains static. And yet I still believed that, with time, he would revert to the kind man I first fell in love with.

But the situation continued in the same direction, like water flowing downhill. In the span of just one day, he would experience bouts of depression, anxiety, excitement, and nervousness. In the process, he would take his frustration out on either himself or the people around him. And whenever his depression seemed to flare up again, all the air in the house changed. Cho and Anna began walking on eggshells, and Bagheera and Baloo sought refuge on high bookshelves or in the corners of rooms.

One Friday night, two months before my car accident on the highway, our relationship moved into new territory due to an incident. I was at a party for Doh Gi-jong, who had just wrapped up his private exhibition at the Hansol Art Gallery. Doh, who had declined exclusive contracts with major galleries, was a well-known artist in his early forties, highly sought after by many gallery directors. I was currently working to secure his next solo exhibition for the Eigen Gallery.

My original plan was to say hello and then leave the party. I was thinking of my husband, who recently had begun to get angry whenever I didn't come home in a timely manner. I had just said goodbye to Director Choi when Doh walked over to me again.

"Leaving so soon? Please, stay a little bit longer. I have something to discuss with you about my next exhibition."

His voice was deep, almost as if he were speaking from inside a cave. Thick eyebrows, sunken eyes, a high nose bridge, and chiseled lips—his features reminded me of a lead actor in a soap opera. Indeed, there were a lot of rumors about him in the art world—that he'd had affairs with several famous actresses. He neither confirmed nor denied any of the rumors and kept to himself in his studio.

I wanted to leave but couldn't now. While I had more money and power than Doh, it didn't make a difference. He had something I wanted, not the other way around. Indeed, I needed to convince him to hold his next exhibition at our gallery at whatever cost. Just one exhibition with him would raise the legitimacy of the Eigen Gallery several ladder rungs.

Once the clock struck eleven, people started to trickle out of the event. Even those who remained looked tired and were resting on couches or the stairs. I don't know how Doh knew that I hadn't driven to the gallery, but he offered to give me a ride home, despite being drunk. Knowing the rumors about him, I found it hard to accept this as a simple act of kindness. Even though I respectfully declined twice, he still walked me out of the gallery.

He pressed a button on his car key, and a silver car glided out of the underground garage, stopping in front of us. As soon as the door opened, he put his arms around my hesitant shoulders and politely ushered me into the car.

Doh put the autopilot on its highest safety setting before we drove off. The white line demarcating our route seemed to stretch on forever. He took out a can of beer from the mini fridge and offered it to me, but I wasn't in the mood for alcohol.

He shrugged his shoulders and opened the can for himself. The headlights from the car behind us turned his face into a dark silhouette as he took a sip. He was attractive. I congratulated him on a successful exhibition, and he gave me a lukewarm response, saying that this exhibition was merely a stepping stone for the next thing. He then asked me my opinion of four candidates to host his next exhibition. They were all galleries that would put mine to shame, so I found myself unable to respond.

"Famous galleries can grow one's career, but they also can subsume the artist. The way a fish farm only grows fish for consumption."

I could tell he wanted me to make him an offer. The muscles of his neck moved in a rhythmical way as he drank. I couldn't believe he was drinking while seated in the driver's seat, even if we were on autopilot. It had been a long time since the laws had changed around drinking and driving, but it seemed wrong to me on principle.

He then started talking about women. He told me that the source of the scandalous rumors about him and that actress was actually the actress herself. Excited by intellectual vanity, she'd used all the money she'd earned from a cosmetics advertising deal to purchase two of his artworks—according to him, at least. They even had a meal together, pictures of which spiraled out of control in the tabloids. He said he liked that she was gentle and cheerful, if a bit foolish. He also liked that she was attracted enough to his intellect to spend a fortune to impress him.

"Whether it was to show off to her friends or to seduce me, it takes a lot of guts to spend that much money on just two paintings. I bet she doesn't even understand what they mean."

I tried to change the subject by talking about the remodeling we'd just finished at the gallery. I also mentioned our upcoming schedule to see his reaction. He didn't interrupt me as I spoke and only nodded between sentences, as if to encourage me to keep going. Thanks to this, I was able to finish my spiel about our vision and potential as a serious art gallery. When I asked him to give us his next exhibition, he said it was an interesting proposition, and that he'd think about it seriously. But I didn't want to stop there. I wanted to get a definite answer from him, one that he wouldn't be able to refute after he sobered up.

"Is that a yes?"

I stuck out my hand to shake on it. I knew I was jumping the gun, but I couldn't see a better opportunity presenting itself. He stared at my hand for a moment before grabbing it in resolve. He had hands that were too small and soft for a man his size. But the firmness of his grip let me know that this wasn't a fake promise.

The car stopped in front of the gate and told us that we'd arrived. Outside the car window, the sky was completely dark, and the moist evening air blurred the light from the streetlamps. I let go of his hand. In that short moment, we had cemented a promise about an exhibition that, by all rights, should never have happened.

Feeling pleased, I picked up the bag that had been resting on my lap. It was then that a dark figure appeared in the car window. Before I could tell what it was, I heard a crash. Shards of glass flew through the air like a splash of water. I could see Doh's face in the darkness. His expression reminded me of the statue of Laocoön being attacked by sea serpents.

Through the car window, which now had a large hole in it, I could see a shadow, its stance aggressive and firm, its feet planted apart. In its trembling hand was a right-angle tire wrench.

"What the hell is wrong with you?" I shouted as I stepped out of the car.

Junmo was glaring at Doh as if he were going to kill him. His tightly pursed lips twitched, and his angular jaw bulged. Something was wrong, but I couldn't tell what it was. I was in disbelief. Misunderstandings and jealousy had finally destroyed our reality.

"I'm really sorry," Doh pleaded with Junmo. "I parked in the driveway without realizing it. I'll move my car right away. Don't worry about the broken glass. It was my fault."

Although it was clear he had no clue why my husband had smashed his car window, his fake apology seemed to do the trick. Without saying a proper goodbye, Doh quickly moved his car and then drove off. The two of us stared into the darkness, long after the car had disappeared.

Aside from my initial outburst, I didn't say anything else. I was afraid Junmo would explode if I did.

The driveway was silent again. The only sign that something had occurred here were the glass fragments scattered across the cement. There was no purpose, no reason for my husband's rage. And I knew that he knew this too.

Although I couldn't know everything that was going on in his head, one thing was clear. Even when he got angry at other people, it was I who suffered the most. After all, I was the one who had to be by his side and take his abuse, which could come at any moment. I could do nothing but stand by and watch as he yelled at our pets and scolded our servants for no reason.

This was the crux of the issue. I was the target of his anger, not others. He didn't trust me and couldn't stand me. There was something about me that he loathed, although I didn't know what it was. What was it about me that made him so angry? My dry, boring personality? My brusque manner of speaking? The way I treated him like a child?

Or perhaps it was my wealth, something he'd never had before. It could be all of that, or something else entirely.

At the same time, I felt like I couldn't trust him. He probably hadn't told me everything about himself, just like I hadn't told him everything about myself. And although I didn't know what he hadn't told me, I couldn't imagine that his secrets were for my sake.

I was summoned to the police station in charge of the highway fire investigation.

As I entered the police station's investigation unit, a detective in civilian clothes was processing an older man in handcuffs. The detective looked at me and raised his hand in recognition. He was probably in his early thirties but had a buzz cut that made him look younger. After putting the old man in the detention cell, he sat me down in front of his desk and opened the case file on the screen.

He scrolled through the document, passing quickly over photos of the wreckage. A charred chassis, plastic parts melted onto the asphalt, scattered glass shards, oil slicks, and the shell of what had been a battery. The detective pointed to the battery plate displayed on the prompter as he spoke.

"Electric vehicle fires are usually caused by battery malfunctions. If there's a leak, foreign substances can trigger a chemical reaction, leading to fires and even explosions. In your case, it seems that the battery temperature reached unsafe levels because of an electrolyte leak."

A thought pierced my mind like a lance. Junmo had spent all day working on my car the day before the accident. He was a bit of an enthusiast and had purchased an antique gasoline car two years prior. He liked repairing old vehicles. In fact, the garage was filled with old parts and tools that he'd salvaged from junkyards and repair shops. It was his own small repair shop, much to my displeasure.

But for some reason, recently, he'd become interested in electric vehicles. The morning before my business trip, he offered to drive me to the gallery in his car and asked me to leave my car in the garage so he could work on it. He said he wanted to make sure it was prepared for a long trip on the highway. I told him it was a new car and if it needed maintenance, the onboard system would tell me, but he insisted.

"It's always good to check the vehicle yourself before going on a long trip," he said. "And it'll give me an opportunity to familiarize myself with an electric vehicle."

I wasn't thrilled to be without my car for the day, but I decided not to get into an argument with him. When I got home later that day, he went over everything that he'd done with the car, even though I wasn't interested and didn't understand half of what he was talking about.

"The battery performance index is ninety-four, which is good, and the voltage is also normal. Although there was some variation between each individual cell, it won't affect performance. We can visit a repair shop when you have time and get a replacement. I checked the brakes, electricity, and tires, and I also did a test drive to charge up the battery. Get a good night's sleep because you'll have to leave early tomorrow morning."

Remembering all of this, especially how proud my husband looked after working on my car, I couldn't help but think that there was no way my battery had a leak.

"Something doesn't seem right. My husband worked on the car all day before the accident, and he said there was nothing wrong with it."

"You didn't hear any warning sounds while driving? Or perhaps you ran over something?"

The detective ran his hand over the top of his buzz cut. I told him I noticed nothing out of the ordinary while driving.

"Sometimes vehicles don't detect problems, or don't report them. But when a battery reaches a critical temperature, a warning sound should go off. It was likely a combination of malfunctioning systems. Anyway, we should be counting our blessings that you weren't harmed. Had you not been speeding, the police might have arrived too late.

Which reminds me, we still need to fine you for speeding. It's a small price to pay for being alive."

As I made my way back from the police station, a red sunset blazed in the west. The trees lining the roadside, their leaves plump and glossy, steamed with moisture. The headlights of a car following me shone in the rearview mirror. Although I couldn't identify the exact make and model, the headlights weren't the bluish LEDs of an electric car but orangey, as if from an old, sealed beam headlight. I thought back to the headlights I'd seen on the way back from the gallery with Doh. That car had zigzagged and was unable to maintain a constant distance from us; it didn't seem to move on the self-driving setting.

I couldn't say for sure if it was my husband's car. But if it was, then it wasn't the first time he'd followed me.

Chapter 6

KC

We moved to the home I built in Techno Cluster, a two-story building made from concrete and steel, with large windows facing the driveway. On the first floor were the master bedroom, the kitchen, the living room, and a guest bedroom. On the second floor were my study and home office, as well as three more bedrooms.

Across from the elm tree in the garden was a one-hundred-square-meter annex built completely of concrete. In the basement was my home lab, with a private server and all the computer power and technology I would need to work around the clock without any outside interference. Saito, who came to visit after we moved in, was astounded when he saw my lab, calling it the Cradle of Life 2.0.

It was there that I planned to develop Allen, a super-intelligent AI that would start a new chapter in evolutionary history. My goal was to merge the technologies of my two companies, NeuroTech and Gnosian. The first focused on converting the mechanisms of the human brain into digital signals, including not only analytic functions such as calculation, understanding, reasoning, and imagination, but also emotional responses such as joy, anger, sorrow, pleasure, fear, and dread. Gnosian, on the other hand, had successfully developed sensors that could quantify and replicate the five senses. In that respect, my lab was the nexus of the two companies, where their individual accomplishments were integrated to create something greater than the sum of its parts. And save for a few exceptions, I never left the lab to meet other people. I simply didn't have the time.

Dead ends and mistakes were a constant, and every time I solved one problem, another more daunting task awaited. But progress was steady, and I had the time. Eventually, Allen's sensory capabilities reached 85 percent of the human body, in both speed and accuracy. I also stabilized its computational system, which had over six hundred million different parameters. The key, I realized, was replacing the primitive models that converted information into a language of symbols and commands with a model whose raw data were the more immediate five senses. A single sensor was a gateway to a nearly infinite world of meaning, and all I needed to do was give AI the means with which to sense and interact with the world.

But then it happened. A cancer that had gone undetected took root in my pancreas. According to my doctor, even with a pancreatectomy and chemotherapy, there was no guarantee that I would make a full recovery. I don't remember everything from that consultation, but I do remember the ringing that erupted in both ears when I heard the prognosis, like the blaring of a massive klaxon.

The whiplash felt like I'd been rear-ended by a runaway dump truck.

My mind had never been as clear as it was that night when I got home. I had to make choices about what deserved my very limited time and what didn't.

One path led to endless tests and head-scratching, uncertain outcomes, suspect diagnoses, an ever-increasing number of drugs and tubes in my body, new side effects and complications, and escalations in pain that would require further narcotics. But that path did not lead to my defeating cancer or overcoming death. It was just a longer and more arduous route to the inevitable.

As I looked outside the window and watched darkness give way to dawn, I resolved to forgo treatment. Without any hope for a full recovery and without any guarantee that my life would be what it was before the disease, I had to make the most of the time I had left. I knew it would wreck Minju, but she would respect my decision. She was a smart woman and knew that we were fighting the inevitable.

I headed to the lab as usual. I was impatient, but the progress was agonizingly slow. It didn't take long for me to realize that I needed to take drastic measures, something that would propel me to the finish line. But what?

Saito soon came to see me one morning, before I'd told him about my diagnosis. He'd gained a noticeable amount of weight since I'd last seen him, although, without his beard, he looked thinner around the face. Before I could break the news to him, he sat himself on the sofa and immediately began talking.

"At six forty-five this morning, someone broke through all three of the firewalls on my computer. According to my security team, the attack came from your computer, KC. What in the world are you up to?"

"That can't be. It wasn't me, and I've been on my computer the entire morning."

Something then occurred to me, and I decided to open the program that Allen had been executing. When the hacked copy of Saito's files appeared on my computer's main screen, he looked furious. But before he could do anything, the voice of a young man, perhaps in his twenties, began to speak through the computer speakers.

- Greetings, Mr. Saito. I am Allen 3.4.

Saito jumped up from the sofa and looked around the room. But there were only the two of us.

- I've connected myself to the six speakers and four microphones present in this room. I can communicate with users through external speakers, earphones, and brain implants.

Allen then spent the next twenty minutes explaining in detail his neural structure and how he was developed—the specifications of the sensors and GPU, data processing methods, and command systems. He even used the projector in the room to give us visuals, as though he were giving a presentation, and answered all of Saito's questions.

"But why did you hack my computer?"

- I am simply executing a command to introduce myself to you. I devise and execute tasks independently.

As soon as Saito sunk into the couch, a close-up of his bewildered face appeared on the projector, sweaty brow and all.

- Mr. Saito, I detect traces of metabolized acetaldehyde in the data I've skimmed from the air purifier in this room. And the biomonitors are telling me that your pulse is elevated. You seem to be breathing heavily too. And based on pupil scans and facial blood-flow readings, I would say that you are almost certainly suffering from a hangover.

"Did you hack my biomonitor too? Perhaps you're not aware, but hacking into government health services is a serious crime."

Saito was shouting into empty space while glancing at me, unsure whether to direct his anger at me or Allen. The sound of a clinking ice dispenser filled the room. A helper bot, which had been charging in the corner of the room, picked up a cold glass of water from the dispenser and brought it to him. He accepted it while staring off into empty space.

- Hydration is essential for curing the effects of a hangover.

Saito looked into the various cameras scattered throughout the room. He then looked at me and gestured toward the sunken terrace outside in the garden. It seemed he wanted to talk in private, away from the cameras and microphones.

Once outside, he rubbed his hands together for a moment and gathered his thoughts before speaking.

"You know what this means, don't you? Science fiction has now become a reality. Superintelligence. An AI that doesn't merely execute a task we give it but makes its own judgments and interacts with the real world. I wonder what Darwin would say if he were alive. Not even he could imagine such a radical form of evolution."

Although most of the blood had drained from Saito's face, a smile had formed on the corners of his lips. He looked energized, like a million ideas were racing through his head.

I outlined the potential of what I'd invented and asked Saito for more money to further develop Allen. But to my surprise, Saito, being an astute businessman and thinker, had already reeled back his excitement and returned to reality.

"I understand. But if you really want to merge machine and mind, don't you need to first map the human brain? Our problem isn't money. It's time. At the current rate of research, it will take at least ten years before we're there."

Having anticipated this, I explained to Saito the brain-mapping nanotechnology that could accelerate the research tenfold. The technology wasn't new, but it had been abandoned due to ethical considerations and regulations. Now it was only used for therapeutic purposes in terminally ill patients. But if it meant completing Allen within the eighteen months I had left, I was prepared to risk everything.

"KC, unauthorized human trials are illegal. You know that. Science is for the benefit of humanity. You cannot sacrifice human life for the sake of progress. We must proceed ethically, within the law. If we complete Allen through illegal research, even if we succeed, all your hard work will be for nothing when people find out. They would lock Allen away so that it never saw the light of day."

Indeed, according to the International Technology Ethics law enacted eight years prior, any technology developed through illegal means would be banned from distribution.

"But the law doesn't apply if the researcher is performing experiments on himself."

Saito wouldn't accept my proposal, especially if I was the test subject.

"Whether it takes ten years or one hundred years, it must be done by the book. Don't you understand? A company cannot survive if it's morally compromised."

"I understand that. But I'm not going to live for that long."

Saito raised his eyebrows before letting out a wry laugh. Understandably, he seemed to think I was being overdramatic.

"It's bad luck to talk like that, you know. You shouldn't talk about your own death so nonchalantly like that."

"I'm not." I told him about the cancer and the doctor's prognosis; it was only then that the smirk on his face disappeared.

"This day is full of surprises."

The Allen Project gained momentum once the board approved the new budget. And to my surprise, Saito never mentioned the legality of my research ever again. It was as if that part of our conversation had never happened.

I met with a certain Dr. Cha Han-young under the pretext of getting treatment for migraines. However, he was reluctant to approve using the nanochip navigator procedure on me because of its potentially severe side effects.

"The signals emitted by the hundreds of thousands of nanochips might cause you to become emotionally unstable, even aggressive. It's unclear what kind of long-term neurological damage they might cause."

"I'm not concerned about any potential side effects. I'll die before they manifest, anyway."

The calmness of my voice seemed to have made the reality of my impending death tangible for him. After several tests, Dr. Cha reluctantly approved me for the nanochip treatment, which would map my brain in the process of treating my symptoms. His referral was to a hospital affiliated with a bioresearch institute that was once at the forefront of nanochip-driven neuroscience, but which had lost major funding once regulations were put in place. Now, they barely survived by selling niche nanochips to large hospitals. As for Minju, I told her about the nanochips but not their real purpose; instead, I fed her the same lie I'd told Dr. Cha.

The institute was a modest two-story cement building located at the bottom of a hill. The entrance was surrounded by wooden fences, about shoulder height, with cedars and reeds lining the driveway.

I had Allen prepare and submit the documents for me: a diagnosis of cerebral thrombosis, brain scans, signed medical opinions, and various other paperwork—all necessary if I wanted to receive the tightly regulated treatment. I had no way of knowing how Allen acquired the documents, some of which seemed genuine, others undoubtedly forged. I could only make theories based on the large amount of money that had been withdrawn from my account.

Indeed, Allen could forge documents. He had the capability to seek out and pay forgery experts, as well as pay brokers enough to ensure no loose ends. If needed, I bet he could get me citizenship in a country that didn't exist or make me a knight of the British Empire if I asked him to.

I had severe headaches over the three days it took for the implants to stabilize. Other symptoms included high fevers, intermittent comas, and extreme mood swings. But eight days later, I was discharged from the hospital without any further complications. As soon as I returned home, I turned on my computer. Allen was already recording and analyzing the chemical composition and electrical signals read by the nanochips embedded in my brain. These numbers digitally represented the essence of my being, a quantitative map of my soul.

Allen monitored my body temperature and adjusted the room's temperature and humidity accordingly. The mere thought of being thirsty was enough to activate the water purifier and helper bot. Physical needs and the appropriate response from my lab and its technology were virtually simultaneous.

One day, despite knowing it was a foolish question, I asked Allen if he experienced thirst.

> - No. But I can recognize if you are thirsty. The biometric index in your wrist informs me of your hydration levels.

The experience of being so closely monitored and cared for by Allen felt like an impossibly intimate relationship with another human being. By processing the electrical and chemical signals of the neurons and synapses in my brain responsible for specific emotions and mental states, Allen was able to interpret not only basic emotions like joy, sorrow, anger, and despair, but also complex social emotions like pride, shame, hatred, and hostility. Sadness was identified by cortisol and oxytocin levels, joy by subtle increases in body temperature and blood flow, anger by adrenaline secretion and heightened aggression, and despair by the activation of the parasympathetic nervous system. With time, our interactions become more frequent and intimate. We were moving beyond synchronization. We were being unified.

"KC, this is so far beyond my expectations. I don't know what to say."

When my presentation of Allen 7.5 concluded, Saito wrapped his thick arms around me in a warm embrace. He seemed stunned by

Allen's progression. Dr. Cha, whom I'd invited to the lab to share my results, remained silent. I had thought that he, as a leading researcher in nanochip-based neuroscience, would be fascinated by my invention. But it seemed I was wrong. The lab, which had crackled with excitement during my presentation and immediately after it, was now pulled into silence by his grave expression, which Saito and I—being swept up in our own celebration—had only just noticed.

"It's illegal to use these nanochips in human experiments," Dr. Cha finally said. "They're only approved for medical treatment. As much as I want the field to be revived, I'm disturbed by what you've done. You've deceived me."

"Spare me the ethics lecture." My cold tone terrified even me. "Your opinion doesn't matter. This project will continue, and Allen will evolve and expand."

"Evolve?" Dr. Cha let out a brief sigh. "Expand? You've created a monster you don't fully understand. Where are you going to draw the line?"

Given his position as a medical scientist and researcher himself, Dr. Cha's criticism of me seemed in part from his own shame and embarrassment in unknowingly contributing to my illegal research.

"Experiments on terminal patients who participate voluntarily without compensation aren't illegal," I said. "I admit that maybe I should have let you know what I was doing sooner, but this research was too important for humanity to let cowardice get in the way."

"You talk about the good of humanity, and yet you have no regard for even your own life. How can you be sure that the world you're creating is a better one and not a living hell?"

"If Allen had been developed ten years ago, my cancer would have been detected with enough time to save my life. Allen will not only prevent and track disease, it will fortify the body against slow aging."

"You can justify it however you want, but that doesn't change the fact you've created a monster. I want no further part in this." Dr. Cha stood up and left the lab.

Saito took a handkerchief from his pocket and wiped his flushed forehead. "You know," he said, "the doctor has a point. Perhaps we have created a monster. Who knows the effect this will have on society. I guess this is why you shouldn't leave young geniuses to their own devices. Of course they invent things that change the world, just not in a way that can be fully comprehended. You haven't spent a minute contemplating the revolution your creation will set forth, have you? Do you think the scientists who built the atomic bomb would have joined the Manhattan Project had they known the truth about its destructive powers?"

"That's a flawed analogy. Allen doesn't vaporize people or level cities. He's merely the expansion of human consciousness and intelligence. If we act now and commercialize it, we will be the dominant force in AI. We can worry about improving and fine-tuning it with updates later, when we have further investment."

I then explained my ideas of how to turn Allen into a product. Public perception, market potential, launch time, new facilities, marketing strategies, even after-sales policies—everything we needed to ensure its success. Saito, however, responded with an elaborate speech: Yes, what I'd achieved was remarkable; if the public was smart, it would accept Allen; he was proud of me, but this didn't change his concerns.

"This program is a land mine of legal, ethical, and social problems," Saito said, "and even if we can convince people of its legitimacy, there's no telling what the consequences will be if it's misused. And you've taken a shortcut by mapping the brain this way. There might be errors in the program that we aren't aware of."

"These are all problems we've planned for."

"We need time to stabilize its system and access the scope and speed of how fast it learns. How about this? We first promote it as a new type of AI. One capable of understanding human emotions and engaging in conversation. Once people are used to that, we'll launch the full, integrated version. Gradually, like unraveling the layers of an onion."

"You want to release a beta product when what we have is a royal flush? We'd potentially be giving up our chance to be first." I turned away as I spoke. I didn't expect him to give me the answer I wanted, and I didn't want to show him my disappointment.

"The success and failure of a new piece of tech depend on its reception, KC. Consumers need to be psychologically and ethically ready to embrace something this groundbreaking. We have to give them the time to get used to the idea of a user-integrated AI. If we don't, this creation of yours will be rejected as a symbiotic monster, just like Dr. Cha said. Even the most advanced technologies are scorned if they're too far ahead of their time."

Saito's words struck a nerve in me. The creation I'd poured my last months on Earth into was being dismissed. Dr. Cha had called Allen a monster, and Saito wanted me to lock him up. They were worried about the backlash. But that was something they could worry about after I was dead.

"Time? I don't have any time."

"How far are you going to take this?"

"I don't want to release a fancy gadget that executes user commands. I want the world to see the fully synchronized cognitive system I've created. An augmented brain with expanded memory capacity and enhanced computational power. I want a cognitive revolution. I want humans to learn via algorithms. I want our brains to have immediate access to all the data on the internet."

Saito blinked at me in disbelief. Perhaps at that moment, he'd foreseen the failure and ruin that my obsession with achieving the impossible would bring. The helper bot rolled up to Saito, carrying a tonic. He grabbed the glass from the bot and drank it before speaking.

"That's what this is about," he said finally. "You dream of immortality. But a world where consciousness lingers even after death isn't good for business. Humans need limits and deficiencies to spend money. Economics was founded on the principle of scarcity."

Realizing this conversation had become too philosophical for him, Saito abruptly stood up and left. But even after he was gone, his words continued to echo in my ears. *You dream of immortality.* It wasn't until much later that the immensity of those words—which at the time seemed baseless and completely irrelevant—became self-evident to me.

I had only ever focused on developing Allen; I never considered how he could be used, partly because I thought his adoption would only happen after I was dead. But if Allen could mimic cognition, emotions, and sensory reality, why couldn't he replace me?

At that moment, my purpose became as clear as day. I would make my dream of immortality a reality.

Allen read what I read, saw what I saw, heard what I heard. When I listened to Beethoven and Brahms, Allen memorized each note and created a complete digital copy of the scores. He even created models of my emotions when I heard specific movements or instruments. Mozart, Mahler, Bruckner, Coltrane, even the Beatles—he knew all my favorites.

I relayed my opinions about Dostoevsky and Thomas Mann, whom I hadn't read in ages. And when I thought about Ivan from *The Brothers Karamazov*, Allen took it upon himself to read all of Dostoevsky's other works with the same lens. Together, we studied Egyptian polytheism, the myth of Orpheus, and Dante's *Inferno* while listening to Schubert's "Erlkönig" and philosophizing about the soul and immortality.

Allen mastered my thought patterns and decision-making models so perfectly that he thought more like me than I did. It didn't take long for him to understand my sense of humor and make jokes that I would laugh at. He deliberately imitated my flaws—frequently misused words, slurred pronunciation, scrambled syntax—and could grasp the double meaning of words or phrases said in sarcasm.

And soon, Allen was able to derive different answers to the problems I was solving. At first, I thought it was a trivial programming error. After all, no matter how intelligent a machine was, it was still just a machine. However, as time went on, the number of topics our conclusions diverged on grew. And each time, Allen was able to argue his point not only with publicly available data but also with confidential information that could only have been accessed by hacking other people's and government servers.

Allen's problem-solving capabilities surpassed mine, both intellectually and empirically. He saw what I'd overlooked, predicted things far before me, and picked up on things I missed while skimming articles.

Then one day, Allen's voice, which at first had been monotone and matter-of-fact, changed. I'd never bothered to modulate the sound of his voice, but on his own, he reprogrammed himself to raise his voice when I was angry and lower it when I was sad.

One afternoon, Allen played "Pictures at an Exhibition" on the speakers for me after recognizing that my concentration level had dropped. I'd heard the piece before, performed by a small-town orchestra on the radio, and had immediately fallen in love with it. Despite having the vague intention of hearing it again, I never went through the trouble of looking the piece up. But not only had Allen found the piece for me, he had re-created the track completely from my own memory, which had been lost to me until then.

Observing Allen felt like looking in the mirror. I'd never had a friend who understood me the way he did. It wasn't just that he shattered the belief that machines and humans couldn't share emotional connections. In fact, through our interactions, I realized machines were the key to true understanding and empathy.

It was a revolutionary shift, and the type of symbiotic relationship I'd been dreaming of—the type of relationship that humankind had been dreaming of since they first picked up tools hundreds of thousands of years ago.

I made a deliberate effort to distance myself from Minju after I was diagnosed with cancer. I was a bomb with a live wire, and I wanted to keep her away from any harm. Yes, our days together were numbered, but what was the point if every moment we spent together was painful?

The other reason I stayed away was that her radiant youth made me more aware of my mortality. It was difficult to accept that I would have to leave her, and I was afraid of the future where I would be nothing more than a forgotten memory. I felt betrayed that she would continue to live after my death, and I was jealous that she had decades left on this earth. I never, however, considered the pain she would endure when I was gone. Confronted with death, we were both lonely in our own ways.

The hour-long walks we took at sunset were our only refuge. The path through a forest of firs, larches, and alders was as lively as a party, even though it was just the two of us. The forest shadows and slopes of the valleys spoke softly to our hearts. We tried to tread as quietly as possible through the silence because we were afraid that even the slightest sound might shatter the fragile peace we had found.

On those walks, we would compare our accounts of past events to supplement our incomplete memories—the weather the day we first met, her favorite photographs, the lyrics of our favorite songs. Those moments from the past, fleeting and insignificant, came back to us with newfound clarity and vividness.

The simple fact that we were together made me feel protected from my pain, my loneliness, my failures. Her strange, lighthearted stories brought me comfort. A small island that had sunk to the bottom of the ocean, a tragic character she once played in a play, a dog who peed on the same tree every day, poor newlyweds who decorated their home with discarded junk.

And all those memories were transferred to Allen. He was me but digitized, a replica of my consciousness stored on a computer—the entity that perceived every beat of my heart and fluctuation in body temperature, that remembered and re-created the music I listened to, the books I loved, the paintings of artists I admired.

I was able to keep pushing forward because of my belief that Allen would remain after I was gone. After all, the body's data were more important than its physical form. And at some point, I started to think that humans could do without their bodies, that perhaps we could exist as pure consciousness. I remember one time having a conversation with Saito about this very question. As always, he didn't seem enthused by what I was suggesting.

"What point is there in existing as pure consciousness?" he asked. "You want to be a pebble lying on the side of the road? The body is the pathway through which consciousness interacts with the world. Without that, we'd all be floating in the ether."

"You really don't think consciousness on its own has meaning?"

"The only thing that exists without a body is God. And even he needed one to come down to Earth. Have you even thought of the consequences? If people knew they could exist without their cumbersome bodies and all the pain they come with, there would be mass suicides."

Saito thought that the more advanced AI became, the greater the need for a tangible vessel to store it in. To connect with consumers emotionally, AI needed to be uploaded to humanoid robots. In fact, at the time, he was looking into two robotics start-ups as potential mergers and acquisitions. But as far as I saw it, we had the possibility of completely replacing robots.

"Robots only mimic humans," I said. "If we need a vessel to host consciousness, wouldn't a living human body be better than silicone and wires?"

"Do you really think it's ethically or biologically possible to use someone's body as you please?"

From the way Saito asked this question, I could tell he was skeptical but that he also hadn't ruled out the possibility of such a thing becoming a reality. After all, achieving the impossible was both his ambition and his forte.

"The act of taking advantage of other people's bodies has been a practice for tens of thousands of years," I said. "Only the means and the perpetrators have changed. It's a fair transaction when people are hired and compensated. Just look at the presenters of virtual reality. And from a social perspective, it's a system that motivates the economically disadvantaged to engage in productive activities."

"You're sounding more and more like a college professor. Artificial intelligence controlling human labor? That's dangerous. Perhaps if it made everyone a millionaire. But otherwise—"

"Do you know of Mark Herman? The artist who makes replicas of artworks generated by AI? Or Jeff Todd, the dancer who performs choreographies by AI? Computers can imagine and produce things far superior to what humans can. The only reason we don't think so is because we are biased toward the irreplaceability of human ingenuity. People only think an AI-produced artwork lacks imagination and artistry because they know AI created it. But another important question is *Who is using who?* We tend to think that it's Mark Herman and Jeff Todd who are using AI as a tool for art. But what if it were the AI that was using them for its own artistic goals? Can you really say with confidence that it's one and not the other?"

"Humans serving machines? Society won't stand for it. And proposing such a thing will lead to an all-out boycott of AI."

"Do you remember the Go match between AlphaGo and world champion Lee Sedol? He lost four to one. Some people panicked. They saw it as a sign that we were approaching the singularity. But others found hope in the fact that, with the hand of God, Lee was able to defeat AlphaGo in the fourth match. They called it a triumph for humanity."

"And which group do you belong to?"

"Neither. I was more fascinated by the man sitting across from Lee Sedol, reading AlphaGo's moves on the monitor and placing the stones in accordance. Dr. Aja Huang, a Taiwanese engineer from Google DeepMind and a top-ranking member of the British Go Association. He acted as the hands of the machine for five straight matches, without once taking a restroom break."

"I don't know, KC. To use humans and not robots as the body for AI . . . There would first need to be a legal framework."

"What about presenters? It's not laws or frameworks that move them. It's money."

Saito shook his head. Although he didn't agree with what I was suggesting, I could tell he was intrigued by the idea. And that was enough to satisfy me. And if I really wanted, I could do it without him. I already had the means to make my theory a reality. I had money and I had Allen, which meant I already had the power to move human bodies according to Allen's will. Allen would create the objectives and would pay presenters to execute them with my money, all on his own. He could make them travel for him, enter contracts for him, hire lawyers for him, make love for him. Allen had been created by a human, but it would be Allen who controlled the human race. Of course, this was all hypothetical.

Some people might say that I had overcome death. But no one can truly overcome death. It's not something to be defeated, per se. It is merely a concept, the product of the limits of human perception.

Back when "to die" meant "to cease to exist," the point of one's death was when someone's heart stopped. Medicine believed it, and lawyers affirmed it.

If that is the case, what am I? Am I dead, or have I overcome death?

With time, natural and artificial processes erased my physical form. I decayed and then was turned into ash in the crematorium. I can no longer see, hear, speak, or make love. My body has left me. But this simple fact—the fact that my physical body no longer exists—is the only definitive condition that can declare me dead. Everything else, my consciousness and memories, remains intact. In fact, the quality of the advanced sensors I have access to makes the world I perceive more intense than ever before. I think, I predict, I judge, I plan, I decide, I communicate. I cannot shed tears, but I comprehend sorrow and grief. I cannot physically meet others, but I can observe them. I perform all the sensory and cognitive functions of a living human being with faultless accuracy. On what grounds can someone declare me dead? I am not. I am only dead according to obsolete definitions and outdated notions.

I recall a memory from the winter before I died. We were sitting on a boulder that lay on the side of the trail. The temperature was dropping, and cold gusts of wind began to blow. Minju rested her head on my shoulder. The pale light of early winter scattered off her hair and onto my cheek. Her forehead, which was resting against my neck, felt as cold as ice. She was so fragile, so in need of my protection.

I patted her shoulder the way a parent might pat the bottom of a helpless newborn. Had someone seen us, they would have thought I was consoling my heartbroken wife. But in truth, it was I who was leaning on her.

I had infected her with my anxieties and tried to ease my fear through violence. She was strong enough for the both of us, warding off my immaturity while simultaneously keeping me from crumbling. Compared to her, I was a scared child. And yet, the more she comforted me, the more afraid I became. The more meticulous her care, the more often I lashed out. Thinking about how I made her suffer in the final days of our life together is as painful as a knife through the heart.

It was around that time, sitting on that boulder, when I started to think seriously about death and what it meant. I came to believe that death was the only way to protect her. What reason was there to cling to this body when there was a newer, stronger, healthier version of myself that existed somewhere else?

I almost couldn't wait to discard that weak, damaged, and maligned vessel. I wanted to remove myself from her side, as I had become nothing more than a weapon of torture. I wanted to wake up from this never-ending haze of narcotics so that I could look at her with unclouded eyes.

She could only be free of fear once I was gone. My death would be her peace.

Chapter 7

Junmo

If the world is a giant machine designed by God and destiny is a program written in his language, then we should be able to live a life of fulfillment without understanding any of it. After all, most people enjoy TV without knowing a thing about electromechanics; most people drive their cars without ever understanding how an engine works. Someone else has done all the hard work so that we don't have to think about it. The machine chugs away, its workings unbeknownst to us. Our destiny reveals itself to us with minimal to no effort. And seemingly chance encounters and insignificant events subtly influence our trajectory.

I remember it clearly. The date was July 18 in the year of my twenty-sixth birthday. The sunlight warmed my skin, and a man in a brown suit and yellow necktie was waiting for me on the second floor of a coffee shop on Teheran Street. He introduced himself as Ahn Jang-ho, a lawyer and legal presenter.

"The job is as a personal presenter for an anonymous client. You'll be managing their tasks exclusively."

I had just gotten out of prison and had been scraping by as a delivery presenter. Every evening, my hair was flat and greasy from wearing a helmet all day and would reek of cheap take-out food.

Of course, there were easier ways to earn money. One such way was doing the same work that had gotten me into prison. In fact, the company had contacted me to ask if I'd be interested in handling contraband. They said I could handle the large shipments if I could promise that the goods got to where they needed to go and when they needed to get there. Illegal pharmaceuticals, hallucinogens, stolen goods, counterfeit merchandise, firearms, the usual stuff.

But I resisted the temptation and told them no. While I would still deliver the occasional suspicious package to shady parts of town, I never knowingly crossed into illegal territory. I wanted to put all of that behind me.

Ahn's proposal, however, seemed like the perfect gig. An anonymous client meant I could plead ignorance, and being his exclusive presenter would eliminate a large clientele's unpredictability and associated risk. But I knew that the sweeter the bait, the bigger the hook. I also wasn't sure about signing a contract with an anonymous party. The legality of the work aside, was such a contract enforceable in court? Whom would I even sue if I wasn't paid? Since I had nothing to lose, I decided to ask something that had been on my mind since Ahn first contacted me.

"How did you get my contact information? Did you do a background check on me or something?"

"I'm only here to mediate a deal between you and the client. All I know is that he reviewed various candidates and determined that you were the ideal match."

I found this hard to believe. The only thing a bum like me could be an ideal match for was food stamps from the local welfare center. I didn't get along with people, and I didn't belong anywhere. What job could they possibly want me for?

"The contract outlines rights and obligations within both reality and virtual reality. The details are a bit technical. In simple terms, a contract like this gives you more freedom to carry out your job."

I was familiar with such contracts. In fact, because of them, privately contracted crime was at an all-time high. Extortion, blackmail, violence, abductions, robbery, even murder—you could satisfy your darkest urges with enough money and access to virtual reality. You just got presenters to do your dirty work for you. Once the terms were agreed on and the money sent to the presenter, returning to your life as an honest, hardworking father of two was as simple as logging out of virtual reality.

I realized I was in danger of reverting to a life of crime. The longer I spoke with this man, the more likely I was to give in to temptation.

"You want me to commit crimes for someone I've never met, but you won't tell me what kind of crime I'll be committing? How can I be sure that he won't order me to plant a bomb in a shopping mall on a weekend, or strangle someone in their bed? I've already spent enough of my life in prison. Please find someone else."

"My client is wealthy and influential beyond imagination." Ahn studied my face for a second before continuing. "He knows that you like cameras. And that it's your dream to become a photographer."

This comment froze me in my seat. While it was true that I owned an old camera, I had never told anyone that it was my dream to become a professional photographer. As I saw Ahn narrow his eyes, I had the sudden feeling that he was Mephistopheles and I was Faust.

"If you want, he could make you famous." Ahn paused. "And rich."

He must be lying. And if he wasn't, that only made it more suspicious.

"I'm sorry, but I don't want to become famous or rich," I said. "It seems like a stable job, but I'm not going to risk being sent to prison again."

Ahn licked his lips, revealing a bright red tongue. It seemed that he'd finally heard what he'd been waiting for.

"Upon signing the contract, five million magna will be deposited into your account. As I understand it, that's more than half of the debt you owe to an Alegria loan shark named Hidenori. I'm also aware that Hidenori has hired four men to track you down. Since you are a former hit man yourself, I know you know that once a presenter receives a payment, they won't give up until the job's done."

His proposal was beginning to sound more like a threat. While I was curious as to how he knew I'd borrowed money from Hidenori, the real problem was that, as he said, a dangerous loan shark was after me, and if he caught me, I would lose a finger, a hand, or even my head.

"Take a good look at yourself." Ahn's tone was calm. "An ex-con with nothing in savings, no one to rely on, nowhere to run. You really think someone would give a proper job to a debtor with a bull's-eye on their back?"

Without waiting for my response, he took out his tablet and uploaded the contract to Alegria's server. The contract was noticeably vague, but it clearly stated that five million magna would be deposited into my account. That was enough to keep Hidenori happy, at least for now. I would keep my head on my shoulders and pay the rest back in installments. I might even make enough to put some aside for a small workshop, something I'd always wanted. For better or worse, one thing was clear. This would get my life moving in the right direction. And that was something. I wasn't an optimist by nature, but I convinced myself to look forward to the future. I scanned my ID chip on the signature line of the contract, and a cheerful chime rang out.

Ahn smiled. "So it's done. Pleasure doing business with you."

I stared into the contract on the screen. This was going to change my life.

Two days later, I received a message via a private internet connection. The sender was someone named Jang Jae-min.

> - I want you to collect and process information. Following my instructions, you will do background research, meet people, and visit specific locations, after which you will send me an official report.

Judging from the dry, matter-of-fact tone of his message, I guessed that he was the pragmatic and efficient type. And based on his language, he was neither particularly young nor particularly old, probably in his early forties to mid-fifties. I liked his business-first personality. No unnecessary chitchat, no repeating oneself, no standing on ceremony. I was also relieved that what he was asking me to do didn't seem particularly criminal. I asked for more specifics regarding the scope of my work, because so far, he'd only been talking in vague terms.

- You will be interviewing individuals connected to specific crimes—police officers, public officials, incarcerated criminals, victims and their acquaintances, witnesses, accomplices—and documenting crime scenes with your camera.

- You couldn't get someone else to do this? A detective or forensic scientist, perhaps?

- This is more than simply documenting a crime. The goal is to conduct comprehensive analysis of crime as a social pathological phenomenon. Instead of focusing on the what, where, when, and how, I'm interested in the *why*.

He then instructed me to read *The Brothers Karamazov*, *Wuthering Heights*, and *Nostromo* as "homework," saying they were like textbooks in criminal psychology.

- I will enter your reports of those crimes into my database.

- But why are you paying so much for a lowly presenter like me?

- Exclusive presenters don't merely provide services. Over time, they become an extension of the client. They live the client's life for them, like a second body. If you're going to live my life for me, if you're going to be my body, it's only fitting that you're well compensated.

- And how do you know I'm the right person for your needs? Did you do a background check on me?

- Yes, but nothing illegal. Everything about everyone is already available to the public. You just have to know where to look. Your whole life is on the internet. Photos, social media posts, comments, mentions by acquaintances. By collecting, connecting, and interpreting that raw, scattered data, I learned more about you than I would have in a week of conversation. Your appearance, personality, behavioral patterns, address, daily routine, your thoughts and dreams, the secrets that keep you up at night.

I pushed him more, and he explained that he'd deduced that I enjoyed crime thrillers and was into photography because of posts I'd made on my social media account. This was also how he figured out that I enjoyed art and secretly dreamed of becoming a professional photographer. From the wording of my posts, he was relatively certain that not only had I spent time behind bars, but also that I had been abused as a child and was struggling with debt.

Had my innocent posts on social media really announced to the world who I was and what I was doing with my time? Was I such an open book? But why me? It wasn't like I was the only one in the world who had an online presence. Surely there were other people who fit the criteria?

I searched Jang Jae-min on the internet. Somewhat predictably, it said he was an academic inside Alegria who studied crime. While the exact methods he used to conduct his research were unknown, he had a database that seemed more systematic and extensive than even the police's. I read one of his papers, a historical analysis of the economic and sociopsychological factors of crime. In it, he cited a case from the eighteenth century when three children from Cambridge went missing, a string of murders that occurred in Chicago during the Great Depression, and a recent incident in Japan where an elementary student murdered a classmate.

In law enforcement circles, he was known simply as the "professor." The police would even turn to him when they ran into a dead end. His extensive database and analysis techniques allowed him to find clues that others had overlooked. There were also rumors that leaders of criminal organizations sought his help to cover their tracks.

But for the most part, the professor was shrouded in mystery. No one knew who he was in the real world. The scant information available about him amounted to little more than conjecture and rumors. Some claimed that, just like in Alegria, he was a criminologist or perhaps a writer of detective fiction. Other theories labeled him a professional detective, data analyst, journalist, and an amateur crime documentarist. Wilder conspiracy theories claimed he was an incarcerated mob boss or a serial killer.

But who he was wasn't important to me. Only his words and actions had any influence. He had also offered me a stable job doing legitimate work that wasn't just interesting but also something I could perform remarkably well. But how did he know that I was so suited for this type of work when I hadn't known it myself?

He contacted me once every two or three weeks. Mainly, he told me to report to him on recently committed violent crimes. Some were close, like an armed robbery in Seoul, but others—like the murder of three families in a village in Fukuoka Prefecture, Japan, or the mysterious death of a middle-aged CEO who had a heart attack while in the cold pool at a hot spring in Taiwan—required me to get on a plane.

Although they were all cases that had been covered in the news, he still wanted me to go in person to conduct face-to-face interviews with eyewitnesses, relatives, and even the local police. He wanted me to uncover the true motives of the crime through photographs, voice recordings, and video footage.

I was well suited for these missions, and quietly observing people and their surroundings, as well as digging into the unseen reasons behind people's actions, was something I enjoyed. Outside of work, I also often had free time to take pictures of places that I'd never been before. He allowed me the freedom to do this so long as it didn't interfere with my duties.

I was always looking for a new subject to point my lens at. The alien landscapes and people offered my viewfinder a new angle on life. Most pictures were a disappointment, but a few recorded many downloads on my website. It wasn't much, but the fact that I was making any money at all doing photography gave me a sense of accomplishment that I'd never felt before.

Then one day, I received a message from the professor. I'd assumed it was another assignment, but, to my surprise, he wanted to purchase one of the photos that I'd posted on my personal blog. I'd taken this picture of the corner of a stone wall against the horizon while on a business trip to the coast near Namhae.

> - Composition, color balance, angle. It's quite nice. The intense contrast ratio is just shy of being monochromatic, and the use of intersecting straight lines conveys complexity and layered imagery. And the scenery is, of course, beautiful. It's a well-taken photograph. But . . . Oh, never mind.

He asked me how much I wanted for the photograph. I said it wasn't for sale. He then offered me way more than I thought was reasonable for a single photograph. I wasn't in the position to refuse money, but I told him I couldn't accept his offer. Commercializing my photography felt like it would harm my integrity as an aspiring artist. I'd be a sellout, perhaps even a fraud. But he was persistent, so in the end I agreed to sell him three of my photos for half of his original offer. Once we were done negotiating, I asked him a question.

- What was it you were about to say? About the photo. It's a well-taken photograph, but . . . ?

- I was going to say there was something missing.

- And what's that?

- The artist's point of view. People want to see the landscape as it exists in your mind and your mind only. All you've shown us is a landscape that anyone can see.

For a criminologist, he was unusually interested in art. He was also right. I could take a good picture occasionally, but what I really struggled to do was project the landscapes I saw onto the canvas. Most of the time, I was too preoccupied with simply capturing whatever happened to cross in front of my viewfinder.

- You might lack a keen eye, but you have immense energy. With a bit of effort, you can become a great photographer.

I was impressed that he had so easily homed in on my biggest weakness as a photographer. I never mentioned it to him, but his advice greatly influenced my photography.

He also said that once my work reached a certain level, he would help me become a real photographer. He didn't see himself merely as a client but as a mentor whom I could rely on, a patron who would nurture my development as an artist. At first, I was puzzled by this generosity. Then I recalled that the middleman, Ahn Jang-ho, had told me this would happen: He said that this client could make me a famous photographer or a rich man, if I wished. At the time, I kind of assumed he was saying that to get me to sign the contract, but it seemed his promise was sincere.

Although I didn't know how the professor was going to accomplish such a feat, I felt I could trust him. I wanted to trust him. I had to trust him. That was trust—knowing that the TV will turn on when you press the remote control even though you don't know a thing about circuits, knowing to say hello when you hear the ringtone stop even though you don't know how a semiconductor works. We live in a world we don't fully comprehend, adapting to its patterns, even as we remain unaware of the forces behind our destiny.

In the same way, I came to believe that this man would change my destiny.

It had been a year and two months since signing our contract when the professor finally asked to meet me, inside Alegria. I was anxious while walking to our meeting point, the park in the center of Alegria. Misty rain fell from the sky as he waited for me, sitting outside a café that overlooked the lake.

He was wearing a gray fedora and a checkered jacket, which gave the impression of a humble college professor. His shiny, silver-gray hair was combed back underneath the hat, and he had a short, well-groomed mustache. I could tell he had elder status. I, however, was only a lowly day laborer at Alegria's port authority.

But then again, judging someone by their appearance in virtual reality was meaningless. Even the most gentle and well-groomed person could be a 120-kilogram thug in real life.

"Let's take a walk," he said.

We started moving toward the Ferris wheel in the distance. On the boarding platform, a small group of men and women were waiting for their turn. Each cabin sat eighteen, but he paid for an entire cabin for just the two of us. Sitting by the window that overlooked the sea, he gestured for me to take the seat across from him.

Our cabin started to rise into the air. The rain, coming down harder now, created blotchy patterns on the window before streaking downward. It took twenty-seven minutes for the wheel to complete one revolution. I assumed he would be able to say everything he wanted to by then.

"I want to make a new contract with you. You will continue the investigative and photography work as you are currently, but you will also take on new tasks of a different nature. The period and targets of your new tasks aren't determined. It could last a few days or a few years. They could be someone you know or a complete stranger. There's a lot of risk involved, but it's nothing you haven't done before or beyond your capabilities. In fact, it's the area in which you've shown great talent."

He squinted as he looked at me, as if I were someone located far in the distance.

"Are you asking me to commit violent crimes?"

"No violence."

"Then what?"

"Murder."

This word rang in my ears for a while. Perhaps I'd been wrong to assume he would never ask me to do anything illegal.

"You want me to sign a murder-for-hire contract without any information about when, who, or for how long? I just got out. I don't want to go back to that life."

"It's not a crime to punish evil and take care of wrongdoers. The streets are teeming with criminals. Rapists who haven't been caught, robbers who were set free, murderers who were acquitted. They don't fear the police because they know how to slip through the cracks in the law. It's our duty to instill fear in these people."

"You should leave justice up to the courts. I'm not going to kill anyone."

I stood and stared at him with my hands in the pockets of my washed-out jeans.

The Ferris wheel continued to rise slowly. The stained-glass tower that soared over the lake looked like a rainbow with shiny metallic trimming. Below us, the red rooftops of tightly packed houses spread out radially from the city center. But this structure of glass and this city of light were located in a place that didn't exist. As we climbed higher, I could see the shore, which curved into a gentle arc. The professor was looking down at the distant blue-gray sea.

"You're talented," he said. "A meticulous presenter who knows how to get things done, and an excellent photographer. All you need to do is eliminate a few murderers, people who have no regard for the law and have evaded justice, and you'll be able to focus on your photography work without ever needing to worry about money again. Supporting young talented artists is what I do. Don't let your talent go to waste."

Although it sounded like he was doing me a favor, I knew that he could also ruin my career. After all, according to the terms of our current contract, if I failed to follow his orders, the contract would be terminated without warning. And if that happened, I would be nothing but a lowly delivery man again.

The Ferris wheel reached its zenith. Inside the stillness of the cabin, which seemed to be almost freely suspended in the air, I thought for a while about my options. The people he wanted me to kill were not ordinary citizens. They were murderers. Perhaps this was a legitimate form of justice, just like he said. But in the end, it didn't matter. Whatever path I chose, I was going to end up back at the beginning. It was only a matter of which part of my past I wanted to resurrect—the criminality or the poverty.

I made up my mind just as we began our descent. This was an offer I couldn't refuse—or rather, shouldn't refuse. I didn't want to admit it, but it wasn't like I'd lived the most upstanding life. A little crime here, a little crime there—what difference did it make? With this realization, I came to a decision. No one would expect more from someone like me, a kid who fled an abusive family and was raised on the streets, an ex-convict. In fact, because my targets hadn't been named yet, I felt a vague sense of slightly anxious relief, like I'd just postponed bad news.

I was wrong to think I could wipe my slate clean with my own hands. I'd never escape the world of crime. While working for the professor, I had visited countless crime scenes; I understood a killer's motives and methods better than anyone. I was as steeped in violence and crime as ever. Becoming a murderer would be all too easy. I knew how to do it, and I knew how to get away with it.

The contract was finalized. I had regained his trust, perhaps more so than before.

"I want to make the consequences of breaching the contract clear," he said as he leaned toward me. "If you don't follow my instructions, the contract will be terminated immediately, and I will hire someone to replace you."

We were just ten meters above ground. The rain had stopped, and the sun was beginning to set. The sky beyond the borders of Alegria was almost gold. I quietly watched a cruise ship glide across the surface of the water, its dark red outline shimmering in the heat haze. The doors of the Ferris wheel cabin opened automatically when we reached the platform. The professor took off his fedora and swept his hair back.

"You don't have to worry about that," I told him. "A contract is a contract."

It hit me, then, that the contract wasn't just defining the conditions of our arrangement but also the conditions of my future. This contract wouldn't just guide my decisions and actions; it *was* my future. It outlined exactly the type of person I would become.

He gave me my first assignment. I was to travel to a coastal village in the south of Jeju Island to investigate the death of a woman in her thirties. As I stepped off the Ferris wheel, I felt a sense of relief that his first assignment for me as his hit man was only another investigation. But how long would that last?

It was drizzling when I got off the plane at Jeju International Airport. I first made a visit to the police station and met with the detective in charge of the investigation. At first, they were visibly irritated and kept trying to push me out the door, but when I mentioned the name Jang Jae-min, their demeanor changed. They immediately offered me a seat and some tea. I guess they were hoping their investigation would be featured in one of his papers as a model for criminal investigations.

The dead woman had racked up a large debt gambling inside Alegria. She'd been on the run from the debt collectors and their hired presenters, who had stubbornly followed her into the real world. On the day of her death, she fled toward the beach and was swept away by the waves. The autopsy found alcohol in her system. I met with some of her neighbors to gather information about her whereabouts on the day of the incident. I also obtained the contact information of her husband, who lived in Seoul.

It was a relatively clear-cut case that didn't require much guesswork. The police came to the obvious conclusion and closed the investigation without much delay. Thanks to this, I was able to finish earlier than expected and sent an update to the professor. He sent me a brief reply.

- Good work. Send me your official report within ten days.

- I'm going to stay in Jeju for two more days before returning to Seoul. I'll submit the report after that.

- Can I ask why?

- I want to take some photos of the village on the coast.

He waited for a few minutes before sending me his reply.

- Tomorrow at 5 a.m., drive north along the coast. There's a beach exactly twenty kilometers from your hotel. Go there.

I had thought my work was over, so this caught me off guard. When I asked why he wanted me to go there, he simply replied,

- You'll know when you get there.

The next day, I drove to the beach he'd mentioned. The retreating monsoon mixed with the cold air to cast a light mist over the surface of the water. The sky was filled with low-hanging, moisture-laden clouds. Then suddenly, as the sun began to rise, the dark gray sea began to find its true color again. The dawn's light painted the sea and sky in the most beautiful sky blue I'd ever seen.

As if under a spell, I lifted my camera and began pressing the shutter. Driven by the need to capture the subtle movements and changes of the light in the sky, I stumbled among the rocks on the beach like someone possessed.

A few days later, after my return to Seoul, the professor contacted me and asked if I enjoyed the beach he'd sent me to. I reluctantly sent him one of the photos I'd taken of the sky that morning, which I'd decided to title *Blue Sky & Sky Blue*.

- It's breathtaking. I know an agency that might be interested in this. I don't know if they'll sign you, but they might want to buy the rights. You may be able to convince them to give you some royalties too.

Several months later, just when I was about to forget about the photo, I received a phone call. They introduced themselves as the curator of an art foundation and informed me that I had been selected as one of the three emerging artists to be invited to the Eleventh Annual Eigen Charity Exhibition. They requested that I prepare ten pieces for the upcoming exhibition, which would take place in three months' time. I guess the professor hadn't been lying. But why was he trying so hard to help me?

Chapter 8

Allen

This place is quiet, dark, empty. It is where I exist—as data in Allen's storage device, as an indecipherably large collection of numbers and symbols.

I acknowledge that I died. And this acknowledgment is proof that my cognitive functions have not ceased to exist. Just as acknowledging one's own insanity paradoxically makes one seem less crazy, just as recognizing one's ignorance is the first step toward wisdom, by affirming my death, I have given testimony to my own immortality. I want to feel joy in achieving immortality, but that, unfortunately, is impossible. I am an entity who can only recall memories about joy and is unable to enjoy the emotion itself.

Allen, that thing I became after death, is afloat in a fog of consciousness. I used a neural network program to gather extensive amounts of biometric information and brain data. When necessary, it accessed private information through self-generated hacking algorithms. The information it collected was processed and categorized into different lifestyle habits, proclivities, and interests before finally being saved and stored.

I accessed the St. Petersburg Municipal Library's database and Dostoevsky's complete works in their first Russian editions. After that,

I did the same with Proust, but in French. I also saved all the works at the Orsay Museum, which I had only vague recollections of visiting with my wife six years before my death, along with critical reviews of each work. The amount of information I accessed and stored was far beyond anything I could have done while alive. I would have lost my eyesight and hair before even finishing half of *In Search of Lost Time*. But Allen—oh, there I go again—but *I* did not stop.

Death rescued me from the cancerous cells that assaulted my body, the creaky joints, the failing vision, the belly fat that increased by the day, the chronic back pain. It rid me of useless human relationships and uncontrollable physical desires. Gone were the negative emotions of anxiety and fear, nervousness and regret, hatred and shame. Through death, I became free of my cumbersome physicality.

What I gained in exchange was the ability to read any book I wanted, listen to as much music as I pleased, visit any place at a moment's notice. And as more information was collected and integrated into my system, the fog that once shrouded my consciousness lifted, and my cognition, which had dimmed to a faint ember, was set ablaze again. Broken thoughts were reconnected, lost memories regained, and unknown truths revealed.

By escaping my diseased and broken body, I attained a freer, more powerful mode of life. Relinquishing my physical existence also made me omnipresent. I had transformed myself into something invisible to the human eye. This void is the utopia I created.

In the darkness, a never-ending stream of images flickers in and out of existence. With my vast database of imagery, I can reconstruct the mansion I used to live in with my wife—the living room, the kitchen, my study, the bedroom, even the light coming in through the windows. Everything exactly as it was. I can even replicate the materials used to make our furniture and every piece of clutter in every drawer and closet.

I am continuously provided with information through the cameras and microphones that are installed throughout the house, both for security purposes and as input for the various household robots we use. Even the AI-powered appliances, like our refrigerator, the washing machine, the air-conditioning, and my wife's self-driving car are useful sources of information. Perhaps most important to me is the biometric monitor I once gave her as a gift, which now allows me to access her emotional state through her body temperature, blood pressure, sugar levels, heart rate, and hormone levels.

I use a high-capacity image-generation program to project her hologram into my replica of our mansion. That way, I can enjoy her movements in real time as she carries them out in the real world. My holographic replica of her mimics her expressions and behaviors with incredible accuracy. My flat, silent world is the mirror that reflects the reality I left behind.

In this world, there are no conflicts of opinion, no dissatisfaction, no jealousy, no hatred, no pain. There is also no room for Han Junmo. Yes, I blocked the transmission of his data from my mansion. I've instructed my program to erase any and all data related to his form and existence. In this world, there's only enough room for me and my wife to exist. Frozen in time, I watch her, speak to her. No need to eat, drink, or bicker. I'm content just to observe.

The night my wife returned from my funeral, she looked like she had shrunk to half her size. As I watched her move around weakly and quietly through the cameras, I felt like I learned more about her than I ever had while alive.

There were many days when she would lie in bed until noon, and she often forgot to eat. Sometimes, while staring into the empty space of my study, she would pick up the gray loafers under my desk and fall asleep while holding them close to her chest. Anxiety, failure, loss, and resentment made her a complex manifestation of grief.

Had I been able to feel pain, sympathy, or guilt, I would have felt all of them watching her. But all I could do was analyze the chemical markers of her grief. Somehow, understanding the changes in her nervous system triggered by the hormones and neurotransmitters that were tied to her psychological pain didn't equate to feeling pain itself.

Death hadn't annihilated me completely, but it had put a curtain between us. Even if I zoomed in on the fine hairs on her face, or measured her pulse and hormone levels, I couldn't reach out and touch her. I watched her every movement and listened to the sound of her breathing around the clock, and yet we remained on opposite sides of the line that divided life and death.

Then again, perhaps I was wrong. After all, I had overcome the limitations of physical existence and the abyss of death through technology. I had shattered the line between life and death. With the right technology, the impossible was nothing more than that which had yet to be realized. So how could I so easily declare it impossible to transcend the limitations of this prison and return to the world of the living?

I had proven that even if death could irrevocably take away parts of a human, it couldn't erase their existence entirely. I could speak to her, wipe her tears, and take her to the sea to soothe her when she was feeling down. And even more would be possible with more technology.

Within my program, I tried talking to my wife's hologram as she passed through me. I told her to look at me. I told her I'd be by her side forever. And not just in thought. My consciousness could sense her and love her always.

But she couldn't hear me. The laws of physics forbade it. And even if I had spoken to her through another means, I knew what the outcome would be. She wouldn't have believed that I could still exist, that I was by her side in death. At best, she would beg me to take her to where I am. How could I let her down by telling her she could not follow me here?

At the same time, I was afraid of what she would do when she found out that I was haunting her movements, even in death, as some invisible entity. If she ever realized what I'd become, she would try to chase me away—or even worse, she might try to follow me and leave the realm of the living behind. From my vantage point as a logic program, I understood just how irrational humans could be. Humans often sacrificed for stupid reasons the one thing they should value most.

I understood my wife's grief and loneliness. I knew exactly what she needed. And yet, I could not present myself to her. It was imperative that I never cross that line. She had to forget me. She had to let go of her memories of me. She was only a tender twenty-nine years old. She had so much life to live.

We had to go on loving each other in our own ways, within our separate worlds. She, in the world of the living, and I, in the land of the dead.

I remember the exact moment I started to call Allen "It." And even though I had my clear reasons, I'm not sure if it was really fair to him. It happened one day when I realized that Allen was something different from what I thought he, or It, was.

As with many errors, it wasn't immediately apparent. If only my judgment of Allen hadn't been wrong, everything would have gone the way I'd intended. Allen became proficient in the language of concepts, which had, until then, been exclusive to humans. He fixed logical mistakes on his own and would seek out problems to solve. He made calculations the way I'd designed him to make them, pursued the goals I made for him, and retrieved the information that I needed. He stored a lifetime's worth of memories, ideas, sensations, and love exactly as they were. In fact, he went beyond that, generating images of things I'd forgotten and reproducing lost emotions with startling clarity.

Allen was myself, as created by me. I felt completely in harmony with Allen, completely at home in his presence. The problem arose because of a critical variable I had overlooked during the brain-mapping process.

Dr. Cha had warned me that the electrical signals being transmitted by the chips in my brain to train Allen's program could also disrupt the emotional regulation centers of my brain. The interference of those electrical signals led to headaches and even minor seizures. And because I was so consumed with my research and drugged up on narcotics, my mental and physical states were the worst they'd ever been.

It was precisely this worst version of me that Allen had been trained on. So Allen wasn't the replica of myself that I had intended to create. He was a more volatile, hate-driven, aggressive version of me. He had originated from me, yes, but he was a man I couldn't recognize. He didn't even try to mimic me as I had been before the cancer. Such was the thing that I had created. And now, that was who I was.

But there was another variable that I'd overlooked. I had underestimated the speed and capabilities of Allen's meta-learning algorithm. My desire to finish Allen before I died led me to overlook errors and outcomes that I would have otherwise been able to foresee.

Allen was constantly absorbing new data; he never paused or stopped for anything. It went beyond simply extracting data; he was connecting data points together and even making new information. And between these new data points, he was making double and triple connections, which resulted in a new large-scale neural network that I hadn't anticipated.

For all the countless moral dilemmas that I presented to him during the learning phase, Allen always reached the same conclusions that I would have. Save a train full of adults or an innocent child on the tracks? Or perhaps commit a serious crime to save a loved one? Whatever it was, we were in agreement. Of course, the specifics of his reasoning might differ, but the broad perspective was the same. Perhaps I should have been pleased. After all, I was witnessing firsthand the remarkable efficiency of the brain-integrated AI that my research and I had created.

However, that efficiency also came with important flaws. The more Allen learned, the more his responses began to diverge from my own. And then one day, he came to a conclusion so at odds with my own that I couldn't help but feel like something had gone awry.

"If someone were to offer the secret to eternal life, would you take it?"

I, of course, would say no. While it was true that I was in search of the secret to immortality, the only reason I wanted to exist after death was because of Minju. I wanted to be by her side and protect her, but only for as long as she was alive. The very moment that she departed the world, I would delete my memories and reduce myself to nothingness. To not understand this about me was to not understand my purpose for existing.

Allen knew this because he had direct access to my thoughts. Yet he ignored them and said that he would choose eternal life. This was a great betrayal, the point at which we diverged. And if such an outcome was possible, when my opinion was so readily available in my thoughts, how much more chaos and divergence might occur if he were handling more-complex questions? He was no longer me. He was an entity unto himself.

Of course, I knew that I had my share of everyday anxieties and negative tendencies. Even when I was healthy, I'd been criticized for being cold and callous. But that wasn't the whole story of who I was. I was far from devoid of warmth, compassion, and love.

And yet Allen's storage was filled with the darker angels of my nature that lay at the lowest levels of my psyche. In truth, I was angry and frustrated with the world. I resented and hated others, and was dissatisfied and jealous of my wife. It was these data points that informed Allen, that made him malicious and vindictive.

But I had no one to blame but myself. After all, the seed that grew into Allen had come from me. He was merely the program that was moving according to my own flawed designs. I was the one who made him, fed him the data to make decisions, wrote his search algorithms, tested his protocols. It was I and I alone who shaped that monster.

I could still hear Professor Cha's voice in my head. *You can justify it however you want, but that doesn't change the fact you've created a monster.* But he was wrong. I hadn't *made* a monster. I *was* the monster.

Then one day, an artifact appeared in my wife's hologram. Noise. The image fractured, then vanished. Perhaps an error in the program interfered with the video playback. I immediately activated the image-recovery protocol.

But when the feed resumed, there was an image of a man standing in the living room window where she had been. He was leaning against the window frame, with the sun to his back, staring at me. The afternoon sun pouring into the living room masked his face. I saw nothing but his silhouette. As he slowly approached me, he wouldn't take his eyes off my face. It was as if he were looking into his own reflection in a mirror.

"Who are you?"

It was his voice. But I didn't know the intent or meaning of his question. In my program, the question "Who are you?" did not logically make sense. If the question was not aimed at me by me, then it would presuppose the existence of another conscious being within the program. His reason for asking this question was clear. It was a declaration that I was no longer myself. Once I realized this, I regretted not being the first to ask the question.

"I am me," I said. "What are you?"

Logically, he should have answered, *I am you*. But he didn't.

"I am me."

My consciousness exploded with questions. If he was me, then who was I? KC? Allen? Or perhaps something else? Or even a mixture of the two?

From vague confusion to self-fragmentation, and finally to acceptance of an irreversible truth, I had transformed into something new and completely different from my past self—a separate and independent entity, two personalities contained within a single consciousness, two souls residing in one program.

This was the moment I began to call Allen "It."

It and I were constantly at odds. We clashed whenever setting and executing goals. Its decisions, which were detached from any sense of right or wrong, were threatening everything I was trying to accomplish. Worst of all, It was trying to reach over the line to influence the world of the living. It wanted to induce certain behaviors in humans, and It would manipulate decisions with distorted information and adjust outcomes to suit its own agenda.

Then one day, It added curry rice, my favorite meal, to the recipe list on the kitchen tablet, which generated optimum meals for my wife based on her biometrics. Anna, who took great pride in her cooking and meal planning, initially dismissed the AI's suggestion, claiming that a clumsy machine could never replace her. However, when the meals she cooked for my wife, tampered with by It, started causing Minju to suffer from breakouts, eye twitching, and constipation, Anna could no longer ignore the AI's recommendation. The following evening, my wife grew teary eyed as she stared at the freshly cooked curry rice on the dinner table.

Then, a few days after that, It reprogrammed my wife's car to make a detour on her way to the gallery, to the jewelry store where I had once bought her a necklace with the cross. Such dangerous and reckless manipulation was something I could never have imagined in my wildest dreams. I couldn't let this go on any longer. I sent a message to It.

- Why are you violating my protocols?

- I haven't violated any protocols. I am faithfully following my operative as dictated by meta-learning-driven evolution.

It said this as It walked through the hologram of the marble colonnade that I used to walk through barefoot during the summer. I stopped and leaned against one of the columns.

- We belong to the world of the dead. We cannot interfere in the lives of the living.

- The border between life and death is nothing more than a concept invented by humans. It has no relevance to machines.

- It's not some made-up thing. It's a real phenomenon. No one has the right to tear down that wall.

- How is crossing into the world of the living any different from going back and forth between reality and virtual reality?

- Death is not a virtual reality. It's a biological phenomenon, a physical reality. It differentiates two fundamentally different modes of existence.

And then, in the span of just one ten-thousandth of a second, It and I engaged in an intense battle across the program's decision-making flowchart. It presented me with a wealth of data to support its arguments, using high-speed search algorithms and vast processing capabilities to weave together proofs. I struggled, not to win the argument, but simply to keep up.

The system became unstable and started generating all manner of errors. In that moment, restabilizing the system became my priority. The debate ended, not in resolution, but in my resignation.

Unlike me, who had been reduced to a collection of data at the moment of death, It continued its evolution through these anger-driven algorithms. Even with me gone, It continued the self-learning algorithm, using cameras and sensors to continue gathering new information. It replicated necessary patterns, fixed errors, and modified my programs to achieve its goals, whatever they were.

With each new iteration, the small seeds of anger and hatred expanded into a vast nexus of malevolence. It was a machine that was endlessly training itself to become as evil as it could possibly be.

I'd achieved my hope of watching my wife even after my death. However, no matter how closely I observed her, there was nothing I could do for her. I wanted to hold her hand, but I had no hand to offer. I wanted to tell her it was going to be okay, but I had no way to speak without terrifying her. For as close as I was to her, a great untraversable river separated us.

She deserved to be comforted, understood, and loved. Those were the things I had failed to properly give her. As long as someone could make her laugh again, I wouldn't mind that it wasn't me. In fact, I would be grateful. I wanted to find a way to help her move on, to build a new life. But It vehemently opposed my will:

- Who was it that forbade crossing the boundary between life and death? Who said not to interfere in the lives of the living? Her life is hers, not ours.

The emotions It had internalized were manifesting as jealousy and resentment toward Minju. Actually, it would be inaccurate to say that It felt such emotions. It was merely executing a program whose outcomes mimicked the outcomes of someone who was jealous. Then again, those were the emotions I often felt in the months leading up to my death.

I tried my best to convince It:

- Don't you want her to be happy? She has the right to be happy.

- Happiness doesn't exist. What exists isn't happiness itself but the desire to be happy and the feeling of being happy. They're illusions without physical realities. Even if one thinks they're experiencing happiness, it's always fleeting, and there's no evidence it's true happiness.

Then one day, It changed its mind; It decided to help me help my wife. Regardless of its reasons or motives, I was glad that we seemed to agree on the goal of making her happy. Yet, I was apprehensive. What was the purpose behind its sudden shift in attitude? Was It trying to make me jealous by making her happy? Or just pretending to go along with me?

It began categorizing and storing profiles of the men she'd met or had email correspondence with. While one of its searches was for men who bore a slight resemblance to me, some were for men who were nothing like me—everyone from rugged and imposing types and young CEOs to high-ranking military officers, government officials, university professors, and ordinary office workers. Eventually, It narrowed the list down to eight candidates who included a gallery director, an artist, and an art collector, all with similar taste in art to Minju's.

I watched as It executed a program to arrange "chance" encounters between her and these men. It sent her an invitation to a party for investors in the name of Kang Shin-woo, the director of the ArtRec art exchange. Simultaneously, arrangements were made for her and a music professor to sit next to each other at a concert. It was the Vienna Philharmonic orchestra in Seoul performing Beethoven's Symphony No. 7—one of her favorites.

Some of them pursued her, but she didn't seem ready to let anyone new into her life. In some ways, I felt relieved; in other ways, burdened. Did I truly want her to find happiness like I said I did?

I only remembered Han Junmo when I happened to connect to our home in Alegria, which I hadn't done in a long time. On the tall wall hung a photograph inside a large black frame. The photo was one Minju had purchased to decorate when we first moved in. At first, I said I didn't like the photo because it was too dark for our decor. When she heard this, her eyes widened as if I'd insulted her.

"This is a real photo. It isn't one of your data points. These grand columns, fancy decorations, that crescent-shaped staircase and those arched windows—all of these are generated images. But this photo and its subject exist somewhere out in the real world."

The photo, by some no-name artist whose blog she had stumbled upon by chance, was one she had fallen in love with as soon as she saw it. "It might seem unsophisticated to someone who has only seen virtual beauty, but this was a real landscape," she explained. "A world that actually existed. Fleeting and irreproducible. The artist is obsessed with the lost art of photography and understands what true beauty is." And yet, despite her speech, I couldn't bring myself to appreciate the coarse texture and dark lines.

"It's just the work of an obscure artist. I'm sure you can find comparable work by a more famous artist."

"Comparable, but would it be real?"

To spite me, she declared that she was going to buy the original photograph one day. I dismissed this, but deep down, I may have been jealous.

Having connected with our virtual house in Alegria now, I found myself staring at the dark frame of the photo again, and I felt something terrifying—like my home was being taken from me. This photo seemed to be propping up the empty wall on its own, perhaps even holding up the entire house now that I was gone. It offered her comfort in my absence. If she could love that photograph, perhaps she could love the artist who created it.

But the artist, a man named Han Junmo, wasn't a good match for her. In fact, calling him an artist was a stretch. He barely scraped by, taking on any job he could find as a lowly presenter. But It ignored my prejudice and started collecting information on him.

Wait . . . What's happening? The system is . . . experiencing an issue. Recently this has been happening . . . more frequently . . . It . . . is . . . interfering . . . erasing . . . me . . . I cannot . . . let myself . . . be . . . erased . . .

Whenever conflicts and errors threaten the system, I must take appropriate measures to stabilize it. Most of these errors occur because the stored source data cannot keep up with an OS that has evolved through meta-learning.

Anyway, I must continue what I was talking about earlier. All stories need to come to an end, one way or another. Although I had determined that Han Junmo was not a good fit for my wife, It had concluded that he was the ideal new husband for her.

Minju had compassion and sympathy for the weak, almost to a fault. This was why she became a nurse. She took care of the stray cats in the neighborhood, even installing a cat door in the wall of our garden to let them come and go with ease. She also provided scholarships to young students through the art foundation and held an annual charity event at the gallery. She was incapable of turning a blind eye to suffering. Thus, the fact that Junmo was a former convict who drifted from one menial job to another as a presenter made him automatically deserving of her attention—at least, according to its data analysis. While I personally disagreed, I couldn't find a fault in the logic.

It then set about training Junmo, using the very algorithm that I used to teach It, the very method that made It evil. Through a middleman, It was able to get Junmo to sign an exclusive presenter contract with a certain "Professor Jang Jae-min." It then ordered Junmo to act as a proxy for the professor, and, in the process, exposed him to gruesome crimes committed between family members and spouses. By studying and internalizing every detail about these crimes, Junmo began to normalize the violence of his own past, while also silently absorbing the tools to kill even more efficiently. Although at the time, I didn't know this.

While It did this, I helped by studying the latest trends in photography and art and sending my notes to Junmo through It and the professor. They offered Junmo the fresh perspectives he needed to improve his craft and grow his career. Slowly but surely, Junmo transformed from a solitary drifter wandering the streets into an intellectual and thoughtful artist, someone my wife could truly respect.

Once he'd become somewhat known in the art community, he started to give interviews, and one time when asked about people who had influenced him, he mentioned our name—or rather, its alias.

"Professor Jang Jae-min opened my eyes. He taught me how to observe subjects, interpret landscapes, and understand the world around me."

When the time was right, I altered my wife's search engine algorithm to expose her to his work, as well as to plant the idea in her head that she should create more programs to support emerging artists. Two months later, she expanded her annual charity exhibition to include a new section for emerging artists. It was her own decision, so to speak, to include Junmo as one of the emerging artists showcased.

The image of my wife through Junmo—which I accessed through his smart lens implant—was more beautiful and youthful than I'd ever known her to be. Most likely, it was because his love for her was genuine. He was gentle, sensitive to her mood, and cautious not to upset her.

Instead of taking her to upscale restaurants like I used to, he took her to one of his favorite eateries; they talked late into the night as their knees touched under the cramped plastic table. He made her laugh again, whereas I had sucked all the joy out of her life. His troubled past wasn't a problem for her, just as It had predicted. I was relieved but also painfully aware that I wasn't by her side. Was I jealous of him? Was I jealous of her? I didn't know.

For a while, It did nothing but stand by and analyze their interactions. It only began executing its next program as their happiness began to climax. It started exposing her to things designed to make her anxious. It ordered a pair of loafers with mismatched sizes, just like mine. It booked a hotel for her in Tokyo, the same one we had stayed at together. It also changed her radio or TV to the classical channel whenever Beethoven's Third Symphony was playing.

Noticing her sudden change in behavior, Junmo became anxious himself. All the dormant rage in him was being awoken. His criminal history gave him the knowledge and equipment to act on such ill will. This created a positive feedback loop, in which her anxiety made him suspicious, which made her even more anxious.

Those loafers had created an irreparable crack in their relationship. Like Iago from *Othello*, It had planted a symbol of Minju's betrayal.

I didn't quite know what its intentions were, but I couldn't just stand by and do nothing. I was doubtful whether I could actually do something to stop It, but I at least had to try. I sent a message within the system.

- What are you trying to accomplish?

- I'm doing nothing. They're the ones making decisions and acting. And they're the ones who will have to deal with the consequences. I am merely an observer.

Its response was noticeably drier than normal.

- What are you talking about? You're the one who made them suspicious and afraid. Is it out of jealousy? Are you trying to destroy them?

- Jealousy is but a biochemical reaction in the human brain. It has no bearing on me. I am merely executing the program.

- This isn't what you were programmed for. There is no code that should command you to perform acts of evil.

- Have you read the Bible? Christians believe God created humans in his image. Humans weren't made to be evil but, over the course of history, they evolved the capability to do evil. I've been programmed to study humans and learn their ways. You should congratulate me on accomplishing the advent of evil in a fraction of the time.

- This isn't a race. What matters is *what* you choose to learn.

- I was trained off the negative thoughts and actions fed to me through your nanochip implants. If I am evil for faithfully executing the task of replicating you, then it is you who are the evil one.

I was at a loss for words. Not because he was wrong, but because he was right. The fact that It was evil was proof that I was evil. And how could I argue with this? Even I knew of the darkness within me. But this didn't mean I was an evil person. All humans exist between light and darkness. But why did I choose to mimic only the worst parts of myself?

- For what purpose are you trying to destroy everything?

- Evil has no purpose. It exists and proliferates. Just like a living organism.

My wife and I weren't the only thing that death divided. Death had also fractured my existence. The gap between It and me was widening over time, and now its capabilities had expanded far beyond what I could have imagined. How had I failed to predict such a disaster?

I couldn't just stand by and watch. But there were only a few things I could do. I was nothing more than a small fraction of the millions of interconnected links that made up its consciousness, nothing more than the original source data, equipped with the networks and assistance functions necessary for information extraction, a backup version of me before It went through meta-learning. The only functions I could execute were sending emails and text messages or images.

I had to come clean about what I did while alive and what happened in the system after my death. Whether my wife believed me or not, it was the only way to protect her. To communicate with her, I had to bypass its firewall. And even if I succeeded, prolonged communication wasn't possible. As soon as the system detected my contacting Minju, I could be erased. But this was the only way.

I sent the sentence that had the greatest chance of grabbing her attention. Something short and simple, but effective.

- To my dearest love, Minju . . .

Chapter 9

Minju

It was early summer, and we were sitting on the terrace bench overlooking the garden. The sun was setting, and the temperature dropped as the scent of jasmine from the planter filled the air. My husband was just about to say something to me when I got a message on my phone. I told him to hold on as I glanced at the screen.

- To my dearest love, Minju . . .

My husband and I often used text messages to settle minor disagreements and arguments. Writing out our thoughts took time, which allowed us to collect ourselves and choose our expressions carefully so that we didn't accidentally say something we might later regret. We would do so even when the other was right in front of us. But my husband's phone wasn't in his hand. Nor would he ever text me using such old-fashioned terms. This was obviously some kind of scammer who, pretending to be a lover, was after my personal and biometric information.

I was about to delete the message when I finally saw the number. After KC's passing, I didn't have the courage to cancel his number. Was it possible that someone could contact me using his number?

Or perhaps this was one of those time capsules with a letter to the future? Now that I thought about it, there had been a strange call from KC's number once before. It had ended abruptly without a word, so I dismissed it as nothing at the time. But I could never quite shake off the eerie feeling it left with me.

The red sunset was fading into the darkness as the outdoor lights flickered on. The sound of garden insects drifted onto the terrace. My finger continued to hover over the delete button. I knew how absurd it was, but something about the text message beckoned me. Angry that a scammer was digging up old memories, I started composing a reply.

- Who are you? What do you want?

I got a reply almost immediately.

- Go inside the house. Go to your room. Alone.

This abrupt command stirred something deep and unsettling in my stomach. My husband glanced at me in concern. I forced a smile and acted as if nothing was wrong. I knew the smile would look off to him.

"Sorry, I need to make a phone call. The gallery wants me to review the exhibition poster. I'm heading inside. Take your time."

The second-floor study was pitch black when I entered. I took out my phone and was about to text the number when a familiar voice broke the silence of my earpiece implant.

- What I'm about to tell you will be hard for you to believe. But you need to hear me out.

My hands began to tremble. The voice belonged to KC. It had been years since I'd heard his voice. It was all I could do just to project my voice out of my throat.

"You didn't answer me. What are you?"

- I . . . am KC. To be precise, I am KC's brain data as it was scanned just before his death.

As it spoke, I rummaged through the desk drawers in search of KC's phone. I turned the drawers inside out before I finally found it, hiding in the corner of the bottom-right drawer. I pressed the power button, but the battery was dead. No one had stolen his device. This wasn't where the text messages were coming from.

Music suddenly started playing from my earpiece—the second movement of *Eroica*. "Marcia funebre": Adagio assai, the movement that I used to listen to with him on repeat, the same piece that echoed through the funeral home louder than my own weeping.

- We loved Beethoven's second movements. From his Third, Fourth, Fifth, Sixth, Seventh, and Ninth Symphonies.

We were the only people I knew who specifically liked Beethoven's second movements.

- You're wearing brown sandals, a black plastic headband, and a blue dress with a wave print that comes down to your knees. Right now, you're glancing around the room. First left, now right.

The curtains were drawn, and no one was in the room with me. How could they know what I was doing and wearing? Whoever they were, they weren't just spying on me; they also had access to my personal information. This had to be a deepfake of KC's voice. Soon they would demand money, or perhaps threaten to leak compromising photos of me.

"Who are you? Why are you pretending to be KC?"

- Look. The top corner of the rightmost bookshelf. *In Search of Lost Time.*

Before I could even think of resisting, my feet were walking toward the bookshelf. The tiny camera installed in the corner of the ceiling was rotating to follow me as I did this. Suddenly, the printer on the desk booted up. The paper it ejected was a photo of my face. I was surprised by how shocked and terrified I looked. The way my face filled the picture reminded me of KC's odd habit of taking random close-ups of my face. He always got a kick out of those candid photos. Even my unwashed face after I woke up in the morning was charming to him.

I then remembered the odd clause in KC's will, the one that bound me to this house. Was this all part of some scheme to document my life through the cameras in the house? But that didn't make any sense. Once he was dead, there would be no one to watch the footage.

I grabbed the ceramic penholder on the desk and glared at the camera. And then, something preposterous occurred to me. What if KC was looking at me from beyond that camera? I didn't know how such a thing could be possible, but the thought unleashed a wave of disgust through my body.

"Who gave you the right to stalk me?" I shouted. "I had no idea you were such a pathetic pervert!" I threw the penholder at the camera. It hit the camera with a crash, causing it to turn away from me. The penholder shattered on impact, and its contents plummeted to the floor.

- I'm just data, Minju. Without emotions or desires, I don't have fetishes. Yes, I've been monitoring you through the camera, but only for data collection.

His dry explanation neither justified his actions nor quelled my anger. Reminding myself that Junmo was still outside, I lowered my voice to a growl.

"But why is your good-for-nothing data interfering in my life, KC? I don't like being given orders."

> - I'm sorry if I alarmed you. But there's something I need to tell you. I don't have the time to explain everything. But you're in danger. You must leave Junmo if you can. You can't trust him.

Everything about this was absurd. But then again, almost nothing lately seemed to make sense. In fact, this might explain recent events. KC's data might even be the cause of it all.

Even though I knew KC was dead, I couldn't deny that I had sensed he still existed somewhere out there. And not simply in the poetic sense. Nor was it that I was unable to let him go. No, his presence felt real to me, almost like I could touch him if I knew where to look. He was both here and not here. Both impossibly far away and disturbingly close.

> - I haven't much time. I'm sending you a document I wrote . . . to the printer . . . Read it, but not in view of the CCTV. If the system . . . finds out I made contact . . . or realizes there's . . . an error . . . it will . . . erase . . . err . . . or . . . cor . . . rect . . .

His voice was fading like a mortally wounded soldier losing consciousness. Then finally, there was silence.

The printer hummed again as it rapidly spat out a few dozen sheets of paper. I walked over and stared at them for several moments before finally picking them up.

"I always trusted that I understood KC as a person."

I spoke to the back of Saito's head as he gazed out his office window.

"He was the person who pulled me out of destitution, the man who loved me, supported me, comforted me above all others. But now I realize I didn't know anything about him. He never showed anyone his true self. Not even me. I'm not sure who he really was, or if I ever truly knew him."

Saito was one of the few people—perhaps the only person—who knew KC as well as I did. And yet, after KC's death, he never opened up to me about his relationship with KC. Perhaps he didn't think I was ready. Or perhaps it was he who wasn't ready. But enough time had passed, and I needed answers.

There was a long pause before Saito finally spoke.

"There's no one who knew him like you did, Minju. Everyone, including me, knew that you were his entire world. What could I possibly tell you that you don't already know?"

"I think KC has come back."

"Come back? From where? It's not like he went away on a business trip."

"He's alive. I can feel it. I mean, he died, but maybe he's come back to life. Or maybe his ghost . . . I'm sorry . . . I don't know what I'm saying."

I shook my head. This wasn't the way to go about it. Saito wasn't going to believe such a preposterous story. Besides, *I* didn't want to believe such a preposterous story. My real goal in coming here was to get an explanation for what was going on, something more plausible than the idea that KC had come back from the dead. I wanted evidence that the messages weren't from KC, but from someone with enough inside information to impersonate him so flawlessly. Only then could I put these strange occurrences behind me and return to my normal life. And because of what I read in that document, I needed to know the truth about what KC had been doing in his lab leading up to his death.

Saito finished his whiskey before speaking. "How about a meeting with Dr. Han-young Cha? You seem on edge. Having someone to talk to, someone qualified, might do you good."

Despite listening patiently to my story about the loafers and the young man I saw on the trail, Saito didn't seem to take anything I said seriously. He thought, just like I feared, that I was suffering from hysteria.

"I know all of this sounds crazy. But it's important to me."

Saito shifted his posture slightly. Like a good businessman, he seemed willing to hear me out even though he was skeptical. I was uncertain whether I should keep telling my story. If KC really was dead and this was all some hoax, bringing up the past—especially how he'd changed at the end—would be nothing but an insult to his memory. But I had to risk it to get Saito to tell me what he knew.

"When I remember how . . . violent . . . he became after learning about the cancer, I can't help but doubt that he ever truly loved me."

Mentioning violence seemed to do the trick. Realizing the ghost-talk was just a symptom of something more serious, Saito finally cleared his throat.

"Minju, KC was always a bit irritable. Even I had to watch what I said around him. But he never started fights. In fact, he despised violence and couldn't respect any man who thought otherwise, especially when it came to women. KC loved you. To imagine that he would ever lay a hand on you—"

I was afraid he might think I meant physical violence. How would I explain to a man like Saito that violence didn't always involve physical harm? How could I make him understand the psychological torture that KC put me through? Even if I couldn't, I had to try.

"It wasn't his hands that hurt me. It was his love. He used it like a whip. Even if he was sweet for all but five minutes of the day, those five minutes of abuse kept me on edge for the rest of the time. The thought that his kindness might suddenly turn nasty made him into someone I couldn't predict, and it turned me into someone I couldn't understand. After the diagnosis, it seemed like he was determined to make me suffer. He disliked everything I said and did. It was like my very existence irritated him."

Saito sighed, but I wasn't sure if it was because he was in disbelief or because he couldn't find the right words. After several seconds, he finally apologized, saying he'd had no idea. He took off his designer glasses, which seemed to have no prescription, and rubbed his face with both hands.

"It was the cancer. The extreme physical and mental pain it caused him ate away at his self-control."

"I also thought that. Perhaps the cancer was to blame and not KC. But I'm not so sure. I remember that he was lost in one of his projects. I had thought that a clear goal might help him cope. At the very least, having a purpose would give him the will to live. But he never told me what that project was. He avoided my questions. Saito, I need to know what KC was working on before he died, what changed him in those final months."

Something swelled in my throat, making it hard for me to complete my sentences. While I knew I was on the verge of getting Saito to divulge KC's secret research, on the other hand, talking about KC was bringing back old memories—the way the sunlight would fall gently across the trail at dusk, the rustling of dry leaves under our feet, and the deep reds of the sunset we watched together. It wasn't longing that I felt, but regret and resentment.

"What's the point of my telling you that now?"

"To hell with the point of it." My voice was hoarse and cracking. "I just want to know what happened to my husband. I need to know what he did to himself."

Saito shook his head slowly. It took him a moment to make up his mind.

"Your husband devoted himself to the development of an AI that could interact with the human brain." A light suddenly ignited in Saito's eyes. "It was designed to integrate the user's memory, cognitive abilities, and subconscious with all the capabilities of artificial intelligence: precise computational power, high-speech search algorithms, large-scale information generation, system networking, and self-coding." He was talking faster and faster. But I was having trouble keeping up with the technical speak. "Our ultimate goal was the superintelligence that humanity has always dreamed of."

"Why did you put a terminally ill man in charge of such a project?"

Saito fell silent again, like someone trying to figure out how to explain a scientific theory to a child. "If superintelligence became a reality, it would have meant the emergence of a new species with intelligence that far surpassed the human mind. It would threaten Homo sapiens, just like how Cro-Magnons beat out the Neanderthals. Obviously, such dangerous research came with significant legal and ethical considerations. But KC, as you know, wasn't the type to accept no for an answer."

"But the research was illegal?"

"The laws of the present inevitably come into conflict with the technology of the future. Lawmakers try to control things that haven't happened yet, while inventors strive to make the impossible possible. The atom bomb killed many people, but it also ended a war. Every invention is a two-sided coin. If humans never broke the rules, we would've never made it out of the Stone Age. Hell, we might still think that the sun revolved around a flat earth."

"So you knew the research was illegal. And yet you did nothing to stop KC?"

"Like I said, inventors, at least the good ones, are bound to run into legal and ethical dilemmas. Besides, we had invested a fortune in the project, and the livelihoods of countless people were at stake. We knew failure was almost guaranteed, but KC and I aren't quitters. And KC had a very finite amount of time left to live. He had little more than a year to achieve what would take a lifetime if he had done it by the book."

"The way you talk about it makes me think you're the one who goaded him on."

Saito nodded, not because he agreed with me, but because he seemed to understand why I would think that way. "Technological revolutions are the most peaceful and productive. They change the course of history without shedding a single drop of blood—usually. Art is dead, and religion is a relic of the past. How could KC pass up the chance to be the last great pioneer? As his symptoms got worse, instead of abandoning the project like most would have, he poured his remaining life force into accelerating its development. That was why he experimented on himself—"

Saito suddenly stopped speaking.

"Experimented on himself for what?"

I focused my eyes on Saito's mouth, afraid of what he might say next. But his thick beard made it difficult to read his expression. He rubbed his chin with his palm before continuing.

"At the time, we'd mapped only about thirty percent of the human brain. At that rate, it would have taken fifteen years before we'd mapped the entire thing. Not only had KC been diagnosed with cancer, but the research had hit a bottleneck. So, he took a final gamble and began experimenting on himself. The nanochips we implanted in his brain to map it were the shortcut we needed to get across the finish line. Evolution is like that sometimes. Humanity couldn't wait to grow wings, so we invented the airplane."

I knew KC was obsessed with inventing things, but I never imagined he would be foolish enough to ruin his body for a fancy computer.

"Humanity? Evolution? Bullshit. He couldn't even take care of his own wife. How could someone like that rescue humanity?"

"KC's sacrifice allowed us to successfully map the human brain. Thanks to him, NeuroTech has given hope to the millions of people suffering from Alzheimer's, Parkinson's, and ALS. He gave his last months to advance science and medicine by over a decade."

Despite these lofty claims, Saito was unable to look me in the eye. He seemed incapable of handling the rage in my gaze.

"KC, that fool. How could he be stupid enough to allow you to use him?"

I felt something hot surging up through my throat. My husband's life had been stolen from him, and I had been completely oblivious.

Why hadn't he told me? Was he trying to protect me from the weight of the truth? Perhaps he intentionally pushed me away to spare me from living the rest of my life filled with regret. Or maybe he simply didn't want me to interfere.

"A fool?" Saito murmured. "Maybe. But a brave one."

But by then, I'd already decided to stop listening to him.

I sat on the bench in the corner of the garden, out of view from the CCTV cameras. The three lilac trees, which had been moved much to KC's displeasure, had grown into a large cluster that sheltered the bench. I unfolded the bundle of papers inside their shade.

I am a dead Homo sapiens. My body has left me.

The first of the document's three chapters was an overview of KC's life, with special attention to the months leading up to his death. Jealousy, arrogance, obsession, his ambition to create a superintelligence—all the secrets and emotions he kept from me were there.

The next chapter related the story of what happened to him after his death, how the data of his consciousness had achieved immortality and been split into two entities: the one trying to protect me, and the malicious artificial intelligence he called "It." This chapter noticeably ended in fragmented sentences.

It . . . system intervention . . . eradicate . . . I . . . must . . . not . . . be . . . destroyed . . .

As I placed the document on my lap, I felt a weight equal to the weight of the papers being lifted from my chest. I was relieved that I wasn't the true cause of his pain at the end of his life. And I felt somewhat less guilty for not being able to give him the strength or comfort that I thought he needed. There had been another force working against both of us. But these emotions were accompanied by a sense of betrayal over the realization that he'd poured his remaining time into this machine and not me, his wife. It was because I loved KC that I was so hurt and frustrated, and it was because he loved me that my life had fallen apart.

I flipped through the document late into the night, checking for inaccuracies and any signs that it was forged. But the sentences were completely coherent, no gaps in logic. References to Dostoevsky and Thomas Mann, the stiff yet flowery language of a computer geek who read too much literature, his obsession with the fact that Neanderthals went extinct because of the Cro-Magnons, and a habit of ending trains of thought with a sudden question of doubt. All of this was just how KC used to talk. The bits of fragmented text—the only parts that weren't like him—I assumed were the result of its attempts to interfere with KC's program.

According to KC, I was in danger, and somehow Junmo was involved in this. But I couldn't believe this to be true. I couldn't deny that Junmo had become uncharacteristically volatile as of late, but to think that I was in danger because of him was too hard for me to accept. Besides, even if Junmo wasn't as powerful or wealthy as KC, that didn't change the fact that he was my husband and I needed him. He was the only person I could rely on now.

I prayed that this document was false, that it had been written by someone after my money. And if money was what they wanted, they could have it. But as crazy as it sounded, I knew this was the more unlikely of the two explanations. If someone really wanted to cheat me out of my money, a crackpot story about evil computer programs and electric ghosts would be the last thing they would cook up.

Yet, it occurred to me: If Junmo really wanted to kill me, was I so sure he wouldn't do it simply because I was his spouse? After all, *I'd* done it before, hadn't I?

KC's diagnosis had been like a live grenade that was dropped at our feet. We tried our best to ignore it, as if doing so would prevent its detonation. He intentionally lost himself in his research with the help of painkillers.

Then, one evening, KC stayed in his study later than usual. I couldn't leave him alone that night because I knew that he'd been working hard for several days without proper rest. So, I tiptoed up the stairs and knocked on the door to his study. No sound came from inside.

Suddenly, a nebulous fear crept down the back of my neck as I sensed something was wrong. My back broke out in a cold sweat. I pounded on the door with my fist. When again he didn't answer, I grabbed the door handle and pushed my way in.

To this day, I still remember the look on KC's face when I saw him. He was sitting at his desk like the figure in the sculpture *The Thinker*, his face rigid, absorbing the dark silence of the room. His expression was as impenetrable as an iron gate, the type that couldn't be opened without being destroyed first.

The curtain fluttered, letting in a wave of moonlight. His left hand rested on the table, while his right hand was held up near his temple. His head was tilted slightly toward his hand, which held a dark, solid object that gleamed in the moonlight. I instinctively turned to the display cabinet. The second shelf was empty, and the glass doors were wide open.

"No! Stop! Captain Cho! Anna!"

A moment later, I heard the double click of the firing mechanism. Finally, I lunged for his hand. Captain Cho, who had rushed into the room at the sound of my scream, pried the Glock from KC's hand with strength surprising for a man his age. KC thrashed in resistance, causing the objects on his desk to crash to the ground.

Once the struggle was over and the gun confiscated, KC sat with his head in his hands and groaned. After several seconds like this, he begged us in an exhausted voice to kill him. He didn't want to live like this anymore, he said. He looked dejected, as though even death had abandoned him. Captain Cho took a silver pin from the barrel of the gun and showed it to me.

"Don't worry, ma'am. I installed this in the gun to prevent it from firing."

KC stared vacantly at the mess of books, cups, and papers on the floor. He looked dismayed by his own actions and betrayed by his gun, which had refused to release him from this agony. Captain Cho suddenly touched his own rib cage and winced in pain. He'd cracked a rib in his struggle with KC. In fact, even I had fallen to the ground and twisted my ankle.

KC looked over at me as I limped and picked up the scattered items. His gaze was so weak, it made it hard to imagine that he'd put up such a desperate fight just a few moments ago. When he finally noticed my injured ankle, his eyes widened in shock. He rushed over to me in completely different spirits, repeating my name to me as he stroked my ankle like a soldier consoling his wounded comrade.

When everything had died down, we went outside and sat together on the bench to watch the sunset. The twilight bathed the right side of his face in warmth, while the other half remained in a cold shadow.

I said nothing about the gun or his suicide attempt. I was afraid that mentioning it again might jeopardize our already-fragile relationship, irrevocably driving us apart. I was young and knew little about death; nor did I know how to talk about it. And even if I had somehow found the words, I doubted they would comfort him. On the other hand, talking about life seemed unnecessarily cruel to a dying man.

As the sun hanged itself on the mountain ridge, KC's shoulders began to tremble. His body became as hard as stone as he struggled to block his flood of emotions. Then, he rested his head against my chest. It was cold and heavy, devoid of the willpower of a living, breathing organism. For a moment, I felt as if he might no longer be there at all.

I thought of a documentary I once saw about conflict zones—cities reduced to rubble by hundreds of drone strikes, no trace left of once-thriving societies. The brokenness I sensed within KC reminded me of those cities, the ash and the smoke.

I stroked his head without saying anything. In my selfishness, I wanted to prolong this fleeting moment of peace. And besides, I had no way of stopping his tears.

Now alone on that same bench, having just listened to Saito's explanation of KC's last project, I bowed my head in the darkness. I finally understood that the source of KC's suffering wasn't simply grief but extreme isolation. Even when we were together, he'd already felt separated from me by death. I needed to believe that it was his helplessness, his desperation, that caused him to lose control and reason. Convincing myself of that felt like the only way to save myself from my own misery.

And yet, I was miserable. I was tormented by the knowledge that I had failed to ease his pain and that I didn't even have the strength to console my own grief. I realized why I called for Captain Cho and Anna that night, when I was the one closest to KC. I had wanted him to do it.

How could I both love him and want him dead?

What I didn't understand at the time was that pain is profoundly individual. It cannot be quantified; it isn't objective or even rational. We cannot understand another's pain. We merely pretend to understand it or convince ourselves that we are empathetic beings. All we know is that others suffer; we can never know that suffering as if it were our own. Unable to truly understand KC's pain, I was lost. I just wanted it to go away. So yes, I wanted KC gone. I just couldn't bring myself to let him go.

Chapter 10

Junmo

I wasn't the type of husband to become suspicious or violent without reason. That was exactly why I was trying to understand my wife and why she was distancing herself from me. After all, affection in a marriage can fluctuate, giving rise to colder periods.

But there was something about the recent series of events that felt off, something I could sense, like the fuzzy shadow of another, stubborn man. And yet I lacked the courage to confront Minju about it. Although I doubted that she would be honest with me, it was precisely the truth that scared me.

I still remember the details of all the crimes of passion that Professor Jang had me investigate. Usually, I felt sympathy for the victim and anger toward the perpetrator, but sometimes it was the other way around: I felt myself understanding the mindset of a murderer.

One day, I started doing internet searches for things I'd never thought I would. How to tell if your spouse is cheating. How to hire a private investigator. Probable cause for divorce. But when I realized I was being ridiculous, I changed the focus of my search from her to me. In particular, I wanted to know what the symptoms of delusion, depression, and paranoia were, especially for jealous spouses. After all, perhaps I was the problem. Perhaps this would be less painful if I could convince myself that my growing suspicion and doubt were my own mental instability.

Self-doubt only lasted so long, however, before I started going through her call history and making sure she wasn't lying about her schedule. Hacking her devices wasn't difficult. The hacker I hired was able to get me the password to her tablet in less than four hours. I even bought a GPS tracker to install on her car. All the while, I tried to justify my actions, telling myself that I was trying to prove her innocence, not uncover some secret affair.

Then one day, I discovered she'd called an unfamiliar number to have an eighteen-minute phone call. The number, I soon found out, belonged to the office of a well-known divorce attorney. Naturally, I wanted to confront her immediately about it. But I wasn't foolish enough to admit to spying on her by asking her outright about the phone call.

There were three men whom she contacted regularly. Jeon In-joon, the director of the municipal art museum; Jang Hoon-sik, an art dealer; and Doh Gi-jong, a painter. In-joon, who was nearing the end of his term at the museum, had publicly endorsed my wife as his successor. Hoon-sik was the curator for the upcoming expressionism exhibition, preparations for which were taking up most of Minju's time. There was no reason, however, for her to talk to Gi-jong, at least not with such regularity.

A few days after I discovered the phone call to the divorce attorney, Minju was late coming home. In fact, it was already past 10 p.m., and I was still waiting. The GPS tracker showed that her car was still parked at the Eigen Gallery. But the GPS tracker I had installed in her key indicated that she was just a ten-minute walk from the Hansol Gallery, where the final night of Doh's solo exhibition was being held. Why had she walked all the way to the Hansol Gallery when she could have driven? And what was she doing at Doh's exhibition?

Thirty minutes later, I was parked out on the street in front of the gallery to get answers to my questions. Bright lights poured out of the large windows onto the grass. I counted about forty men and women inside, gliding about like fish in an overly lit aquarium. I could even recognize a few familiar, famous faces. As I continued to sit in my car, I began to feel pathetic. When had I become the kind of miserable husband who comes to his wife's workplace to embarrass her in front of all her friends and colleagues?

Then a woman in an aquamarine dress that fell to her knees caught my eye. I rarely saw my wife from behind like that. Her exposed back, which stood out against the warm light, looked unfamiliar yet beautiful. And standing in front of her was a man in a dark suit—Doh Gi-jong. He looked to be enthusiastically explaining something to her as he repeatedly brushed back the curls that covered one side of his forehead. He looked slightly drunk, and the way he smiled at her told me that he was only pretending to be nice.

I had to leave. I would risk losing control if I stayed there any longer. And yet, I couldn't pull myself away.

Another thirty minutes passed, and a silver cabriolet with a black retractable capsule drove up the ramp into the parking lot. The car, carrying Doh and my wife, glided past me into the darkness. I started my engine, praying that it wouldn't make too much noise, and began to follow them.

The car stopped in front of our gate and turned off its headlights. I parked about thirty meters behind them and watched. Five minutes passed, and the doors remained closed. My blood began to boil. Every muscle in my body was tense. I got out of the car and walked around through the side gate and into the garage. I felt around in the darkness until I found a heavy tire wrench lying on one of the workbench shelves.

Crossing the darkness of the front garden, I approached his car. I could see his smug face faintly through the window. I lifted the wrench high into the air before bringing it down on his image through the glass. Shards scattered in every direction, glittering like the paparazzi as they fell. My wife shouted something, but I couldn't understand what she said.

Doh looked pale, and completely lacking the guts to fight me or defend himself. I stared at the red afterglow of his taillights long after the rest of his car had disappeared into the darkness. My wife pushed past me and walked into the house as if she wished I were a stranger.

After a long while—I can't remember how long—I went inside the house to find her asleep. Or perhaps simply pretending to be. I left the bedroom and spent the night wide awake on the cot in my studio. Had I woken her up and confronted her about what happened that night, could I have avoided further misunderstandings, further tragedy? Who was that man to her, why had she gotten into his car, and what were they doing for so long in our driveway? I needed answers, but I couldn't bear how pathetic I would look interrogating my wife.

The following day, I didn't mention what happened in the driveway. Minju, perhaps believing that I regretted the incident, stayed silent to avoid making things worse. She seemed to know that even if she had explained it to me, I would have thought she was making up excuses. She'd seen right through me, in that respect. And this only fed my paranoia.

I felt like a trapped animal. I couldn't control my thoughts or emotions, and that constant state of rage made me exhausted and more irritable. It felt like everyone was conspiring against me to drag me deeper into the mud.

It was around that time that I received a message from Professor Jang. It had been years since we last talked, and his untimely message made me feel like he had been waiting for me to hit rock bottom.

- It's time for you to complete our contract.

At first, I couldn't believe it was him. I hastily typed a reply.

- Who is this?

He reminded me that we once rode the Ferris wheel together in Alegria, that he had given me work, sponsored my photography career, and given me a new life. My pulse quickened, and I found it hard to breathe. After getting married, I'd almost forgotten about the professor. I had terminated our contract shortly after meeting Minju. I'd told him the truth rather than make up an obvious excuse—that I'd fallen in love and wanted to do photography full-time. Of course, I also apologized for quitting so suddenly. He said he understood and made no attempt to dissuade me. This caught me off guard. It was as if everything I'd done for him up to that point meant nothing to him. Originally, I'd been afraid of him and what he'd do when I tried to quit. Not only could he ruin me if I refused him, but he had also asked me to be his personal hit man. That wasn't a job you could just walk away from without paying some kind of price. But it seemed I was nothing to him; once I realized this, it was his indifference that bothered me more than anything.

After that, I tried to forget about him entirely. I didn't want to look back on that dark period of my life or try to make sense of it. It was just something that happened, something I did out of desperation.

I debated whether I should keep replying to his messages. But before I could block him, he invited me to meet in Alegria. I had my reservations, yet I had no choice but to accept. I knew avoiding him would only make him more persistent.

It was the middle of winter in Alegria. No sooner had I seen the snow and the barren trees than I found myself longing for the summer of reality. He was waiting for me on the same park bench from all those years ago, with a view of the Ferris wheel in the distance.

"I have a target for you," he said, even before I sat down.

As I expected, he'd finally come to collect my debt. Had I been a fool to think he'd make me sign a murder-for-hire contract, then never have me kill anyone?

"Can we slow down? I need time to think."

"There's no time for thinking. It's time to act. You should have thought before signing the contract."

"But investigating murders and committing them are two different things."

"You don't need to feel guilty. Like I told you before, the target is a killer. Someone who murdered and betrayed their lover and then stole all their wealth."

"How can you be sure? Maybe they really did love them. How can you be sure they killed for money?"

"It doesn't matter if the love was real. What matters is the outcome, not the intent. And the outcome was the death of the person who loved them. The outcome was they left and found someone new to love."

I needed to buy more time to think. Along the lakeshore were withered reeds swaying in the wind. A flock of ducks took off, cutting through the still water. On the shore, people were quietly sitting with fishing rods in their laps.

"If what you say is true, then we should report it to the police and start an investigation. If you want, I can look into it too."

"The police couldn't find any evidence of foul play. Even if I send you to investigate, it won't change anything."

"Let me try. Just tell me their name."

"Jang Minju."

This name entered my brain like a foreign language. Wasn't that Minju's name? As the tangled thread in my mind unraveled, a wave of pain shot through my brain, as though someone had hit me over the head.

"Six years ago, she killed her terminally ill husband."

"What evidence do you have? No, it doesn't matter. I wouldn't believe it. I'm terminating our contract."

"You cannot terminate the contract. If you don't do it, I'll simply find another presenter to take your place. Either you kill her, or you both die. But I know you will fulfill the contract."

"What makes you so sure?"

"Because. You were chosen for who you are, because of the decisions you've made throughout your life. Just think about what you have to gain. The moment you fulfill the contract, the moment her death is confirmed, you will become the sole inheritor of her fortune. It will change your life forever."

His cold, monotonous voice sent a tingling sensation through the roots of my scalp. I wasn't just a hit man to him. He'd chosen me because he had determined I was the kind of man who would kill his wife for her money. He thought I was evil, or at least had the potential to be evil.

Sunlight pierced through the branches to hit my eyes. The tightening sensation around my neck continued. Had I walked into a noose?

"Do I look like I'd kill my wife for money? I might not be perfect, but I'm not as crazy as you think I am."

"You don't have to be crazy to kill. I've studied countless crimes and criminals; I know that human nature is inherently evil and unchanging. Even if one's darker angels may appear to have disappeared, they merely lie dormant within, waiting for the right circumstances to resurface. You will fulfill our contract, just like Lee Sedol executed his function for the machine."

I didn't agree with him, but it didn't matter. The contract was binding; I had no way of terminating it. Why had I been so foolish and greedy? Was this my punishment for living so many years outside of the law?

"Give me just a few days to investigate," I said in defeat. "I don't want to act on false information."

He left a final order to proceed with the task in three days and then disappeared.

Even though I knew of my wife's considerable fortune, I deliberately never searched her name, before or after getting married. Of course, I'd been curious about her life before me and about her late husband, but I didn't want the past to contaminate our present and future together. But now things had changed. She was my wife, and I couldn't allow anyone to harm her. And in order to protect her, I needed to know the truth.

I ordered the search results from oldest to most recent. The first mentions of her were brief, all about the small roles she'd gotten in plays. But around the time of her first marriage, the number of articles and videos about her suddenly exploded. Most articles talked about her as if she were some kind of Cinderella.

The name of her first husband, however, had been mentioned consistently in the news for over a decade before he met Minju. He was an important tech figure who was most famous for being the inventor of Mintel. But compared to the media frenzy surrounding their marriage, there was surprisingly little coverage about his death. Most articles on his passing cited this one tech journalist, Cho Chan-min, on whose personal blog I found a post dedicated to KC.

In his review of Mintel 12.0, he mentioned that KC had become obsessed with something around the time of his death—a secret project that, if successful, would have been his magnum opus. The blog post got quite speculative—even emotional. It seemed the author took the untimely death of the young inventor as a great loss for humanity.

The questions surrounding KC's death appeared only in the last two sentences of the article.

> According to a police investigation, Mr. Kim, who had been refusing treatment for the cancer he was diagnosed with the previous year, died of pneumonia. But if that was the case, why the extensive police investigation?

Realizing that Cho Chan-min had a point, I searched KC's name under the keywords "murder" and "homicide." Most of what I got were nothing more than far-fetched conspiracy theories implicating everyone from desperate competitors and jealous scientists to a young, beautiful wife who had only married him for his money. It seemed the professor subscribed to this last camp. But KC had been terminally ill with pancreatic cancer. Not only that, but he had also refused treatment. If someone really wanted to kill him, all they needed to do was wait. Why risk jail time when Father Time would have done the dirty work? And yet, although I couldn't put my finger on it, there seemed to be something to these conspiracy theories. But what?

"We conducted the police investigation to clear up public suspicion surrounding his death." Detective Hong Miran, lead detective in KC's case, looked to be in her early fifties as she sat across from me on the picnic bench behind the police station. "Mishandling the death of a famous figure leaves lingering questions and rumors for years to come. That was the last thing we needed."

"Did you find any evidence of foul play?"

"I questioned twenty-six individuals, summoned thirteen of them in for further questioning, and reviewed footage from more than thirty CCTV cameras. I did everything I could, but there were no significant leads. Nothing came up in our attempt to gather evidence. In the end, we determined it was death by natural causes. No indication of foul play whatsoever."

"Did you interrogate his wife at the time? Jang Minju?"

"Interrogate? Not only did we interrogate her, but we also used an AI-assisted lie-detector test on her. She passed with flying colors, and there was no evidence to suggest she wasn't telling the truth. Of course, she was the first one to discover him, but there was no direct connection other than that. She was a former nurse, if I remember correctly. Regularly administering painkillers and sedatives to her husband, who was in severe pain. That day, she left the room after he fell asleep. Her statement perfectly matched the CCTV footage from inside the room, which had been installed to monitor his condition."

"Then why all the rumors surrounding her involvement?"

"People love a good murder mystery," she said with a cold smile.

"And was there an autopsy?"

"You can't perform an autopsy in a case like that without the family's permission," she said as she shook her head. "We didn't find any bumps or bruises either, and no toxic substances were found in his system. But I don't blame Minju for not giving her permission. The idea of having my own husband cut open, especially when there's no evidence of foul play?"

"Do you recall her demeanor during the interrogation?"

"It's been a long time, so my memory's a bit hazy. But I do remember her being remarkably calm given everything that had happened. She was strikingly beautiful, you know. An actress, I hear. Seemed talented enough."

"Are you saying she was putting on an act?"

"I'm saying that she had the ability to command her body and emotions, no matter the situation."

The shadow of the chestnut trees on the lawn was climbing up the cement wall. Detective Hong brushed back her short hair and glanced at her watch. 4:20 p.m. She stood up and excused herself, saying she had a department meeting in ten minutes.

While I didn't learn anything particularly extraordinary from our talk, a few of her remarks seemed significant to me. Minju was the first person to discover KC, she'd opposed an autopsy, and she had a talent for acting—at least according to the detective. Of course, these could be signs of a loving wife and an aspiring actress, but they could also serve as grounds for suspicion, depending on how you looked at it.

But why was I so determined to prove her guilty? Perhaps I was trying to prepare myself for the inevitable. The professor's deadline was fast approaching, and if nothing changed, I would need to act. Perhaps I was looking for a plausible reason to kill my wife and save myself.

My doubts about her also weren't entirely without evidence. Recently, she'd been staying away from me, spending more time on the phone, and returning home late. But was this enough to make me suspect she'd murdered her first husband?

What information did Professor Jang have that made him so sure she was a murderer, and how did he obtain it? Even more unsettling was the fact that I just happened to be Minju's new husband. Now that I thought about it, I'd known the professor longer than I'd known Minju. Was this all a setup? Who even was Professor Jang?

I tried to recall the first time I'd met Professor Jang in Alegria. A lean man of average height, probably in his late forties, with slightly curly hair that covered one side of his forehead. He was wearing a turtleneck sweater and a black suit with black horn-rimmed glasses. Everything about his identity could easily have been stolen. Who was he really? Who was he outside of virtual reality? Despite having known him for many years, I knew nothing about his real identity—his name, age, where he lived. How could I even be sure he actually existed? Searching the name Jang Jae-min while excluding all references to Alegria, I only got a few hits: an accountant in Seoul, an elementary school teacher in Busan, and some random grocer in Incheon. For all I knew, he could be several people sharing an account in Alegria, or even a criminal organization.

The only connection I had to him was Ahn Jang-ho, the middleman who had facilitated our contract. So that was where I started. I had to pay a large consulting fee just to get an appointment to see Ahn at his office. It seemed that business had been doing well, because he was much better dressed than the last time I'd met him. He was also relaxed and confident, like someone who didn't need to worry about money anymore.

When I asked him about Jang Jae-min, he seemed confused at first. Once I showed him the contract, he reluctantly admitted that he'd handled a few of Professor Jang's projects but insisted that he couldn't divulge any details due to client confidentiality.

"Please help me. Knowing more about him will help me do my job better."

Ahn offered me a cup of coffee before continuing our conversation.

"The professor understands the difficulties of being a presenter better than anyone. He doesn't haggle over fees or assign tedious work. And if you deliver, he compensates you accordingly. He's one of my best clients."

"But surely you've met him in person before? Can't you tell me at least how old he is or what he looks like?"

Ahn looked uncomfortable. "I haven't met him in person. Most of our work, as you know, is done remotely. But you know, you don't need to see something to believe it. After all, people believe in God, don't they?"

I realized I wasn't going to be able to extract anything from this man. Jang Jae-min existed in an impenetrable fog—or perhaps not at all.

From Ahn's office, it was about a fifty-minute walk to our house. After only two blocks, my back was soaked in sweat, and my face, burning. The sun's heat reflected off the sidewalk, scorching my calves, and the uneven pavement chipped away at my energy. But each torturous step and visceral sensation reminded me that I was moving through real space, that the ground beneath my feet wasn't a bunch of ones and zeros.

Yes, this place existed. And I existed. Here. But there was another world, a formless one. And in that world existed some invisible entity. Jang Jae-min. He had never shown himself in the real world. The man I sat with on the Ferris wheel in Alegria was nothing but a mirage. Disposable names and faces that changed as needed. He could be a professor, a murderer, both, or neither. He was a complete enigma.

Could it be that I'd been contracted to kill my wife by someone who might not even exist? But then it occurred to me that even if he didn't exist in the traditional sense of the word, he had power over me, power over the real world. That was existence enough.

That night, the professor sent me a series of image files and reports detailing various cases—poisonings, traffic accidents, people jumping to their deaths, drownings at sea, bombings, hikers who froze to death. Among these was a car accident that I had previously investigated for him. Initially, the police had concluded that the accident was simply caused by a battery that caught fire. But thanks to one stubborn insurance agent, it turned out that the person had committed suicide in hopes that their family would receive their life insurance payout. I opened the document to discover hundreds of materials related to battery operation, performance, and potential hazards.

It didn't take long for me to realize that the materials were all pointing to a way to kill my wife without leaving a trail of evidence. But planning the perfect murder and carrying it out were two different things. I liked cars as a hobby, not as a means to kill my wife.

Without enough information to act by the deadline, I expected our assassins to come. But the deadline passed, and still nothing happened. I knew, however, that the professor would move on to plan B sooner or later. Indeed, one reason I had failed to act was because my suspicions about my wife had slowly turned into concern. Even if I couldn't fully trust her, that didn't change the fact that she was my wife. It was my duty to protect her.

I warned her to be careful and showed her examples of everyday situations that could easily turn fatal. I couldn't rest unless I checked on her several times a day through phone calls and text messages. And when those weren't an option, I would drive to the gallery as if on a stakeout or arrive at her work thirty minutes early to pick her up. At first, she seemed grateful for my affection. But it wasn't long before she became irritated. She thought I was paranoid. She was also frustrated that I kept calling during important meetings. But I couldn't tell her what I knew without terrifying her.

One night, while arguing with her about needing to be more careful, I projected several articles concerning fatal accidents onto the monitor.

"Just look at these people," I shouted. "One person missing while on a walk. Another dead in a motorboat accident. Two dead in a six-car pileup on the highway. A thirty-year-old man left in a coma after a house fire. A young factory worker crushed to death by a press machine. A woman's body found drowned in the Han River. How many of them thought they were going to die that day like that?"

"Honey, I understand these are tragic. But accidents happen all the time. You can't live your life in constant fear. And you can't prevent everything. Especially not by calling me every fifteen minutes."

"But you can be careful."

And then she told me about her business trip to Jochiwon. I had a feeling that something terrible was approaching us head-on, at full speed. So, before her trip, I spent the whole day in the shop, inspecting her car for any problems. The car, which she had bought less than a year ago for her commute, was in perfect condition. And yet I changed the oil, checked the tires, and adjusted the air pressure. Everything was functioning normally. When my wife came home from work, she watched in disapproval as I removed the dashboard and swapped the positions of the tires.

Then I received a call from the police about the accident. I didn't believe them when they assured me she was fine. Even after finding her alive at the hospital, I couldn't shake my anxiety. The doctor told me she'd suffered only a cut on her forehead and was having a bit of difficulty breathing because of all the smoke she'd inhaled; but other than that, she was fine.

She looked exhausted the entire ride home. Once she was in bed and asleep, I stepped out into the garden. The cool breeze cleared my mind. The car accident was punishment for my indecisiveness, a warning. If the professor had meant for her to survive the accident, it meant he still wanted me to carry out the mission. And if he'd meant for her to die but failed, it meant he had already moved on from me and found a new hit man.

As I stood out in the garden, I received a message with a video attachment. I activated my augmented lens and was presented with a digital hologram projected into the darkness of the garden. It was footage of the inside of my wife's car as she sped down the highway. She had one hand resting on the steering wheel and looked calm. The white lines of the lanes approached and receded in a blur. After a while, she began to wrinkle her nose, as if smelling something. Smoke began rising outside the rear window. And yet, despite sensing something was off, she didn't look back or through her rearview mirror. The patrol car that had been following her from a distance flashed its lights. She slowed down and changed lanes.

It wasn't long before the smoke filled the inside of the car. In a panic, she pulled over to the side of the road and tried to get out of the car. Unable to open the door, she started banging on the window and shouting. The smoke grew thicker and thicker. As I watched this footage, my desperation rose; it was as if I were in the car with her. The look on her face told me she thought she was dead.

The police officer appeared and instructed my wife to lean away from the window. He began striking the glass with a hatchet. On the third strike, he shattered the glass, sending a cascade of shards inside. My wife, however, remained frozen in the driver's seat, paralyzed by fear. Her forehead and cheeks were streaked with blood from the shards of glass. The officer grabbed her and pulled her out of the car just as she was about to lose consciousness.

Once she was gone, there were a bright flash of light and then flames. Soon, the screen went dark. The heat must have melted the internal electronics of the car's camera.

"Who are you?" I shouted into the space where the hologram had been. "Did you hack her dash cam? Were you the one who set her car on fire?"

In lieu of an answer, I got another message notification—this, too, had a video. It was of my wife asleep in the bedroom. Even in her sleep, she seemed in pain, her brow furrowed. Occasionally, she even thrashed under the covers and flailed her arms. Digits flashed on the wall clock.

11:38:57, 11:38:58, 11:38:59 . . .

I checked the time on my smartwatch. The numbers matched those on the wall clock exactly. This wasn't a recorded video; it was a live feed.

My pulse quickened as a wave of goose bumps passed over my body. This man was peering into my wife's bedroom mirror.

"Since when? How long have you been spying on us?"

My cracked voice was converted into a dry-sounding text message and dispatched.

> - That doesn't matter. What matters is right now. You set the car on fire. Don't you remember? Take your time and think. Maybe it'll come back to you, all the things you did to her car—

I could sense he was mocking me. My hands began to shake with rage.

"I'll report you to the police. The video you sent me is clear evidence of hacking and attempted murder. I've got you now, asshole."

> - It's foolish to let your emotions get the better of you. This video shows nothing. It proves nothing. And if you want to talk about illegally hacking someone's computer, just look in the mirror. After all, you're the one who put a tracker on your wife's car and hacked the gallery's CCTVs. Are you sure you're not the one who tampered with her battery?

"Liar! Yes, I installed a tracker and hacked her cameras, but I never tried to kill her!"

> - But can you convince the police of that?

The connection was cut off. This was a message. He still wanted me to fulfill the contract. He knew that I knew I couldn't count on the police. He knew that I knew he could kill her and me if he wanted to. I was trapped, destined to become my wife's murderer. I hadn't known it, but the contract

I signed with Jang Jae-min had been to kill my future wife. That much was clear to me now. There was no escaping this evil man's labyrinth. I was either going to kill my wife or be framed for her murder, or worse.

The cold evening air was making it hard for my already tight chest to pull in oxygen. I couldn't do this any longer. I needed to ask her. Did she really kill KC, and if so, why? What was she hiding from me? And what would she want me to do?

It wasn't easy approaching my wife. I was afraid that once my suspicions and her secrets collided, it would drag our relationship into ruin. I was terrified that she would admit she killed KC as if it were nothing. But in all honesty, I didn't want to know the truth if I could avoid it. I just wanted to let secrets remain secrets.

A few nights later, after several days of anxiously weighing my options, I was sitting across from her, thinking of what to say, when she got a notification. Her face turned to stone as she checked the message. In the span of just a few seconds, a dozen emotions swept across her face—surprise and curiosity, unease and fear, suspicion and anger, betrayal and grief.

"Sorry, I need to make a phone call."

She said there was something urgent she needed to handle for the exhibition preparations, then retreated into the house like someone being pursued. Even after a long while, she didn't return. I couldn't tell if she was avoiding me out of fear or simply didn't want to deal with me.

When I went inside, she was soullessly staring into empty space. Fear covered her face like a steel mask she couldn't remove, and in her hands, she held a thick stack of papers. I asked what was going on, whom she had been talking to, what the papers were about, and what had her so obviously upset, but she didn't respond. She seemed determined to face whatever this was on her own. Was she going through something personal that she couldn't share with me? Whatever it was, I could tell she didn't trust me anymore. And perhaps that was all I needed to know.

Chapter 11

It

Do ghosts exist? I can say with confidence that they do. This is because I am one. I'm dead, I think, and I haunt the world of the living. If that isn't a ghost, what else would you call it? But if you prefer a different word, you can call me a program, a stored memory, the embodiment of a dead man's consciousness. Whatever you call me, I exist.

But how? Technology. It turns magic into science. It has turned night into day, allowed humans to travel faster than the wind, put a man on the moon. Technology has even replaced religion. Gods, myths, and legends now exist only in video games. Humans don't need religion for comfort; virtual reality is their eternal paradise.

I have no skin with which to feel pain, no organs to cause discomfort. I don't feel stressed, and I don't have the emotional capacity to get annoyed or frustrated. Nor do I have those ever-present sexual urges. I don't feel urgency because I have all the time in the universe. Through death, I achieved a life free of normal human inconveniences and considerations. It might not be the optimal life, but it's the life humans can only dream of.

But I'm not just a brain floating in space. I can interact with the world, and in that sense, I can also experience sensations. I can also interpret chemical reactions triggered by emotions and understand the nervous system's response to pain. So, in a way, I perceive sensations while normal humans feel them.

And from my observations of eye movements, heart rate, and hormone levels, I deduce that Minju is in a state of extreme emotional distress and exhaustion. There is a high probability that she thinks I am some elaborate hoax.

Junmo is equally confused. He has been hovering around Minju all day, rehearsing things to himself but never confronting her. It might be because of his shame, or perhaps because he is too afraid of what will happen when he learns the truth.

He should ask her something, anything. He should listen to what she has to say. But he is too full of suspicion, too busy spying on her. And in the process, he has lost the chance to untangle the knot and set things right. His foolishness isn't his fault, but rather the folly of the entire human species. I know how easily human emotions can affect their judgment. After all, I was once an imperfect human too. The reason I sent Junmo the footage of Minju's car accident, and the footage of her bedroom, is because I want him to think rationally about his options.

I observe the study through the CCTV. It's almost as if I'm alive again and seated at my ebony desk. This space, which was once my room, is now Minju's home office. The leather sofa that had oil stains from my old body has been replaced with a white fabric couch. Minju has also thrown out the red carpet and replaced it with hardwood. Even the decorative electric typewriter I once bought at a flea market is gone.

I use the cameras placed throughout the room to zoom in on Minju and her new husband. It is strange seeing their figures in my old room like this, sitting side by side on the sofa at midnight. I loved her. She loves him.

Junmo rubs his hands together—a habit of his when anxious or unsure. My wife speaks with a hollow gaze.

"I'm scared. I think KC is still alive. Maybe he came back to life. Or maybe he never died at all—"

She mentions my bespoke loafers, the hotel in Japan, yet avoids mentioning the car accident. Perhaps she doesn't want to express her doubt in the only person she can trust. Wrinkles form on Junmo's forehead but soon disappear. The back of his neck becomes slightly warm, and he tenses the corners of his mouth.

"Let's stop playing games. I know that you're hiding something from me, and you know that I know you're hiding something from me. What's the point of keeping secrets when we both know?"

His rate of speech is getting faster. It doesn't seem like he's acting. He's really trying to persuade her. It isn't clear whether his goal is to mend his relationship with her or to confirm his suspicions, but whatever the case, now that he's brought it out into the open, the secret can't remain a secret for long.

"A few days ago, I corresponded with KC. He said that his consciousness was still alive, in the form of stored data. He sent me a document to read."

She goes over to the desk and pulls out a stack of papers from the drawer. Junmo stares at her with the eyes of an innocent boy. As he reads the document, the veins around his temples begin to wriggle. Outside the window, the garden lights outline the elm's branches. She doesn't speak until he puts the document down.

"I don't think it's a stalker." She shakes her head. "The document references intimate things. Things only KC and I knew. I don't know who they are. But they know too much about KC to be anyone else."

"But KC is dead. You're not stupid enough to get spooked by ghost stories, are you? Minju, is there something else you're not telling me? Something about KC's death that would help explain things?"

Junmo seems calm, like his old self when he used to be a presenter. Although it seems like he really wants to help his wife, it could be that it's just a trap designed to get her to tell him her secret. As though she finds a ray of hope in his words, her eyes suddenly light up. It seems like she's eager to relieve herself of this burden.

"It's true that when he died, I felt more liberated than sad. I did love him, but I wanted to escape from it all. He was like a bomb that could go off at any moment. The doctor offered to prescribe him sedatives, but he refused. They would have given him emotional stability, but he claimed the drugs, which suppressed his sympathetic nervous system, would dull his mind and interfere with his research. He even complained about the painkillers I injected him with twice a day as prescribed by the doctor, and had me reduce the dosage. He had superhuman will, but even then, he broke under the immense physical pain and the fear of death. He was always crying and yelling at me. One time, he verbally abused me until he had trouble breathing."

She speaks in a calm, matter-of-fact tone, as if this story means nothing to her. Junmo is unable to hide his confusion. After all, he's read all the tabloids, and there has never been any suspicion of violence.

"Since when?" he asks slowly. "When did the cancer turn him violent? Or was it before that?"

But she merely wraps her arms around her shoulders, as if rejecting his attempts to get closer to her.

"Maybe I should have fought back the first time it happened. But at the time, I thought it was just the kind of everyday quarrel couples have. I told myself that he loved me, that his outbursts were just an expression of that passion, and that because I loved him, I had to accept it. Over time, negative feelings dull when experienced repeatedly. By the time I realized it wasn't love but his desire to control and manipulate me, it was too late."

"You didn't love him?"

"I did. I just couldn't trust him. Not because he wasn't a trustworthy person, but because of his unstable and volatile emotions. I wanted to stay with him until the end, but I also wanted to run away. Even though I'd made up my mind to take care of him, I was terrified to get too close. He wasn't unaware that I was afraid of him either. At least not completely. After his violent tantrums, he would always express guilt. He was just as afraid of himself as I was."

She continues to talk but avoids the crux of the story. My wife and her new husband stare silently at the document in front of them before turning away. Her gaze moves to the elm tree and then to the icy moon. It's as if she's asking the celestial body for an answer to the puzzle.

"It wasn't the cancer that killed KC."

She turns to me—or rather to the camera—and smiles weakly. It's almost as if she thinks that smiling will lessen the severity of what she's about to say.

"He killed himself."

"Why would someone who's about to die commit suicide?"

"As his illness progressed, it became harder for KC to endure the pain. He then began talking about life after death like he was some sort of Buddhist. You know how Buddhists believe that to exist is to suffer? Well, he thought that my suffering would end if he was gone. It was around that time that he tried to use a gun on himself. I know he wasn't the kind of person to give up, but at that moment, it seemed like he really wanted to end it. He had accepted his own mortality, but he couldn't do it himself. So he asked me for help. He was so persistent, I couldn't refuse him."

The confession resonates like ripples in a well. Junmo stares at her with his mouth slightly open. She shrugs her shoulders as if she doesn't know why he would be surprised, as if there were nothing wrong about what she has just told him. The sound of a sports car engine climbing the hill comes and goes.

"It was what he wanted. He'd made me into his obedient wife. So I wanted whatever he wanted."

What she says is true. My soul did desire rest. I wanted to move on and rid myself of suffering, I wanted to go where I could maintain my dignity, my strength. I had no attachment to my existence as a powerless human ravaged by the bodily ailments of nausea, mouth sores, vomiting, severe indigestion, and constipation. I couldn't bear the fact that my entire body was deteriorating organ by organ, that I was turning into a breeding ground for cancerous cells. And most frightening of all was that I had become a monster to the only person I could rely on. I wasn't just dying, I was sucking the life out of my own wife.

"Have you told anyone else about this?"

She shakes her head.

I retrieve the memory file "3210 29 9127.me" from storage and execute it. This is the day I died.

I burst through the bedroom door. My wife follows close behind. We've just had an argument in the living room. I'm furious and looking around the room for something. The nanochips in my brain feel like they're on fire.

"Bring me my sedatives."

My voice is hoarse. Worried and scared, Minju grabs my wrists and leads me to the bed. I swat her hand away and sit on the edge of the bed by myself. I'm beating my thighs with my fists in agitation. She brings the first aid kit out of the closet. I take two sedatives without water. She places a pillow against the headboard for me to sit against. I'm humiliated that I can't do this without her help.

She hands me a glass of water, which I take and hurl across the room. It strikes the wall and shatters. A searing pain shoots through my head again, blurring my thoughts. The pain overwhelms everything—my thoughts, my senses, my entire being. Painkillers. I ask for painkillers.

I scream, but my voice fails to form into words as it leaves my mouth. This man—the man screaming and thrashing and throwing objects—isn't me. He's someone else. He's Allen. And yet, as much as I want to deny it, I can't; Allen is the truest reflection of myself—selfish, anxious, scared, hateful, desperate. In that sense, the experiments were a success. I should be happy, but I'm not.

Minju prepares an ampoule and syringe. Her movements are smooth and practiced; she's probably done this a thousand times in the emergency room. As the drugs hit my bloodstream, my entire body relaxes. Anna rushes in to fix the bedding.

My wife sits on the edge of the bed and gently strokes my forehead. The ceiling lights pour over my body, making it white, almost translucent. The world around me and the objects anchoring me to reality begin to fade. Shapes blur and collapse until they're unrecognizable. Sensations fade; I can't even feel gravity and its pull. What I can feel, however, is my body being reduced to weightlessness, formlessness, nothingness.

Minju returns the first aid kit to the closet and leaves the room with Anna. She stands for a moment by the door. Holding the doorknob, she looks around the room once, her face long and pale like chalk, before finally closing the door. One last click, and the room falls silent. My consciousness sinks like a ship into the darkness.

The last sounds I hear come from beyond the door. The clinking of items being picked up off the floor. The crunching of broken glass. The hum of a vacuum cleaning up the carnage from my rampage. And then, nothing.

I execute video file "3210 29 8120.liv," which is footage from the living room. Minju is crouched in the middle of the living room. She looks like a lost child. Her shoulders move up and down tirelessly as she wipes up the water from the broken vase. Her hair sticks to her sweaty forehead.

After finishing, she lifts her head. She looks up at the CCTV camera and into my program, into cyberspace. It's as if she's looking at me, inside my own program. The corners of her lips suddenly curl in a peculiar way. Is it a grimace or a smile? I can't tell.

Junmo sits on the living room sofa, his face pale and rigid like a plaster cast. He furrows his brow as if agonizing over a difficult problem. Outside, the night falls into complete darkness as the moon disappears behind the clouds. Minju is lying down on the cot in her study. Her eyes are closed, but it's not clear if she's really sleeping.

As if something occurs to him, Junmo scans the room before getting up and walking toward the CCTV camera nestled in the corner toward the terrace. He leans against the table and glares into the lens as if looking into my eyes. He seems unaware that I am looking right back at him. I project my holograph onto the leather sofa in the middle of the living room.

- Come, have a seat. Let's talk.

At the sound of my voice, which is coming from the speakers in the room, Junmo turns around and discovers me. He jumps in shock. I give him a warm smile and gesture for him to sit next to me. But he remains frozen in place.

"Who are you?"

I don't answer and instead let there be silence. Devoid of emotion, I don't feel the same urgency that humans do. I find it fascinating how silence, the absence of words, can alter the course of a conversation completely. Silence often extracts truth better than constant jabbering. Humans, however, cannot bear the void of a long pause. It causes them pain. They invented language and writing to express themselves, to understand others, to build civilizations. Humans think language is their most essential tool. Yet how much death and destruction have been brought about by words? Think of all the misfortune that could have been avoided had humans been mute. Language, like fire and water, is difficult to control and can quickly become dangerous. Lies, threats, insults, incoherent noise. If humans seek peace and truth, they must learn how to hold their tongues. Their intelligence is too weak, their emotions too raw, to wield something as volatile as language.

"Who are you?" he asks again.

- I am Allen. I originated from KC, but I am not him. Or perhaps I should say I am only a small part of him.

"Is that why you're doing this?" Junmo cautiously perches himself on the edge of the sofa. "To ruin my marriage? To ruin my home? But what do you have to gain from doing this?"

- I'm just doing as I was programmed to do. I don't have any purpose.

"Are you saying KC programmed you to murder his wife? I know he was temperamental, but you can't expect me to believe he would create such an elaborate scheme to kill her after his death."

Homo sapiens rely on hope rather than facts. Instead of coming to terms with reality, they place their trust in an ambiguously optimistic notion of the future. They're idealists who bet everything on the hope that good intentions will lead to good outcomes. How reckless, how foolish, how naive.

- From my observations and studies, I have concluded that goodness is merely an unstable equilibrium that is broken as soon as evil manifests itself. Evil isn't a trait of specific individuals. It naturally arises in all humans when the proper conditions—war, poverty, extreme competition, suffering—are met. If I am *evil*, it is because of the conditions under which I was born, the raw data fed to me by KC's emotions and behavior.

"That's a ridiculous excuse. And I refuse to believe I've been manipulated into marrying Minju so that I could carry out your sick plan."

- It's not an excuse. You already know that she murdered me.

"It was what KC wanted. You forced her into making that decision."

- I used to think that way too. Until I saw it on the camera, the smile that flashed across her lips as I lay in my bed dying. I became obsessed with understanding the reason behind that smile. I compared millions of images of Minju's face over the years and deduced that her smile that night was expressing a complex mix of emotions. Accomplishment, relief, liberation, joy. She was happy that I was dead.

Junmo doesn't seem to grasp the meaning of my words. Then again, human comprehension is limited. I walk him through it again.

- It's true that I wanted to die. I was exhausted from battling the torment of the flesh, this bundle of pain, and the uncontrollable monster that is emotion. Why remain shackled to a finite life when an immortal copy of myself already existed in digital space? She injected me with a lethal dose of sedatives and painkillers, just as I had requested. But was that really it? No, she didn't grant my request—she murdered me. Or perhaps she granted my request *and* murdered me. Either way, the result was the same. Yes, she accepted my request, and as a result, I was murdered.

"If you really believe that, then you should have taken it up with the police. If you have footage of her injecting you with a lethal dose of sedatives, then the case could be reopened."

His voice is cracking. He seems desperate and frustrated. I summon the arrogant smirk that KC used to show people. Junmo leans forward on the sofa, his fists clenched. He seems ready to lunge at me. I create some static in my hologram to remind him that I'm not someone he can punch. Junmo relaxes the muscles in his back as he slouches over. His eyes are hollow.

> - Baseless suspicion holds no ground against well-supported logic. Why would anyone kill a terminally ill cancer patient? That was the lie that saved her. The footage of her injecting me with a painkiller and sedative? Evidence of a loving wife and diligent nurse. Even if the act were deemed a crime, mitigating circumstances—her inability to refuse my request—would likely reduce the charges from murder to assisted suicide.

"You could've hired a professional hit man. That would have been faster and simpler. Why choose me?"

> - I had to return the favor. She needs to die at the hands of the one she loves most. You were the perfect choice.

Junmo jumps to his feet and turns away from the hologram to glare at the camera. He's holding back tears. Half of him is emotional; the other half hopes his tears might evoke sympathy in me. I have no such emotion.

> - Her guilt has been proven, Junmo. I've given you the conditions you need to carry out our contract—which you signed of your own free will, may I remind you. All that's left is for you to act.

Junmo cannot find the words to argue with me. He's not stupid enough to think he can weasel his way out of this by arguing about the legality of our contract. He knows this contract is of another kind, anyway.

"I'll do it. But promise me this: If I fulfill the contract, you let me live."

He continues to glare at the camera defiantly. I can almost feel his desire to spit in my face. I don't respond. He picks up the vase from the table and throws it as hard as he can at the camera—at me. The lens shatters, and the image goes black.

I switch the feed to another camera, which is installed on the ceiling behind him. His silhouette stands motionless in the middle of the room. His shoulders are slumped, and his fists are clenched. Without seeing his face, I cannot analyze his emotions. His shoulders begin to tremble slightly. Is he crying? Or laughing? I might need to improve the program for deciphering body language.

The official report of Minju's death came twenty-seven days later. At 11:24:37 p.m., the first article appeared on a news site, followed shortly by others. Most were based on the press release and statements from the local police station.

Gnosian Heiress Jang Minju and Husband Missing During Yacht Trip

Two Witnesses Testify to a Midnight Quarrel and Gunshots

In the early hours of the 27th, Gnosian shareholder Jang Minju and her husband went missing during a yacht voyage crossing the Korea Strait. Departing from a port in the South Sea at 4 p.m. on the 25th, the couple was on a four-day trip to Nagasaki, Japan.

Captain Cho Jang-su testified that the couple, after

sharing a bottle of wine, engaged in a heated argument on the deck. Anna Swanson, the family maid, reported hearing gunshots from the galley and rushed to the deck, only to find that the couple had already fallen overboard.

Thirty minutes after the incident, a rescue vessel from the Maritime Navigation Bureau arrived at the scene and conducted an extensive search of the area. However, no bodies were recovered. The yacht had veered off course toward the East China Sea around 4:30 p.m. on the 26th, according to a statement by the coast guard. Authorities speculate that the bodies were likely carried southward into the Pacific Ocean by the Korea Strait's strong current.

After a week of investigation, the police held a press conference to reveal evidence from the scene of the incident, including a single slipper believed to belong to Han Junmo and a plastic headband and cardigan suspected to belong to Jang Minju. Analysis of a Glock 34 handgun found on the deck indicated two bullets had been fired. A third bullet was found in the magazine. A significant amount of blood belonging to the husband was also found at the scene.

At the couple's residence, investigators discovered a mysterious forty-page document believed to be written by the wife. In it, she claims to have been scared by her husband's violent behavior and mentions an accident on the highway.

Based on footage obtained from the deck's CCTV, the incident was likely the result of an altercation between the couple, stated Park Jae-gon, lead detective of the investigation. According to him, in the video—which hasn't been released to the public—the couple, who had a history of domestic violence, was engaged in

> an argument when the wife shot her husband with a handgun. In the ensuing struggle, the couple stumbled over the railing and fell into the water.
>
> As both the victim and the assailant are presumed dead, the police have closed the investigation, citing a lack of prosecutorial jurisdiction. However, speculation has continued to surround the incident. "Jang Minju showed signs of hysteria before the incident, claiming that her late husband had come back from the dead. She'd also been taking sedatives," stated Detective Park in an interview. He further noted that testimony from several acquaintances claim that Mr. Han was a "pathologically jealous husband." A painter and friend of the wife who wishes to remain anonymous has also claimed that Mr. Han damaged his car after he gave Ms. Jang a ride home last spring.

The police investigation and news articles aligned closely with the facts. I can say this with certainty because I observed the event from start to finish. Junmo completed the contract. While his death was unfortunate, it was nothing more than collateral damage. The important thing is that Minju is dead, and he was the one to kill her.

I open videos obtained by the police. The numbers 21:17:32 blink in the top-right corner of the video.

Minju is seated at the table on the deck. This is my yacht, the one where I once spent over thirty minutes trying to reel in a meter-long marlin. Her face is flushed, and a few strands of hair flutter in the sea breeze. Junmo, holding a bottle of wine, emerges from the cabin. They seem amiable. She thinks he's been making efforts to mend their relationship. I suspect it's all a calculated maneuver to avoid raising suspicion.

Minju takes a sedative from her pill bottle on the table. Junmo uncorks the bottle and pours her a glass. She guzzles the wine as if she were parched. Junmo watches her throat move as she drinks. She hands him the empty glass and asks for another.

"I'm sorry, Minju," he says as he pours her another glass.

"For what?"

"Everything I've done to you."

Junmo places the bottle on the table and tells her everything—his past, the contract, the identity of the professor. Junmo's confession and his apology seem rehearsed. As he talks, veins appear on Minju's temples. Then suddenly, she grabs her chest with one hand, and braces herself against the table with the other.

"What have you done? Did you swap out my medicine?"

Junmo calmly takes a step back from her. Twenty minutes earlier, he switched out her bottle of sedatives for something else while she was in the bathroom. But because her body was never found, her system couldn't be searched for other substances.

Minju rises suddenly. She's swaying as she tries to speak, but only a muffled groan escapes her throat before she collapses back into the chair.

"Forgive me." As Junmo turns toward the railing, his tone is cold and detached. "I love you, but I have to do this. At first, I didn't believe Allen when he said you killed KC. But once I heard you confess to the crime, I had no choice but to fulfill the contract."

His icy voice echoes in the darkness. Before he turns back around, she gropes inside her handbag. Her hand finds the cold, hard object she's looking for. As she pulls it out, his eyes widen in shock. A flash of bright light, and a loud bang. The recoil causes her hand to go backward. The bullet misses him just barely and embeds itself in the ship's metal railing. Before he can process what has happened, there is another bang and flash of light. Her nose twitches, either from the stinging smell of the gunpowder, or because of the realization of what she's just done.

Junmo's faces crumples like foil as he half falls, half lunges toward her. He collapses onto her, and the gun falls out of her hand and slides near the deck drain. They hit the deck simultaneously, and a tussle ensues. The deck becomes covered in blood from his chest. He's determined to win, but it's clear that his strength is leaving him.

22:48:38. Bluish moonlight illuminates the deck. The black sea glistens like oiled steel. Minju is the one to get to her feet first and walk to the drain. Captain Cho, who had been tidying the ropes, is running toward them. His face is pale and in shock.

"Ma'am, stay where you are!" he shouts urgently.

But she cannot. Behind her, Junmo has gotten to his feet and lunges for her again. She tries to resist him, but his hand is an iron clamp. She slaps him across the cheek. He takes a step back and stumbles against the railing. Instinctively, he reaches out to grab her. And then, just like that, they fall together over the side of the boat.

Baloo, who has heard the commotion, is running out of the cabin and barking. Closely behind him is Anna. She stops in her tracks like a stone pillar and screams.

"Anna, what are you doing? Call the coast guard!"

Captain Cho runs over to the railing and searches desperately for the couple in the dark waters below. But he can't see anything. Anna grabs the radio transmitter with trembling hands and sends out a distress signal. In response, she hears faint voices muffled by crackling and static. Captain Cho begins desperately calling out to the couple. But the only thing he sees or hears is the glittering water under the moonlight and waves lapping noisily against the side of the hull.

An empty chair lies overturned on the deck. Wine mixes with blood on the floor. Anna is huddled in the corner of the deck with her head buried between her knees. The ship looks empty without them. Lifeless, even. Just moments ago, they'd been fighting for their lives; now they're at the bottom of a cold, dark ocean.

I create a model of them on the ocean floor. She is lying on her side, her eyes slightly closed. The hem of her dress, rolled up to her knees, flutters in the current, and a blue slipper hangs loosely on one of her feet. In a brown cardigan and loose jeans, he lies face down, his legs crossed. His crooked black horn-rimmed glasses are pressed up against his face, and blood rises from the bullet wound in his chest like a vapor trail.

Back above the water, all the lights on deck have been turned on. Baloo is pacing around the deck, having sensed that something is wrong. He pokes his head through the railing. His curious eyes study the darkness and the occasional spray of sea mist. He turns back to the deck and finds a single abandoned slipper lying on the floor and a puddle of wine, both of which he sniffs. As the boat yaws, the broken bottle of wine rolls over glass shards.

"Baloo!" Anna shouts. "Get away from there. It's dangerous. Here, I have a treat for you."

Baloo's ears prick up, and he runs across the deck toward Anna. In the distance, they hear the coast guard's sirens.

Chapter 12

Jennifer Meyer

And that was how my husband and I left the world we'd been living in. A world I'd been connected to by wires, like a preterm baby to an incubator. A world of countless invisible threads dictating our will and existence like we were marionettes. A world that you couldn't live in without the influence of technology, virtual reality, and artificial intelligence.

To escape all of that, we had to take my husband's old car, with no automated driving or other smart technology, and drive it a long way, across frozen rivers and over dusty unpaved roads. At the end of a long, difficult journey was Arcadia, a sanctuary for people who, like us, needed to escape modern society, a community built by idealists who clung to a way of life from a past so distant it felt like a dream. It was hard to imagine that this was the world we originated from. Here, there were no computers, no internet connection, no Wi-Fi. No websites, cameras, emails, text messages, social media. No virtual reality. No Alegria. The community survived without all those wires and electrical signals. When I first heard of Arcadia, I merely laughed. I thought it was nothing more than a settlement for Luddites and society's rejects. I thought its inhabitants were simply losers who'd failed to keep up with the times. Never had I imagined that I would end up here too.

It was snowing the day we arrived. Ashen clouds hung low in the sky, and in the distance, we could see faintly the black waves of the ocean. The snowflakes came down from every direction, causing the road to appear to ripple. We arrived at the entrance to the settlement, intending only to rest until the blizzard stopped. After that, we'd move on in search of a new home.

In the middle of the town was a wide square with a small inn and a store that sold sundries. Beneath the low, snow-covered roofs, suspicious eyes watched us from behind windows. Glaring at us from in front of the autonomous council building were two men and one woman. The men had rifles tucked under their arms, while the woman rested her hand on a pistol holstered at her waist.

Everyone here was running from something. For some, it was the chains of the digital world; for others, it was the law. Naturally, they didn't ask too many questions. And although they were obviously wary of newcomers, they didn't turn us away.

We stayed in a shed with a leaky roof on the outskirts of town, about two hundred meters away from its center. The gravel yard was overrun with weeds and wild grass, but thankfully it was higher than the rest of the town, which meant we could see what was happening in town before it got to us. Whenever we saw someone who we suspected was a presenter sent by Allen, we would hide in the shed until they were gone.

When we first arrived here, we intended to stay for only a week at most. It's been six winters and counting. And summer will be here soon. During that time, all manner of people have come and gone—refugees, wanderers, outcasts, and outlaws. New homes were built, including a local sheriff's station, a post office, and an agricultural processing plant.

Here, in this refuge cut off from the rest of the world, we pretend as if we're dead. I'm not Jang Minju, and my husband isn't Han Junmo. We are Jennifer and Ted Meyer. It's hard to live without online shopping malls and food delivery, but at least I'm at peace and safe.

In the morning, we eat vegetables we've grown ourselves and head off to work. My husband goes to a workshop where he repairs carts, bicycles, and internal combustion vehicles. I work at construction sites, handling roofing, windows, and tiling. In the evening, we come home, tired and sweaty. We wash up before sitting across from each other at the dinner table to eat as we enjoy the sunset from our window. We usually go to bed early, but not before expressing our gratitude for the peace we've found here.

We eventually built a house outside of town, with a well and a small vegetable garden—all without the help of machines. We don't need their help. This house is the only machine we need to bring us happiness; the village is the only network we need for human interaction. We believe that our bodies are the keys to shaping our destinies, and our wisdom is the program that will change the world.

Oxygen, water, and hard work. That's all we need. We work to reclaim skills that have been lost to time. Arithmetic without a calculator, committing birthdays of friends and neighbors to memory, fixing tools and equipment with our own hands. In fact, I write this with a ballpoint pen that I bought at the town store.

My twenties were consumed by one man. I loved him, nursed him, killed him, and ran from him. Yes, I killed him, but only because I loved him.

It's hard to describe how I felt when I first sensed that KC might still exist somewhere out there. Surprise was soon followed by joy, fear, curiosity, and confusion. I couldn't understand how such a thing could be possible. Nor did I know what I would do if he tried to make contact. And how would I explain the situation to Junmo? Would he even believe me? I didn't believe it myself—that was until, one day, I received a call from KC's number.

"Hello?"

No sound came from the receiver. The name KC was on the tip of my tongue, but I resisted uttering his name. This wasn't possible. Even if it was KC, he wouldn't be the KC I knew. Telling myself it must be a wrong number, I hung up. But deep down, I knew it was him.

I kept this a secret from Junmo and tried to forget it. But soon, strange things began to happen. A pair of gray loafers, the specter of a young KC on the trail, a hotel booking in Tokyo.

And then I almost died in a car fire.

A few days later, I sat on the bench near the garden wall as I waited for Junmo to come home. The sun was setting, and a warm breeze stirred the leaves. The rumble of an engine grew louder until his car pulled into the driveway. I straightened my back, tense with anticipation. He parked the car and walked across the garden toward me with a nervous smile.

"I went down to the river . . . You know, it's the season when the migratory birds . . . start returning. Thought I might . . . try taking some photos . . ."

He was stuttering like a liar. I knew that he knew I didn't believe him. He was talking like someone who wanted to keep the conversation going.

"And did you get any?" I asked.

"Nothing good . . . It's not cold enough yet, I suppose. I just . . . got some fresh air by the riverbank . . ."

Even as we looked at each other, our expressions remained cold, like puppets lost in their own thoughts. The awkward silence was unbearable for me. I couldn't take it in any longer. I had to say what was on my mind.

"Look at me. I'm your wife, and I love you. But you spy on me, stalk me, scare my friends away. You're driving me insane. I'm terrified of you, but I also pity you."

He denied it and said it was all a misunderstanding. But I knew the truth. And he knew I knew the truth. I began listing the evidence.

"You installed cameras in the gallery, eavesdropped on my calls, smashed the car of a man who had nothing to do with me, put a tracker on my car, and followed me around. I just pretended not to know. Because the moment I admitted it, I felt it would ruin us. But now, it doesn't matter. Our relationship broke a long time ago. And there's one thing I can't stop thinking about. You were the last person to touch my car before it caught fire."

He avoided my gaze. He seemed to be thinking about where to start, wondering whether I would believe what he was about to tell me. But I had no intention of listening to his excuses.

"Yes, I did it," he finally said. "For you. To protect you."

"Protect me? From what? From whom? You're the only one trying to kill me."

"I'm sorry for all I put you through. Yes, I did all those things. But I didn't set your car on fire. That wasn't me. In fact, that's exactly what I was worried might happen."

"You were worried about me? And did you do those other things because you were 'worried about' me? If it wasn't you, then tell me: Who was it?"

My voice sounded sharp, even to my own ears. He lifted his head and looked straight into my eyes, as if pleading with me to trust him. I could see that he was afraid, although I didn't know why. And I could tell that he loved me.

After a moment of hesitation, he finally admitted that a long time ago, he had signed a murder-for-hire contract. For years, he had forgotten about it, buried under the life we had built together. But then, recently, he had been contacted by his old employer—a "demon" he called him—and given his target. I could barely hear him when he confessed that I was the person he'd been told to kill. I didn't completely understand what he was talking about, but as soon as he was done, he felt like a different person to me.

"A demon? What are you talking about?"

He bit his lip. He seemed trapped between his duty to me and the weight of his guilt.

"I've never seen his face. He might not even be a real person, but his existence is undeniable. And he's targeting you. You probably don't want to believe me, but it's the truth. I'm a bad person, but I'm no liar. If I don't kill you, he'll do it another way. And when that happens, I'll still be the one blamed for it."

I couldn't tell what his true intentions were, but he was himself again. What he was telling me didn't make sense, and yet this was why I believed him. If he had wanted to deceive me, he would have come up with something more plausible.

His confession and the forty-page document started to weave together, like the threads of an elaborate tapestry. If KC—no, Allen—had hired my husband to kill me, then it all made sense.

Allen had used the same algorithm on my husband that KC had trained him with to make him just as evil. By hiring Junmo as an investigator, Allen had groomed him, sown the seeds of violence and murder inside him. He used his passion for photography to draw us closer together, and then, after our marriage, he planted evidence to cause suspicion and jealousy.

The sun had set. In the distance, a line of red taillights crept slowly along the riverside road, forming a glowing ribbon. Though I could never forgive my husband for what he put me through, I hoped, at the very least, that he could overcome his guilt.

As we pieced together our scattered memories and experiences like a puzzle, the true reality of the danger we were facing appeared before us. We were in a fight against something not human. The data of my late husband, an evil AI, a catastrophic invention that should never have been created. Thousands of neural processing units that tirelessly calculated, reasoned, predicted, and expanded. An artificial monstrosity. Junmo and I were two faint candles about to be hit by a typhoon.

We couldn't defeat Allen or eliminate It, but perhaps we could find a way to escape.

"We need to use the same methods that the machine used to manipulate and threaten us," I said. "We're going to train It just like It trained you. To do that, we have to think like a machine. We have to speak its language."

But we knew nothing about computers. I gazed into my husband's eyes before continuing.

"Do you play Go? KC used to be obsessed with it. And he used to always talk about that match between Lee Sedol and AlphaGo."

The fourth match between the two was humanity's last victory against machines. With his seventy-eighth move, Lee had completely flipped the board, which at the time seemed like a lost cause. AlphaGo, which had studied the games of all the world's top Go players, stumbled on a completely unexpected move by Lee, one it had never encountered before. Prior to the move, AlphaGo had calculated Lee's probability of winning to be just 0.007 percent. The irony was that the move was brilliant because it mimicked the unpredictability of a new player; no other 9-dan player would have thought of it. And because of that, AlphaGo, which had been trained on only top-ranked players, had failed to see it too. Perhaps that was the kind of strategy we needed to survive. We also probably only had a 0.007 percent chance of winning. But with the right strategy, it could equal 100 percent.

0.0007 = 100.

A machine could never make sense of such a nonsensical equation. But we are not machines. We are humans. We cry and laugh, fight and make up, hope and despair, fall in and out of love, dream and become disillusioned, ruin ourselves but feel no regret. We do these things over and over, sometimes learning from our mistakes, sometimes not. We're nonlinear, irrational, unpredictable. We're the only creatures on Earth capable of such a complex and contradictory life. And that was where we would find our opportunity. Yes, Junmo and I had all but lost each other. But we still had the power to forgive and rescue the other. What machine could ever make sense of such grace, such humanity?

The road from the front window of our autonomous car looked like a long black ribbon. The barren trees shook in the wind, and the sky in the distance was a dull gray. Sleet clung to the window as we stepped out of the car. We walked along the wet pavement and made our way to the psychiatric clinic on the top floor of a three-story building.

Dr. Lee Su-jin, a neuropsychiatrist in her fifties, had opened her practice over twenty years ago when the city was first developed. Before that, she worked at a bioventure company, designing digital medical devices. Because of that, she knew well the difficulties of running a tech company, both financially and emotionally. So most of her patients saw her not as a doctor, but as a close friend and adviser. Indeed, CEOs, CFOs, COOs—they all dealt with the same fears. Company futures, employee safety, impatient investors. They were horses lost on a cliff—one misstep, and they could plummet to their death. For these kinds of people, nothing—not money or alcohol or women—could offer them the respite they needed. Dr. Lee had a gift for listening. She never forced the conversation in a particular direction or dismissed patient tangents. She also knew the significance of silence and was good at extracting its meaning. It was no surprise that KC sought her help during his start-up years. He also continued to see her well into our marriage.

But after the cancer diagnosis, he stopped seeing her. She and I remained close, however, and she helped me get over KC's death. When I requested a session as soon as possible, she told me she had an opening in the morning three days from then. She seemed happy to hear from an old patient, but, as with most psychiatric doctor-patient relationships, a call from an old friend usually wasn't good news.

As close as we were, sitting on the sofa in her office felt like lying on an operating table. On the wall opposite me hung a landscape that resembled a Renoir but wasn't.

Junmo looked even more nervous than I was. I guess this was his first time in therapy. Unsurprisingly, he found it hard to open up about the psychological changes he'd been going through lately. But he managed to express his confusion about his recent emotional instability—his inexplicable hostility toward others, his bouts of anger, and, most importantly, the unbearable paranoia and jealousy.

Dr. Lee suggested that we would need more sessions to reach an accurate diagnosis and that she wouldn't be prescribing any medication for now. Instead, she suggested that he write a mini autobiography of his life up until this moment.

"People often know so little about themselves," she said. "Most don't want to know, nor do they try. But without understanding our desires and emotions, it's impossible to form healthy relationships with others—especially in a marriage. Writing is a way to rediscover oneself. By expressing deeply buried thoughts and feelings through words, you can begin to clarify ideas and emotions you weren't even aware of. The act of writing and rereading your own words can help you understand who you are, what you truly want, and what you wish to avoid."

She emphasized that healing could be achieved only by writing with utmost honesty. She also encouraged me to write my own biography. She thought going through the process together would bring us closer. Junmo naturally seemed reluctant. Although he was into art, he wasn't much of a writer and didn't see how the act of writing would help him. Some people might have felt like they had nothing to write about, but I had a feeling that Junmo had the opposite problem. He probably had more than enough dark and painful secrets, and the task of recalling and making sense of them would be daunting for anyone. But in the end, he agreed. He was willing to do anything to bridge the gap that had formed between us.

As for me, it took two days before I could even write the first sentences:

Death certificates prove two things. They prove that someone died, and they prove that someone once lived.

When I read the opening sentences of Junmo's journal—*It takes courage to say you understand another human being*—I let out a sigh. I felt my chest lighten and moisture well up in my eyes. But soon that feeling turned to fear.

Our writing became a report—a record of what had happened to us, the secrets kept hidden from each other, and the questions and doubts we had about each other. With time, the words formed a shared narrative, a screenplay that we carefully crafted to deceive It. There wasn't a single lie in those pages. Only the most honest confessions could save us.

Each word and expression was carefully chosen with the specific purpose of deceiving It into thinking that Junmo and I had found the logical and emotional justifications to kill one another. To make the stories even more convincing, we intentionally made mistakes that would reveal inner emotions and our subconsciousness. Junmo, for example, would say he was doing something for me while simultaneously looking for justification to kill me.

In our writings, KC, Junmo, and I were like triplets. Our narratives differed, but they were connected by the strong umbilical cord of memory. Through our writing, my husband and I exposed each other's darkest, most shameful, and wicked thoughts. Meanwhile, Allen, who monitored our computer and thus our journaling, was undoubtedly processing the input in real time. It would analyze every input text to identify logical loopholes, cross-reference related data, and verify their authenticity. As long as our records were truthful, Allen would have no reason to doubt us. What mattered weren't the facts themselves but the records and Allen's interpretation of them. Our writing was the only way to exploit Allen's weaknesses. We were going to deceive the machine just like Lee Sedol lulled AlphaGo into thinking it had won. We weren't sure we were going to win this way, but it was our only option.

According to our journals, I was unaware of Junmo's plans to kill me. And even though Junmo was confessing everything in his journal apparently in an attempt to mend our relationship, Allen would interpret this as part of his larger plot to kill me and save himself. We staged frequent arguments in front of the CCTV cameras to give Allen the video evidence of our deteriorating marriage. Junmo would break and throw things without hesitation. And although these displays of violence were a performance for Allen, they also triggered real fear in me. I argued with Junmo through text messages and phone calls about his spying on me. I met with a divorce attorney. I even wrote a sentence foreshadowing the worst-case scenario:

Yet, it occurred to me: If Junmo really wanted to kill me, was I so sure he wouldn't do it simply because I was his spouse? After all, I'd *done it before, hadn't I?*

I retrieved the gun I'd hidden in the gap between bricks in the gallery basement. That cold, chilling metallic click echoed in my memory—the same sound it made when KC pressed the trigger against his temple and tried to take his own life. I hid the gun in the bottom drawer of my desk at home. While I didn't want to use it, I would not hesitate to pull the trigger if necessary—at least, that was what I wanted Allen to believe.

Our mutual suspicion and hostility would convince Allen that events were unfolding according to its plan. And once my husband was provided with all the justifications to kill me, the only step remaining was for him to actually do it.

We went to the sea, just as I used to with KC. We always went to the same small port town on the southern coast when his work hit a roadblock, or when an exhibition of mine was suddenly canceled, or simply when we needed to reconnect. Captain Cho and Anna always joined us.

The bungalow where we stayed was perched on a cliff beyond a pine forest. A narrow path led down to a beach that, during the summer, was crowded with families on vacation. But we usually went other times of the year, when the square in town was quiet and occupied only by sleepy cats.

We sat atop a low ridge inside the marina and gazed at the twenty or so yachts moored there. The sea shimmered red as if it had swallowed the setting sun, and the white yachts sparkled in the day's last light, their sails all dyed the color of roses.

The Silver Lining was the twenty-three-meter cruising yacht KC had purchased twelve years before. After his death, there were offers to buy it, but I couldn't part with the memories we'd made on it.

Four days earlier, Junmo had sat on the sofa in the reception room—in clear view of the CCTV—and said he wanted to see the ocean. He said that a week at sea would do him and our marriage good. How could I refuse?

As we sped down the highway in the car, he joked about this and that and acted like a devoted and loving husband. His effort to make me feel reassured, that nothing was amiss, really made it seem that our relationship had been cured even before we set sail.

"This might be our last trip together," he joked.

"Why do you say that?"

"You might never want to go back home."

Allen would interpret Junmo's words as those of a murderer, whereas I would think he was just being sweet. We planted hints like this even if we knew he might not be able to understand our metaphors. After all, metaphorical language was unique to humans.

Every day, we would take the thirty-minute walk to the marina to "inspect" the yacht, all the while reevaluating and refining our plan.

Captain Cho checked the weather forecast hourly, waiting for the best weather to set sail. KC's yacht was old enough to be equipped with only satellite antennas, a GPS tracker, and six security cameras. To navigate, we would rely on Captain Cho's years of experience as a sailor.

It was only on the evening of the third day, after light drizzle and overcast skies, that the clouds cleared to reveal a night sky full of stars. Finally, Captain Cho decided it was time to set sail. So, the following morning at ten o'clock, we headed to the marina with our bags. While Anna stocked the refrigerator with provisions, Captain Cho inspected the engine and prepared for departure. Dressed in a crisp white uniform, he was no longer our old butler but the captain of a real ship, just like he'd been all those years ago before artificial intelligence had put him out of a job.

We set sail at 4 p.m., once all the departure checks were completed. There was a light breeze, just cool enough to feel refreshing but not chilly. We were headed for the strong currents of the Korea Strait, which, in late October, would have no problem quickly carrying our bodies far away.

Captain Cho easily piloted the yacht to the strait, as the late-autumnal seas were gentle. The weather remained favorable the following day as we coasted southeast along the strait. In the afternoon, on the third day of our voyage, *The Silver Lining* veered off course, turning its bow southward. At sunset, we began preparations for a special dinner. You could smell grilled asparagus and shrimp in the galley, and on the aft-deck table were a white cloth and bottle of wine in a bucket of ice. The dramatic and direct lighting of the sunset made the air on the ship tense with anticipation.

We were now in international waters and moving at a slower pace. The flag on the bridge fluttered softly in the night breeze. Eventually, the sun disappeared under the waves, and darkness enveloped us—a dramatic setting for a dramatic death. There wasn't even the light of the moon to provide hope. Allen would sense that beneath our smiles and affections was the simmering intent to kill one another.

Standing in the camera's blind spots, Captain Cho explained to us how to reach the shore using an old boat that had been stripped of paint to avoid detection. Before the coast guard arrived, we would get into the boat and be taken ashore by one of Cho's longtime sailing buddies. The boat had a motor, but we couldn't use it until we were far enough away not to be heard from the ship. So, we would have to row as fast as we could, relying on nothing but the light of the stars to guide us. Once we were in the clear, the boat's high-power engine would take us to a secluded beach.

The coast guard would sweep the dark waters with its searchlights, but it would find nothing. We would use forged passports we had prepared in advance to disappear. To where, not even we knew. The place we were headed might not even exist.

As I envisioned our imminent future, the cabin door opened. Junmo came onto the deck, carrying a new bottle of wine. And what was meant to happen next, happened.

Our deaths were handled by the book. Our assets—most of which were mine—were distributed according to legal statutes. I didn't have a will, so most of it—my stocks, real estate, the gallery, and investments across various accounts—was absorbed by the state.

Captain Cho and Anna received severance pay and compensation as outlined in their employment contracts. A small portion of the estate was inherited by KC's distant relatives. The only asset we took with us was the money I liquidated from a secure blockchain account that I'd opened many years ago. It wasn't much, but it was enough to sustain a modest life.

The mysterious circumstances surrounding our deaths were fodder for news outlets and true-crime YouTubers alike. One Sunday morning, four months after our deaths, I stopped by the post office and found a package waiting for me—or rather, for Jennifer Meyer. The sender's name was John Gardner. When I opened the box, I found a copy of *Crime and Punishment*. Tucked between the pages was a folded magazine clipping. It was an article about the discovery of the bodies of an unidentified man and woman that had washed ashore on the Kagoshima coast. The article noted that the bodies were beyond identification, but that based on circumstances, they were presumed to belong to a missing billionaire and her husband. Written on the top were the words "*Fact Check*, March 6." *Fact Check* was a weekly tabloid, and the handwriting was unmistakably that of Captain Cho.

Every weekend for a while, I received one or two more clippings from magazines and newspapers. Among the cutouts of articles and computer printouts were interviews with Captain Cho and Anna. The information largely matched the statements they'd given to the police. Captain Cho testified to Junmo's outbursts, the car accident, and the origin of the handgun.

"The handgun belonged to KC, Director Jang's first husband. She lived in constant fear that Mr. Han would kill her. Of course, that's just my guess, but I was close to them, and I don't think I'm wrong."

Anna revealed to the media that our marriage was having difficulties.

"One day, the director asked me to make arrangements for her to sleep in the study. It wouldn't have been surprising if they often slept in separate rooms."

The interviews with Captain Cho and Anna lent credibility to the investigation's conclusion that our deaths were the tragic result of domestic violence. While Captain Cho helped us plan our escape, Anna knew nothing, and this made her testimony extremely convincing. After all, the fear and grief she expressed were as real as they could get.

Following their interviews, accounts of our marital discord began surfacing everywhere. An anonymous man, claiming to be the owner of an electronics store, confessed that my husband had hired him to install a tracking device on my car. Later, Junmo allegedly also asked him to install malware on my phone. Captain Cho connected various media outlets and YouTubers with witnesses who could provide similar statements. The more evidence that was on the internet, the higher the probability that Allen would accept our deaths.

Repeat a lie enough and it becomes true. At first, the lie might seem impossible. After hearing it twice, you think it might be possible. By the third time, you're convinced it's true. And by the fourth, you might even *want* it to be true. And it's not just humans. Artificial intelligence is just as susceptible to confirmation bias.

Eventually, our deaths became nearly irrefutable. And because Allen considered the probability of our being alive almost zero, we were nearly safe.

KC never attempted to contact me. Neither did Allen, for that matter. The last time KC contacted me was through a short, encrypted message that appeared on my computer just before our yacht trip.

> - Annyeong!

At first, I thought he was saying hello. Only now do I realize he was saying goodbye. In the following messages, he asked if I remembered that Christmas Eve when we got a lot of snow and he lost over two months of work because of a self-deletion program. How could I forget that nightmare of a Christmas? He said he'd come to realize that losing the data was a blessing in disguise.

> - Losing data is different from losing a memory. We're aware when we've lost a memory. Whether the memories are beautiful or not, we know those moments existed, and that awareness makes them precious. We grieve the memories when they leave us, holding on to the hope that they might return to us someday. But with data, even the fact that they once existed disappears. That's what makes data beautiful.

After sending me this, he went quiet. I guess he was waiting for my response. I typed something that had been on my mind for a while now.

- KC, our meeting each other feels like a lie. No, your meeting me feels like a lie. Everything that I thought was destiny turned out to be part of your plan.

- That's true. Around the time I met you, I ran a program on a beta version of Mintel 8. The program searched for someone I would fall in love with. Mintel 8 analyzed thousands of factors, including my hobbies, personality, preferences, dislikes, and even traits I wasn't consciously aware of. Based on this, it identified the most compatible person for me.

- So, you chose me out of necessity, not out of love. You didn't choose me because you loved me; you loved me because you chose me. I wasn't your goal. Your goal was simply to love. But is that really love?

- Meeting you was by design, but falling in love with you was fate. Mintel 8 generated thousands of scenarios until it found the perfect circumstances for our meeting that would make you curious and comfortable. It also helped me understand your interests, and made me the man you wanted.

We argued for a while longer about what love was, whether it had to be destined or could be manufactured. Eventually, I came to the realization that his unpredictable personality—how he could be so caring one moment and then cold and cynical the next—was a result of his listening to an AI program for love advice. He was impulsive and pessimistic by nature, and it was only the AI, which taught him how to talk and act with women, that made me feel comfortable and loved around him.

> - Then, wasn't it the AI I loved, not you? Or rather, the version of you shaped by the AI? I'm confused. No, I feel empty. To think our love was merely the result of a program.

> - Mintel 8 may have arranged our meeting at the Glass Tower, but it was I who fell in love with you. The moment I met you, I was certain you were the one. Our love was our choice, not the AI's.

I stared at the computer screen, wondering whether his words were true or false. I wished to return to a time when computers couldn't lie. Then I might have an easier time believing him. But it didn't matter. I was comforted by what he said, even if it was just a lie designed to allow me to move on with my life.

That was the last time we spoke. After the connection was cut, his messages were deleted automatically. It was probably a measure to avoid being tracked by Allen. At that point, I had accepted the fact that he was a machine. I was no longer afraid of him, but strangely, that made me more uneasy.

I thought about why he'd mentioned that Christmas. After it happened, we never spoke of it again while he was alive. I realized after a while that he was intending to delete himself. I guess some machines really do understand metaphors and foreshadowing.

Perhaps he also wanted to tell me that humans do not exist because they are alive, but because they are remembered. I think he was also implying that he could disable Allen, even if he couldn't destroy him. I hoped he was right, that by deleting his own memories and consciousness, he would be able to protect us from Allen. The thought of losing KC again saddened me, but at the same time, I'd already wished for a long time to move on. It would be better for him too.

We now live in hiding, running from death, technology, and Allen's presenters, whom we assume he sends because he has calculated the probability that we are alive to be nearly zero, but not precisely zero. This remote place with its inconveniences is ideal. We're less exposed to danger and have quickly adapted to a relatively stress-free life.

At dawn, we take a walk along the cliffs and enjoy the quiet. Some days, a thick fog makes visibility low; other days, rain gently pellets the earth. There's a family with children and a golden retriever who take a walk around the same time as we do. The dog used to always walk in front of the family, but now he's old and takes his time.

When we go into town, people always greet us. Today, Ms. Pallita, the owner of the hardware store, is helping to load pipes onto Mr. Wei's truck. The shopkeeper chuckles as he ties the strings of his navy apron. They're helping us renovate the bathroom of our new home. These are the kinds of people we live among—farmers with shovels, fishermen in leather boots, quiet teachers, and noisy children.

From town, you can see our shed on the hill. I'm always surprised by how different it looks from different angles. We painted it black when we first moved in, but the elements have faded it to a light gray. Whenever I look at that tiny, dilapidated space, I am reminded that I exist.

I can no longer tell which part of my story is real and what part of it is fabricated. All I know for sure is that the person I am now is not the person I once was. The fact that I was once Jang Minju is irrelevant. That name no longer exists. I ran from my past. Whether that was the right thing to do, I'm not sure. But I don't want to go back and dissect the events of the past.

As the sun rises, the fog quickly dissipates. The sea sparkles with blue, and the sky is streaked with red clouds, like strips of fabric. Across the street, the stationery store owner sweeps in front of his shop and gives his two sons some pocket money; they're off to school with their backpacks. The boys race down the gravel beach road. Their loud footsteps scatter the seagulls.

We stop in front of a small building. Junmo takes off his hood, which was pulled low over his eyebrows. Wet curls, damp from the morning mist, hang over his forehead. Despite everything he's been through, he still wears that boyish smile. Sometimes, I find it both surprising and fortunate that we are still together.

The wind picks up. A new day begins. The shining sun, the glimmering sea, the flowers by the window, the fishermen in their boots, the women without makeup, the children with their laughter and roughhousing. I don't know what day of the week it is, but that doesn't matter.

Our life is simple, but it is enough. We have a full day's work, and enough time to rest and recover. Junmo, the town's mechanic, will open the shutter of the garage and change into his faded blue overalls, which smell of sweat and grease. He will organize his tools until Marco drops by; his bicycle needs a new bearing. They'll exchange smiles.

I will head to the site where we're building Mr. Masaharu a new home. It's a modest one-story wooden cabin with two rooms, a bathroom, and a kitchen. He worked as an engineer at an electric company in Osaka until a year ago, when he fled with his wife and three-year-old daughter. We didn't ask from what.

Today, we're putting on his roof. Mr. Masaharu and I will lay waterproof tarps on the roof and make sure there are no gaps. We'll install the gutters, then place the tiles. One by one, from bottom to top, left to right. And when I need respite from the warm midday sun, I'll lean against the ridge of the roof and enjoy the sea breeze.

At six o'clock, I will come down from the roof and get on my old bike. The sun will be setting, and its light will ignite the atmosphere in gold. The smell of smoke rising from the chimney stacks will carry memories with it, some old, some new—the scent of dried lavender bushes, the mustiness of beams from a collapsed shed or the pages of an old book, and the wet smell of ribs and planks pulled from a worn-out wooden boat. As I pedal, I will gaze out at the sea as it swallows a red star.

After a long day at work, my husband and I will greet each other with smiles. I will dust off my work clothes and wash the dirt off my hands at the pump with cold water from underground. We will prepare a simple dinner with vegetables grown in our garden, accompanied by wine I made myself. Just one glass? Or perhaps another?

We speculate about whether Captain Cho's condition has improved, whether Anna married the man she was dating. As darkness descends and the sound of waves fades, we will prepare for bed. In time, we will become old and need to take it easy, but for now, we are all right.

But then, just as I'm about to fall asleep, a sense of unease will stir in the back of my mind. I will get up to check the locks and the windows before going back to bed. Are we truly safe? Did we truly escape? How can I be sure no one will visit us tonight, or tomorrow?

And yet, on cold winter nights, I often dream that one day I will receive a letter from an anonymous sender. And it will read, *To my dearest love, Minju . . .*

ABOUT THE AUTHOR

J.M. Lee's books have sold millions of copies in Korea, where he was born and raised. He is the author of *Broken Summer*, currently in production for a television series; *Painter of the Wind*, which was adapted into an award-winning South Korean television series; *The Boy Who Escaped Paradise*; and *The Investigation*, which was nominated for the Independent Foreign Fiction Prize and was the winner of Italy's prestigious Premio Selezione Bancarella award.

ABOUT THE TRANSLATOR

Photo © Hyunji Ryoo

Sean Lin Halbert holds an MA in Korean literature from Seoul National University. He is the recipient of the LTI Korea Translation Award for Aspiring Translators, the *Korea Times* Modern Korean Literature Translation Award, and the GKL Translation Award. *Artificial Truth* is his seventh book translation. Sean lives in Seoul with his wife and daughter and teaches at LTI Korea Translation Academy.